CREEK CREW:

KINGDOM OF THE CREEK

Drew Bale

ISBN: 9780648868531

To Richard, Mitchell, Ben, Mat, Lahne and Ashleigh.

Without you I would never have enjoyed my weekend childhood anywhere near as much.

CHAPTER 1 - A DOZEN YEARS, A DOZEN HOUSES

"House number twelve," Hunter sighed as he slumped into the family's old cream coloured Holden. "This will be the twelfth house we have moved to, and that is only counting those that I can remember." The car rocked from side to side on its almost ancient suspension. The interior was a rough and scratchy brown shade that made entering the vehicle even worse than looking at it from the outside. Hunter was joined straightaway by his mum in the front seat, as well as his younger brother, Alex, in the back. They were all joined by a small six month old Scottish terrier, which was clipped into his seatbelt between Hunter and his brother, who immediately reclined into an oversized basket. The dog wagged his tail and rushed around excitedly, bouncing his container around harmlessly. Hunter's dad, who had been the one to throw the dog in the back, untangled the tiny pup as it promptly became entangled in its small belt.

"Look after him will you?" their dad stated before jumping in his seat. Everyone held on tight as the car jiggled around with the big man's movement before appearing to sink a couple of metres into the tyres. The car struggled to reverse down the short driveway, and everyone braced as the car slumped over the edge of the curb with the front of the car dragging savagely on the concrete. Dad patted the dash, and Hunter was not sure if it was in apology at what had just occurred, or with pride that it continued to take such torment.

"Where are we going?" Alex asked almost instantly as the car lumbered into life.

"We told you, we are going to see something special," Mum replied, not really answering the question.

"It's a new house," Hunter grunted, "Number twelve." Hunter rolled his eyes, receiving a shake of the head from his mum and a glare from the ever watching eyes of his father in the rear-view mirror. The number didn't affect Alex, nor did Hunter think he cared about where they were going, as sometimes he just liked to ask questions to be annoying. No, Hunter thought, not sometimes, frequently.

Mum waved at a house at the end of the long street, which exited the extremely stretched out cul-de-sac in which they lived. They never went to the other end because it was at the top of a long hill, in which their house was about halfway up, and the car would have struggled to make it to the summit without spluttering and ultimately failing. The house their Mum waved at though was that of Hunter's grandparents, who, surprisingly, were not just randomly standing at the front of their house waiting for the car to go past at any moment. This time.

They were lovely people, and Hunter's family had lived in their house for a short period of time when they last moved between places. His grandfather was a war veteran and told frequent stories from his past. Hunter would listen to all of them, but sadly forget some of the tales, while Alex would just spin around on one of their swivel chairs oblivious to the treasure trove of knowledge he was passing by. Their grandmother would indulge them, in between having what she thought were very posh parties with her other older friends. It seemed alright to be spoilt, except instead of a hoard of toys and lollies they would get a mixture of homemade foods. This would have been great as both Hunter and Alex loved food, but a lifetime of wine and smoking had left her taste buds basically burnt out. That resulted in her food containing copious amounts of extra spice and ground, but more like whole, pepper. Hunter remembered one time imagining that while he was eating a massive serving of meatballs he was actually a minesweeper. His tongue was the detector and his eyes would revolve as if being able to see inside his own mouth. He was searching for a big chunk of unground pepper and as he found them he would quickly send them to the back of his throat and swallow them. He had learned the hard way that this practice was necessary, getting pepper ground down in your teeth (especially more than one) would result in discomfort for the rest of the meal and possibly the night.

Due to the run down nature of the family car Dad would take what he deemed to be the best route to anywhere. Usually this was so he didn't have to slow down at lights, wait at stop signs or give way on roads with more traffic. His chaotic driving would have been concerning, if not life affirming to most people as there were some definite close calls, but Hunter was used to it. There were small moments when you thought you were going to die, but those were only heightened by the fact that their mum would lean heavily into the windshield, expecting it to break, while hanging on to the door handle as if she was going to be propelled around the inside of the car and holding the front window might help provide some sort of safety. After she had stopped yelling at their dad it would all calm down again, until the next time.

That second nature was entirely a result of Hunter's early life and the journey he had already taken. Hunter was almost twelve and his younger brother would be ten at the end of the year, both had been to more places within Australia than most people had seen on television. Their dad was a bank manager and had been made to travel between different branches as demand required. Which means in that time they had travelled to Rylstone, Goulburn, Crookwell, Griffith, Canberra, Hillston, back to Griffith and a few more remote communities before eventually landing back in Orange. The distance between those places and the last were extensive, and the distance between some of those places and the nearest shopping centre could be just as vast. That lengthy distance travelled in the car was occupied with a few different activities. Talking to one another in the car, listening to his parents' choice of terrible eighties music, playing his brand new Gameboy (but only sometimes), or using his imagination.

Hunter had an amazing imagination, it had been essential to develop one quickly. Without enough time to develop long or meaningful friendships, or by spending an obscene amount of time in the back of a car, there had to be something to fill the void that was being occupied by nothing but loneliness. Books were the greatest outlet, whether it be at home or travelling. But when you had a bike and a whole lot of country all around, you didn't really need anyone else to provide entertainment when you could simply explore that space and create your own environments and stories.

As his dad pointed out the window and towards the school that both Alex and Hunter attended, Hunter slipped into playing one of his own simple independent games. Inspired by playing some video games, and by the prospect of seeing the same uninteresting things out his window, Hunter had devised a game which he called Super Finger Man. In Super Finger Man Hunter would look out his window holding up his fingers as if they were legs. His fingers could then seemingly jump between various buildings and objects but were never allowed to touch the ground. In town, shops and buildings were easy, they were so close together and the three second limit that his fingers could stay in the air was definitely manageable. When you turned to cross roads it became harder. You could jump on trees but no bushes, that was cheating, and the objects had to be beside the road and not in the near or far distance. It wasn't realistic for his fingers to be next to the road and then all of a sudden over a kilometre away. The challenge was what made it fun. Powerlines were some of Hunter's favourite things. His fingers could sprint, glide and leap easily along and between them. But sometimes in those country areas when powerlines disappeared they were gone for good, with very few objects left to jump on. That ate up lots of lives, and with only three to begin with the game would soon end.

It wasn't long before Alex would start playing as well, but, to Hunter's irritation, his fingers had powers like a super pogo stick or flying to keep his fingers in the air. Sometimes they took on abilities of characters from television shows or video games to stay in the air. Hunter didn't mind this, in fact sometimes he did it himself, but Alex would always turn it into a competition and Hunter would always lose, simply because in his head he played the game correctly whereas Alex had to win at all costs.

Hunter had managed to keep all of his lives in the game until they turned down a street and headed into a new development area. The buildings became fewer, in some instances they were only frames of newer developments, and the powerlines were nothing but big poles of newly cut timber that lay abandoned on the roadside. Hunter lost his last life just as the car pulled up. He told himself that he had somehow survived that game, but then shook his head because he had only really been competing with himself and he knew it was a lie.

Hunter's parents jumped out of the car first, before helping Hunter unbuckle and remove the still excited Scotty dog from his hold. The small pet had wet whiskers from all the drool he had released in the relatively short journey. They had discovered that he, Buster, would get car sick very easily and quickly so it was best not to take him on big journeys, and that was before you factored in how erratic their dad's driving was. They had learned this about their dog the hard way, but luckily Alex had been the recipient of that knowledge before anyone else.

When Hunter finally stepped out of the car he had a quick look around as he followed his parents. They were once more in a cul-de-sac, albeit a short and stumpy one unlike the one they currently resided in, and within it there were only a few things to see. The first was a house that was complete, with driveway and nothing else. The second was a cleared block revealing that there was another development about to be erected to the right of that house, and in between the two there was a long path stretching from the very end of the road to the area beyond. Back at the road entrance, which was only about twenty metres away, there was nothing but completely vacant blocks with for sale signs and big tufts of grass growing around and through them, suggesting they had been there for a long time. Further on down the road that they turned off to access the cul-de-sac, there was a small street which ended in a dead end. Big concrete barriers stood there but they were in part useless as the road didn't continue anyway. Trees, bushland, mountains of thorns and pastureland were all you could see in that direction. There was one other block being built down that road, which became the one behind the piece of land that Hunter and his parents had stopped at.

It was a weird shaped block, instead of being square like Hunter had imagined it looked like a crooked pentagon, judging by the boundary pegs which were easily seen by their fluorescent pink streamers floating in the overcast and windy day. The house which they had been coming to see was nothing but a single slab, nowhere near completion. It was odd shaped too, more like a boomerang than the square he had envisioned.

"What is that?" Alex demanded, managing to somehow put into words exactly what Hunter was thinking, but adding a mountain of extra disgust. He had walked Buster into the long and wet grass that sat at the curb edge. The dog was playfully sniffing around and marking its territory in multiple places.

"Try and keep the dog on the grass," Hunter's dad suggested before answering, which made sense because the grass that probably existed there before the block had been turned over was now gone, the grass present was rare to find and patchy at best. This absence of greenery was replaced with dirt, but after a recent dumping of rain this had been transformed into thick claggy mud. "And that is the start of what will be our new home."

"Until the next time," Hunter spat the statement, which was far more aggressive then he usually responded to his father. It had more sting than Hunter had intended, but his parents both seemed to ignore the comment mostly.

"Hopefully not," his dad replied. They all started walking on the various planks of wood which had been extended to allow some sort of passage way from the road to the large slab without getting anybody dirty, especially your shoes, thus leaving the slab relatively clean. Alex found the task hard. Despite Buster still being very young their small pet had a mind of his own and was already very stubborn, where it wanted to go it persisted to try and drag the person holding his lead in that direction. Mum shook her head as Buster finally made it to the slab under protest. His small paws covered in mud, as well as the long black and brown skirt of fur that had been dragged along underneath, amongst the wet grass and cruddy mud.

Hunter's parents started stepping out rooms that had no boundaries as of yet and talking to each other about where invented things would go and what it may look like upon completion. Hunter hadn't seen the plans to the new house so could not follow what they were saying, nor did he have the vision of an architect at this point in his life. He could see and understand basic things from the layout. He could tell where the driveway would be, the deep gouges in the mud from where one or a few trucks had been parked in the days prior still existed in front of the slab and leading out to the curb. He could also tell where some areas might be, like the bathroom, laundry and kitchen, but that was only because of the pipes which stood up randomly through the concrete.

Before Hunter could explore anymore a single car pulled into the street and parked in the garage of the house next door. Before Hunter saw who they were he assumed that one of the parents was a locksmith, as a white and blue van with advertising all over it sat in the driveway beside a big cage like trailer. He was quietly excited to see who actually emerged from within the garage, but he turned away to hide his interest. There was a man and a woman, who Hunter presumed owned the house together, and then following them came three children. Two were boys who looked like they may be similar in age to both Hunter and Alex. The third was a girl who was easily younger.

Both sets of parents came together on the roadside and introduced each other. The trip back along the planks proving to be a little more difficult for Hunter's dad than the original trip down to the slab. Hunter watched as the boys disappeared from view for a moment before re-emerging. The oldest had a soccer ball in his hand, and the younger had a scooter. From their driveway it was nothing more than a small leap over to the concrete slab.

Alex was at the far end of the area already, with the dog, and that is where the younger boy took off with his scooter. He attempted a few small jumps over the very limited steps that were present in the structure as he went. The other boy dropped the ball with a wet slap onto the concrete, dribbling it remarkably well between his feet, and came towards Hunter. Hunter suspected he was showing off, lowering his opinion of him for a first impression, but a moment later the new boy held out a hand to Hunter.

"My name is Shane," he offered and Hunter took the hand trying not to seem too eager or reluctant.

"Mine is Hunter," he replied. "My brother is over there. His name is Alex, the dog's name is Buster, he is only a pup."

"My brother is over there too, his name is James. He is a pain. Thinks he is real mad," Shane explained. "My little sister is over there." He pointed to the girl who was huddling around the legs of her mother. Shane's parents contrasted in the same way that Hunter's did. Both the Mums had their arms wrapped around their own waists, hiding shivers from the slightly colder day than usual. Winter was approaching but it hadn't really arrived yet. Both of them wore long woollen track pants and multiple layers of jumpers. The dads, however, both wore shorts and rugby jumpers. Shane's dad had thongs on despite the chilly breeze, where Hunter's had old school whiter than white sand shoes with his socks pulled up covering most of his shins. Both had a belly hanging over their shorts, but despite this they still stood very straight and erect with no sign of slouching.

The two boys wore similar daggy clothes like Hunter and Alex, although with designs that Hunter hadn't seen before and their shoes were replica basketball style with big thick tongues. James was smaller than Shane, and both Hunter and Alex as well, whereas Shane was the same size as Hunter but was hunched slightly forward so it looked like he was constantly shrugging towards Hunter. They had a slightly darker complexion, but it was only mildly darker than Hunter's skin as he seemed to have an almost constant tan.

Shane started juggling the soccer ball on his foot, scooping it over and over again until it eventually fell. At this point he looked at Hunter before attempting to do it again.

"So where are you from?" Shane asked Hunter, returning to focusing on keeping the ball in the air.

"From Orange," Hunter replied, "but we have only been here for a couple of years, maybe."

"Oh yeah," Shane replied. "What school do you go to?"

"My brother and I both go to Orange Public," Hunter answered. "You don't or I would have seen you."

"Nah I don't," Shane agreed. "We all went to Calare. I don't anymore. I am at high school, but I should still be in year six. I am a year young for school."

"So you are the same age as me?"

"If you are the right age for the end of primary school, then yeah I am," Shane replied. "So what else do you do?" He managed to keep the ball bouncing for longer that time but once it fell he just trapped it under his foot.

Hunter thought about it for a moment. This new kid seemed nice, he also seemed really cool. Hunter didn't want to say something that might not be liked by the other, so he remained silent. Shane looked at him for a moment and smiled. Hunter even thought for a second that Shane knew why he didn't reply. He started walking over to where his younger brother was still riding around Alex at the far end of the slab. Buster was trying to chase the scooter, more excited every time he went past. All it achieved was getting Alex to spin around quickly as he attempted to keep the lead from trapping him as it wove its way around. Hunter followed and smiled as Shane laughed. As they got closer it was clear that Shane's brother James was asking similar questions.

"We have moved heaps," Alex said before Hunter could get him to be quiet. "Hunter says we have been to over ten homes and places, same amount of schools. I can't remember them all but I reckon we have been to more." Hunter shook his head, more to get his brother to be quiet rather than telling him he was wrong, but that didn't stop Alex from talking. "Yeah," he continued, "in some of the places I remember we moved between two or three houses. Remember that two storey one? Remember that old Italian house? I think there were definitely more." Hunter's teeth were grinding visibly, but still Alex spoke on. "Hunter isn't excited about this place. He says as soon as we move in we will be moving out again." Hunter felt his face for the briefest of moments, imagining that his face was turning red, full red like a beetroot or tomato, with embarrassment. Shane continued to smile, James stopped riding his scooter.

"I don't think so," Shane eventually said after scratching his chin. He pointed over to where all the parents still stood. "Were any of those houses built by your parents?" Hunter put up one finger in reply. "One, probably a while ago. I don't think that your folks will want to build a house for you guys and then move away again. I might be wrong." Shane then dragged Hunter around by the shoulders warmly and faced out the back of the slab and pointed to what lay beyond.

Beyond the non-existent line of fences of both Hunter's and Shane's houses was a vast paddock. From where Hunter stood he could see what seemed like endless grass to the North at his left, and to the South at his right. There were tall mounds of grass and reeds at the base of a hill face in front of him, suggesting something that was hidden beyond. On top of that hill to one side there were houses, but they were hardly present in that area. There was a big grass mound and a couple of tall eucalypts standing before him at the base of that hill. Some of those trees were alive, but some were very much dead.

"With all those moves though, I doubt you have had many good neighbours," Shane said as they all looked. Hunter thought about it. There had been some good neighbours, very few that were kids, but he realised sadly that as good as they may have been he couldn't even remember their names.

"There have been a few," Hunter replied glumly revealing nothing more.

"You have never had any like us," stated James with a big smile while he twirled his scooter as he stood nearby.

"He is right," Shane agreed, and then swept one of his hands over the vacant paddock. "You have never had any neighbours like us, and when you finish moving in, or your parents start coming around more to check it out, we are going to show you just how good this place is." He clapped Hunter hard on the back.

"We will see," Hunter, not entirely convinced but still happy to hear the other boy's enthusiasm, added with little conviction.

"We will," said Shane, once more slapping Hunter at the base of his neck. "So not only will you be building a house, which will eventually be your forever home, but you will be able to build something that you haven't been able to yet."

"What?" asked Alex.

"Memories," Shane said once more following his hand as it swept across the scenery.

"With us," added James. He stuck his hand out in front of him, palm pointed down to the ground, and nodded at everyone to take it. "Together."

"Together," proclaimed Alex as he stacked his hand on top, still struggling to hold Buster still with the other.

"Together," Shane agreed, before standing face to face with Hunter, looking deep into his eyes. Finally Hunter bowed to the pressure, in his head thinking that he had nothing to lose anyway. He finally agreed though didn't believe the claim for even a second.

"Together," he said at last.

CHAPTER 2. KING SHANE

That winter was wet. Hunter had never seen a time where he had seen so much rain and so much water. It hindered the building process only marginally, but it also meant that the only time Hunter and his brother would ever visit the block they would be sitting in the car for what seemed like an eternity until their parents returned. There wasn't one occasion when he saw the new neighbours in that time, and he was surprised that he cared at all about that. The prospect of exploring an unknown area which seemed to offer so much promise, and with the possibility of doing it with friends, was quite warming. Hunter became fond of the idea over the duration of that wet season, but it remained only an idea.

Hunter and his brother were forced inside, which was remarkable because wet weather would usually see them both outside continuing to do the things they usually would. There was so much you could still do outside if it was wet. They would climb trees and shake all the droplets out of the leaves, which had somehow refused to fall despite autumn being left well and truly behind. You could jump on a wet trampoline and watch as water came up to meet you in the air as it was propelled up from the black mat. Sliding on the trampoline was more fun, even if you had it leaning on its side, but the boys were still aware that the prospect of a burn or getting any part of you stuck in the spring was still very high. Slamming into it as it stood on its side was just as fun, taking a ride as it tipped over dangerously before landing safely with a thud on its base.

They missed that they couldn't ride their bikes. Even though they were only allowed within the street they found more games to do out there. Starting at the very top of the hill, going as fast as you could while your tyres skidded initially due to the water, and then hitting the breaks at a designated tree at the roadside and seeing how far you skidded down the road. The boys had only gotten into trouble once before doing that. Alex locked his breaks and kept skidding, then a car came around the corner and he had panicked. He was unable to turn or start peddling his bike to safety. Luckily it had been dad's car, which hadn't been going all that fast, but not by any lack of trying. Alex still ran into it as dad had slowed down. He got the biggest growl of his life that afternoon.

There was another game they had invented with their bikes. They would place the back wheel in a puddle and one of them would peddle as hard as they could while the other just had to stand there and get covered in mud. The winner was the person who got in the least amount of trouble. That game didn't last very long.

But none of these, as well as several others, continued in that onslaught of water. Hunter and Alex protested frequently, but not with a massive amount of passion. The street which had come to resemble something between a river and a waterfall most days, definitely was reason enough to abandon the thought of outdoor play. They were also able to play the old original Nintendo for almost as much time as they wanted, only on weekends of course and never through the week. Hunter thought he played so much that the next time he played Super Finger Man in the car he would automatically hear the sounds of jumping from several different video game characters.

Hunter found that he started to read more in his solitude. Their two storey rental house in which they lived had several rooms which were usually out of bounds for play because they either had too many valuable or special items held within them, or they had a high percentage of hard or pointy surfaces in which their dad had said could result in injury of impaling, broken bones, and decapitation. But as long as Hunter was reading he was allowed to sit and do so in these areas, where Alex hated to read so he was never allowed in them.

Hunter changed position every time he read a different book. Sometimes he sat on the front veranda under cover, despite the constant deluge, and pull one of the heavy white metal chairs around to face a certain house. That house then became the focal point of many of the places in his book. One became a haunted house from spinechilling book he read, another became the house of Atticus Finch

12

simply because it had something that resembled a tyre swing in the front yard, and the house at the top of the hill became the hideout for a gang of thieves all because it had a flagpole in the front yard. Hunter's school had become both a fortified abbey and castle for teaching magic at the same time, and while he was there he would also read in different locations to expand his universe constantly; bringing more locations from fiction into his reality.

Then there was the discovery of what his grandfather called a grindstone wheel. The property in which Hunter lived had two backyards. One, which was closest to the house, was where they played predominantly. The other, further away and surrounded by fences, contained a couple of trees, which they climbed frequently and ate the fruit; one was a peach and the other a fig. In that second yard was an old and tiny abandoned shed. Within it there was a rusted old frame resembling an upside down bike, and held within that frame was an enormous wheel. However that big wheel wasn't made from rubber with metal spokes. It was made from solid grey granite or stone and from its centre to its edge it would have had a radius that measured half a metre. It took a lot of strength to move the heavy wheel regardless of how much you tried. Alex couldn't sit on the old chair and pedal hard enough to make it move so he had resigned himself to kneeling on the floor and pumping the foot pedals with his hands. Even then the stone had stopped moving by the time he tried to press something against it. Alex had also learned the hard way that he couldn't stop the big wheel from moving with his hands. Hunter had been using it more, mainly because Alex could hardly turn it at all, and in Alex's jealousy he tried to stop Hunter from doing so by grabbing the wheel as it spun. He was lucky to have his fingers left after that, but his long fingernails didn't fare so well. Dad had joked that Alex could have robbed a bank if his hands weren't so tied up in bandages, simply for the fact that his fingerprints were non-existent and they would never identify it was him.

Hunter would, on some days, and with permission to go outside despite the rain, run quickly through the unrelenting weather and hide out in that old shed. It was surprisingly warm and was built on a small mound so the water didn't dribble through underneath its ancient corrugated iron walls. There weren't even many spiders in there.

Hunter let his mind run wild in there and he would never have to leave the chair. There were days where he would spin the wheel and attempt to sharpen something, and on those days he became more scientist than dreamer. He tested out how well things like his mum's pruners or the old shearing scissors worked under the force of the sharpening device. As far as Hunter could tell he just scratched the metal harshly, rather than sharpening them with the devastating edge he had desired. There were other days where he tried numerous abstract things. He resolved that the grindstone wheel was not a useful pencil sharpener, nor potato peeler, or even dirty sock cleaner. Those attempts were all failures.

The other days, where he was just dreaming, the wheel wasn't used and in some instances it didn't even move. Those days were more interesting for Hunter as he himself transformed into many things. A blacksmith was an obvious choice, making armour for great knights, sharpening blades for sword wielding myrmidons, nurturing the tip of the most dazzling lances wielded by halberdiers and cavalry. There was a week where he made weapons only for villains. Sharpening fangs and claws, creating the darkest jewels for abominable acts, or simply smiling mischievously as some non-existent tyrant paid for his silence. Some dreams turned the wheel into something else entirely. It became a time machine, the golden loom for a sleeping beauty or even some odd kind of space age hover bike with blasters. Isolation and imagination were usually a great path towards creativity and fun, in any situation.

Finally the family made a return to the block with the promise to be able to actually get out of the car this time and walk around. The day was overcast but it wasn't raining so Hunter and Alex were excited about the prospect of being able to get out and run all over the vacant slab. That was not the case when they arrived though. Yes they could get out and check it out, however it was no longer a slab as Hunter had remembered. Despite the rain a lot had been done to the house. The frame had gone up, the charcoal coloured roof tiles were in place, the exterior brick walls were erected and the inside plaster board was nailed over fat yellow insulation strips in the walls. Hunter actually found that he was amazed at how much had been done in the torrid and torrential weather conditions. Inside was relatively clean as well, there were virtually no muddy footprints across the still concrete floor. The outside was a different story. Mounds of mud that had been transitioning between wet, dry, slop, then repeated several times again, were smeared across the ground and against deserted brick and timber at every entrance to the building. On the southern side it was virtually inaccessible due to the pool of dirty brown muck that lay there. Clearly someone had tried to gain entry that way, and failed, which was evidenced by a couple of leg sized holes and one of those containing a large abandoned boot.

The heavy slapping footsteps coming from Alex echoed throughout the house. It was clear that he wasn't overly keen on listening to their parents talk about which rooms were which as they all entered the house, but rather more focused on finding and claiming his own room. Hunter didn't blame him, it was forefront of his mind as well, especially considering the two of them had been sharing a room ever since they had arrived back in Orange. It wasn't unbearably bad, but the prospect of your own room was always exciting.

"This one is mine," Alex proclaimed as he ran into what looked to be the kitchen area, before realising that was in fact the case. "No probably not." He ran through all of the big living areas claiming each one, as Hunter travelled through them quietly, before dismissing the idea and shuffling quickly to the next. Eventually he came to the end of the hall and sighed triumphantly.

"This. This is it," he said and sat down on an upturned plaster bucket.

"I don't think so," echoed the voice of his mum from down the hall.

"It's not fair," Alex complained. "So you're telling me that you guys get your very own bathroom and walk in wardrobe and I don't."

"Don't forget the spa," his dad added smugly. "And yes that is exactly what we are saying." Alex got up and slumped on every wall down the hallway, covering his jumper in a layer of white dust. No sooner had he gone a handful of steps then there came a knock on what could have been called a door, but was instead a large bit of timber with a large nail hinge.

"Hello," boomed a voice. Hunter's parents quickly moved away to intercept who it belonged to.

"Hey neighbour," Hunter's dad replied when he recognized who it was.

"Phil," the man corrected.

"Come in Phil," dad waved the other man in. He was accompanied by the rest of the family as well. The daughter still clung to her mother's trousers as the boys strutted past looking around the inside of the house. Hunter suspected that they would have been inside before. Why not after all? There was no temporary fencing around the outside of the construction site, but perhaps now that they had been invited they could look at things with a bit more detail.

"Hey guys," shouted Alex. "Come check out my new room." James and Shane followed Hunter up the hall to where Alex had yelled from. Upon entering they saw Alex constructing what could only be described as a poor attempt at a drum kit. Alex smiled proudly before grabbing a couple of loose cut offs of wooden dowel and some discarded electrical wire. He struck all the varieties of improvised drum that he had assembled, ranging from near full plaster buckets, half empty paint tins, a dirty water container and a large packet of metal power point holders. James and Shane smiled at him, which Hunter suspected had more to do with his comical show rather than his complete lack of skill.

"What is that horrible racket?" called out Hunter's mum. This was greeted with a massive laugh from both Shane and James. "If that's you Alex you need to cut it out."

"She always blames me," Alex whined as he stopped striking the objects.

"That's because you are actually doing it," Hunter stabbed back.

"But someday it won't be me," he snarled at his older brother.

"Yeah, but then she won't be calling out at all because there will be no need," Hunter responded. Alex moped about on his makeshift seat, clearly not liking being told off, but he was greeted by yet more laughter.

"I have an idea," Shane's dad said popping his head around the corner as the parents arrived. "Why don't you two show these guys the back paddock?" Shane and James shrugged, nodding their heads in agreement. Hunter looked over at his parents and they gestured that it was okay.

"Make sure you come back as soon as we call," Hunter's mum stated.

"And don't get muddy and wet," added his father. The comment was greeted with a large smile from Phil and his two boys, and a look was shared between both of Hunter's parents. Nonetheless they all went to venture outside.

The quickest and easiest way to get outside was through the room which would become their parents' bedroom. Luckily the sliding door which formed the window was not yet attached properly, and the ground outside was not covered with the same level of muck as everywhere else. Despite the slab being level this spot seemed like the highest point of the house as the ground outside fell away after being excavated and a large two metre drop lay below them. Beyond that drop was everything they had seen all those months before when they had first arrived at the site.

Hunter and Alex just stood there staring. For a moment the other boys simply let them observe what was in front of them, before not long after, and rather abruptly, Shane hit them both hard on the shoulders and beckoned them to follow him. Hunter noticed how both Shane and James stepped on massive tufts of grass to avoid touching the mud which still had the look like it could turn into quicksand at any moment and suck them down beneath the surface, ending in a similar fate to the forgotten boot at the side of the house. Hunter let Alex go first and noticed that he stumbled on the solid trunk of some weeds and smaller tufts of grass. He observed that if you missed the middle and ended up standing on nothing but slim leaves or the tips of the blades you would definitely be touching the mud. If you jumped away to quick you would slide a little and your loss of balance could result in you landing in the muck. If you stood too long the sole of your shoe would suction and leave a big dirty stain halfway up which would be hard to remove. There would be no way that his parents wouldn't notice that. Hunter took even greater care.

"Welcome to my Kingdom," Shane declared from the front of the group, still hopping from grass patch to grass patch before standing strong with hands on hips as he surveyed what lay before him.

"Your kingdom?" scoffed James. "Since when? It has never been called that."

"This is," Shane started, jumping back to almost land on James. He grabbed his younger brother by the loose neck of his shirt as he threatened to let him go into a large pile of water filled mud. "My kingdom," Shane finished, leaning closer.

"Okay, okay, whatever," James reluctantly agreed for the moment. "Keep moving your majesty."

After a few minutes they finally came to the edge of the block's boundary, which was no further than ten metres but the precarious journey over the mud had been slow. Shane stopped hopping all over the place and started walking normally. The grass that the paddock had seemed to be filled with was different to what it appeared from the house. It did cover the majority of the land, with only a few small paths between the patches. However those patches were bigger than all of them.

"Those things are huge," Alex announced as he caught up with the two brothers. "They must be at least two metres tall each."

"At least," Shane agreed. He then kicked the nearest massive grass bush and watched as a huge curtain of water exploded from it. "We call this the labyrinth," he broadcasted, eyeing off his younger brother as if daring him to say otherwise. James, wisely, said nothing. "Try not to get wet." Shane and James both sniggered at the comment.

"And don't get lost," James added as they both disappeared.

"We are so dead if we go in there," Alex stated. The directive of not getting wet could usually be understood as having the words 'or else' added to the end. "What do we do? Follow them or go back?" Alex was concerned, and Hunter shared the same level of worry. He didn't want to get in trouble, especially because it was obvious that they were going to get wet amongst the towering grass fronds. But he didn't want to seem like he wasn't someone his neighbours could hang out with. That he wasn't cool enough.

"We're going in," Hunter stated simply.

"Okay, but you are wearing this if we get in trouble," Alex negotiated.

"Fine," Hunter agreed. "But you don't have to come in if you're too scared."

"I am not scared, I'm just not stupid. I am happy to go in, especially if it is your fault how we come out," Alex responded and followed Hunter into the depths.

Almost as soon as they stepped in the feeling and the surroundings changed. They were completely enclosed on all sides, the only obvious sign that showed they were outside was the swirling grey sky above them which appeared where a ceiling should have been. The route was easy enough to follow as there weren't too many trails leading away in different directions, but Hunter realised quickly that Shane and James had disappeared almost as soon as they had entered and Hunter had not caught up yet. He strained his ears, listening for the rustling of the grass up ahead. Hunter purposely kicked a grass patch nearby which shook water all over him. He heard his little brother laugh from behind him but he drowned out the sound as he listened for a somewhat similar noise up ahead. He followed the path like a tracker. Alex shook a clump of grass trying to mock Hunter but yelped suddenly looking at his hands.

"Aw man," he cried out. "That really hurts." Hunter could see that tiny blood droplets were beading their way along Alex's hands. The grass was razor like on the tips and tiny cuts had appeared all over Alex's fingers.

"We have to be careful," Hunter suggested turning back towards the path he was following. "Be quiet. We don't want to stay lost in this labyrinth."

"Labyrinth?" Alex exclaimed in disbelief, but the next moment he raced to catch up to his older brother, pressing almost into his back. The idea seemed to have startled him. "Just because Shane said that doesn't mean it is true."

Hunter was the opposite, he was actually enjoying the prospect of exploring the grass labyrinth. He wasn't even worried if he didn't find his neighbours, though obviously that was the ultimate destination and goal. Hunter remembered the old Greek legends he had read in the bookmobile when he used to live far out west in Hillston. That bookmobile would come into town every few weeks and share an assortment of books that the school didn't have the space or money to possess. Within the trailer walls he remembered finding several books based on legends and myths from all sorts of cultures based all over the world. All varieties of creatures lived within those stories, he remembered, but at this exact moment his mind couldn't go past what he had learned about the guardian of the labyrinth. The guardian creature which was called a Minotaur.

"Beware the Minotaur," Hunter surprisingly said out loud.

"A Minotaur," wailed Alex. "What's a Minotaur?" Hunter could feel his brother tremble alongside him despite his supposedly brave outlook.

"A beast that guards the labyrinth," he explained, "half man, half bull." Hunter wasn't sure if Alex believed him that such a thing existed but his younger brother didn't protest against the explanation. They continued to creep through the grass maze, Hunter finding that the ground itself was far damper in some areas than others. His feet sinking down slightly as he trod on water logged straw, the cold damp rising up to grab at the bottom of his socks from within his shoes. A quiet squelch and gurgling sounded from his feet, a moment later he heard that his brother had stood in a similar spot as he started sharing his own sounds. An extra sound emerged from somewhere nearby.

"What was that?" Alex asked, confirming that Hunter wasn't just hearing things.

"It sounded like a cow," Hunter replied truthfully.

"You're just saying that to scare me," Alex growled, "to make me think that there is actually a Minotaur in here." Almost as if summoned the call came again. This time there was no mistaking the unique sound of an animal mooing. Hunter heard his brother's loud gulp, before starting forward again with slightly more caution.

Hunter's thoughts jumped to other creatures he had read about, those that might also occupy the maze. A centaur crossed his mind, but he felt like they would be too big for these passages, and their tracks too obvious. A griffin was dismissed with similar thoughts. There were smaller creatures that could occupy the areas, or even more dangerous ones that Hunter couldn't remember the size of. Hunter turned his eyes to the ground lest a gorgon appeared and turned him to stone by simply looking at him, but once his eyes were there he found he was searching for signs of other creatures including big foot or hoof prints. They had walked only a few more metres before a crashing was heard suddenly from beside them and both boys were pulled into the thick razor grass.

"Aaaargh," yelped Alex startled. Hunter made no such sound, but that didn't mean he wasn't shocked. His alarm quickly subsided as he looked up and saw the smiling face of Shane, chuckling happily to himself.

"Sorry for grabbing you, sort of," said Shane pulling Hunter to his feet. "It was pretty funny to see your faces. But you have to be careful in here, you almost stepped right into the creek."

"The creek?" Hunter asked this time, immediately following from behind as Shane started to lead on. The grass was not as tall here and Hunter found that they were beginning to walk at an incline. Shane pointed off to the right through the thick reeds that seemed to appear out of nowhere. A few more steps and Hunter could clearly make out a divide and within that gap a heavily flowing waterway. The bubbling sound of it flowing by made him alarmed as to why he didn't hear it sooner. Hunter looked back to where he had been hauled over and noticed that he would have been maybe only one or two more strides away from stepping straight into that water. Shane seemed to read what Hunter was thinking and simply shrugged. This time James was behind both Hunter and his brother, as Shane led on in front he made sure they were safely together from the rear.

"This is the ramp that goes to the top of the grass mound," Shane explained, "this is my castle, though sometimes we call it Ayer's Rock because of its appearance, and you can see a whole lot from on top of my walls." A sarcastic laugh was heard from behind, and it was joined by another. No doubt James was rubbing off on Alex. Hunter and Shane both ignored them. Hunter instead understood immediately what Shane was talking about.

The tall grass became shorter by almost a metre. There were still huge clumps of it all over the wall like mound but they were easy to avoid and the whole world, it seemed, could presently be seen. Off to the left stood Shane's house with the timber skeleton standing beside it that was becoming Hunter's own dwelling. The long paddock seemed to stretch even further to the south than Hunter had thought, but then again it had seemed to expand endlessly in multiple directions. Hunter bought into the idea of this being a kingdom and the prospect that he was now standing inside a castle. Back behind him and off to his right the creek continued to follow alongside. There was a lower grass ledge shelf below them that was several metres wide and at the same level as the original labyrinth, and beside and below that ran the creek. A couple of tall eucalypt trees stood on the other side where a hill ascended to meet both a couple of old houses eventually with a street hidden beyond, as well as farm land and more seemingly endless paddocks. These paddocks contained multiple cows, one of which had decided to become the Minotaur in the labyrinth earlier. One of the trees had long since died but now lay out across the creek gaining access, although awkwardly, to both sides.

"A drawbridge and a moat," Hunter whispered to himself, but as no one else was really around it was no surprise that Shane heard him.

"A drawbridge and a moat?" Shane questioned. His confused look quickly transformed into a smile. "I can see that. You are buying into this idea of a kingdom aren't you?"

"If you are going to play why not imagine all the way?" came Hunter's quick response. He stopped as Shane halted in front of him. They had almost walked the entirety of the grass mound wall, which was probably only about thirty metres long but had felt like the Great Wall of China. Shane pointed down below them on the left of the mound, which was the side closest to their own houses.

"Below us, there is a big dam which stretches the entire length of the mound. It is grass almost all the way to the edge so if you don't know it's there you will probably fall into it without ever knowing what's happening," Shane explained, then turned his attention back over towards the end of the mound where they were walking. There was another big tree standing there but it was a light grey colour, with no visible leaves. It seemed to be very dead and used only as a nest of sorts for various birds, which was shown by the array of twigs and sticks gathered above its fractured trunk.

"See that tree?" Shane pointed it out, not waiting for a response. "Don't go near that tree." Before Hunter was able to ask why, Shane continued to enlighten him. "It looks like the grass continues to go all the way up to it, but it doesn't. The creek continues to flow hidden through that long grass and it is not strong enough to hold most people up. But even before that there is a swamp area, which is more like a bog. You step in there and you aren't going to lose a shoe, you are probably going to lose a leg and it is near impossible to get out of. As fun as this place is, and will be," he added looking excitedly at Hunter. "You never play out here alone. Do you understand?" Despite it feeling like he was being chastised by a parent, rather than warned by a friend, Hunter nodded his agreement.

"Seeing as this is a castle, I have one more thing to show you," Shane shared eagerly. "You can see it first, just take a few steps that way." Hunter obeyed. He was interested as to what it could be, especially as he would see it before his brother did. He followed the direction, but all the while he was thinking of turrets, canons, flag poles and towers. The last thing he expected was to fall.

Down he tumbled, almost as soon as he took one step too many. He was slowed somewhat by the long grass which still protruded from the side of the mound. Despite his fall being broken on the way Hunter still hit the ground hard. His face felt like it was being stabbed by knives made from straw, several of them invading his nostrils, mouth and eyes. He spat them out as he rose to his feet, feeling at all the patches of his open skin where the razor grass had serrated his flesh and in some places his clothes. He turned and looked back up to where the other three boys smiled and laughed openly at him. Hunter was shocked, he must have fallen almost five metres.

"Beware the trap door," Shane called down. Hunter replied with a sarcastic smile as he continued to wipe broken foliage off of his body. The three boys followed a slim track down the side of the mound. Whilst it was still steep it was also easily negotiable and far more ideal than simply falling off the edge. Shane walked down and gave Hunter the familiar tap on the arm before beckoning him to follow once more. Hunter resisted the urge to hit his brother as he smugly walked by. Hunter was glad they had taken so long to come down to him, it gave him the time needed to compose himself and force away the tears that had started to rise.

The long grass became shorter here as it made way for harder dirt that had been scraped from the blocks. They skirted the edge of the construction sites before starting to climb a large hill, but this one was all brown and grey with no green. Shane waited for them at the top which took far longer than originally believed. It was a steady but steep incline and all of them were puffed by the time they got to the top.

Shane stood cross armed at its summit as if in some sort of trance. The man made hill stood taller than all the nearby houses by a good couple of metres but Shane wasn't looking that way. He stood facing an expanse beyond which was filled with a steady downward slope, an opened creek, more trees, shrubs and blackberry bushes than you could count and an expanse of mystery.

"One day this will all be my kingdom too," he said finally. He pointed over towards where the road stopped. "One day they will continue that road and when that happens all that you see before us will be unlocked. It will all be part of my domain where we can do whatever we want." His short speech was inspiring, as was his long pause. That lasted right up until the point where James burst out laughing, unable to hold back any longer. Shane turned and growled at him, and then he smiled.

"So you guys weren't supposed to get wet or dirty huh?" he questioned both Alex and Hunter. Hunter didn't have to look down to know that his clothes were wet, dirty, covered in blood and ripped in several places.

"Don't worry," said James, "our old man would have told your parents that there was no chance that you guys were coming back clean."

"Maybe," Shane added, inviting concern to come rushing straight back at his new neighbours. "So how about a race then?"

"A race," queried Alex. "Where to?"

"From here back to your place of course," James answered. Hunter looked down at the proposed track down the hill they had just climbed, which although not long was covered in rocks and dirt. He also noticed where it had split, as rain had created little canyons all across its surface and streaked down to the hill's base. That told him that someone was definitely going to roll their ankle. Again Shane saw the look that was showing on Hunter's face.

"Come on, it will be fine," he cheered them on. "Plus if you win I will proclaim you King for a year."

"That's not even a thing," protested James.

"Then don't race," offered Shane.

"Oh I am racing," James scoffed. "And I will beat you and be called King for a year. Don't think I won't rub your face in it either." Shane smiled at the statement, then looked at Hunter and Alex.

"What about you?" he asked. Both brothers looked at each other and then nodded. They made a makeshift starting line before abruptly Shane yelled out 'Go'. Shane took off quickly, despite his slumped posture he could move pretty fast. James was right behind him and Alex tailed James. Hunter had been caught off guard and started last. He quickly gained speed as they all did and it wasn't long when he turned his focus from sprinting downhill to simply trying to stay upright without falling over. Hunter's running stance changed from leaning forward to bending backwards as he tried to slow the pace of his feet while gravity forced him down.

Alex was the first to go down. He slipped on some rocks, almost hyperextending his leg in the process, and jolted dangerously before being propelled into a roll down the hill. James, startled by Alex's fall turned to see what had happened. He never saw the small canyon he stepped in as he seemed to twist his ankle, falling hard shoulder first into the ground a moment later. Hunter ran past both of them, the thought of helping the other two not once crossing his mind, and catching up to Shane as he descended. Hunter started believing that he would reach Shane and pass him, which meant he would win and be named King, proclaiming to all that he was now ruler of the Kingdom. His delusions of grandeur were short lived. His foot sucked down and was stuck fast into a deep pocket of mud. His shoe was tugged clean off of his foot. Hunter felt his whole body leave the ground and tumble forward into an almost perfect front flip. He seemed to fly through the air for an age before landing harder than he had done previously down the trapdoor. Air escaped from him and he struggled to obtain it again as he lay winded on the ground. He slid maybe a few metres on the steep area of the lower hill as he continued to search for breath, he couldn't talk, he couldn't suck in air, and it felt like an elephant was sitting on his chest. He had a massive headache and a moment later he was starting to panic, thinking that he was not going to get any oxygen back into his lungs and he would die. Then the pressure gave way and he was relieved by the sudden cold gush that exploded into the space behind his sternum.

Alex walked down the hill as Shane pulled Hunter to his feet, throwing the retrieved shoe that was completely encased with mud.

"Good luck with that one," Alex sniggered, knowing full well that regardless what Shane's dad had said Hunter was definitely going to wear it for that.

"Are you alright?" Shane asked Hunter with concern. Hunter simply nodded, tucking his hands behind his head and continuing to draw in deep breaths. "That's good to hear, but unfortunately being alright doesn't make you the winner." James groaned as he limped the last few steps from the hill.

"Here we go," James said, rolling his eyes.

"There can be only one King," Shane seemed to stand straighter than Hunter had thought possible, his slouch disappearing in the moment. "And that person is me. Now because you all lost you must tell everyone."

"We aren't doing that," James protested.

"Say all hail King Shane," Shane demanded.

"No," replied James angrily.

"Say it," roared Shane. There was silence for a moment as no one else spoke.

"Fine," James finally agreed. "All hail King Shane."

"Louder," commanded Shane, "and all of you." The three remaining boys looked once at each other. Then all together, with about as much excitement as a lawn mower in water, they yelled with satisfaction showing from Shane.

"All hail King Shane."

CHAPTER 3 – ONLY GO WHERE I CAN SEE YOU

There were some tell-tale things that changed after the last events at the block and within the back paddock. The first was that now Hunter and his brother had to ask whether or not they were allowed to go and spend time playing out in the paddock either by themselves or with their new neighbours. They usually didn't have to ask though, and that was because of a second stipulation. Which was that Hunter's parents, or more accurately his mum, had gone and purchased a whole bunch of ugly, disgusting and cheap clothes that could be, in her words, trashed. These were to be used whenever they were allowed to go roaming in the paddock, the fact that they were rarely permitted in them suggested that there was no point in asking in the first place.

They were also advised to bring either homework or a book to read while on site or sitting in the car to pass the time. That amount of time could be a small amount of minutes or numerous and lengthy hours. In one instance their dad had been talking to the builder for so long that the sun had set and, considering there were no street lights erected yet, both Hunter and Alex had absolutely no chance of achieving the task they had been given. Due to the lights diminishing and the inability to read both boys would eventually engage in a light brawl, which was usually started because Alex could not do anything but annoy others when he was bored and Hunter would only put up with so much before he snapped.

The time always seemed longer still despite the waiting, because while Hunter would gladly read for hours Alex would not, only doing so under duress. What he would do, however, was squirm and grunt and groan until Hunter developed overbearing murderous intentions.

Luckily, in most instances, their parents would return shortly before those intentions were put into actions.

One thing that didn't change though was the weather. It was still bad, in fact it was possibly worse. It meant that regardless of wanting to go and play in the new landscape, which they had only just started to discover, they had no choice but to stay inside. The paths in the tall grass through which they had previously trekked became flooded. The creek rose so high that you could see it bubbling up, from the safety of the house, flattening all the tall reeds in its wake and making it completely obvious as to where its location actually was. That same water flooded downstream as well. Hunter observed the water surrounding the still standing dead tree that Shane had pointed out. It had become more of a dam than a creek with sticks and litter scattered all through that space as the debris attached to the sinking grass patches wherever possible. That same water tried approaching the house as it flooded the paddock, but as the house was already built up those extra few metres, as well as being on a block with slopes that gently fell away from the building, there was very little concern.

Hunter became even less concerned to play over the next few weeks. The rain stayed constant for a while, but when it eventually subsided Hunter was away on a school camp. He travelled to a place called Point Wolstoncroft, just North of Sydney in New South Wales, and the drive took five hours by bus, or, as the driver insisted frequently, by coach. All of his year six cohort went and it was one of the things they had been looking forward to for most of the year. Even in the short time that Hunter had attended the school the trip had taken on a legendary status all its own so the students really wanted to attend regardless of their connection to the school. On the trip he was able to explore, partake in interesting and new sports, and just generally enjoy himself. Apart from great memories he brought back a boomerang as a souvenir, but like most things Hunter possessed it was more of an ornament than a tool for using. His focus on preserving what he owned and taking great care in its longevity was something he took pride in.

He had also been able to hang out with his friends. Although he hadn't been able to keep many in the past he had accrued some fantastic ones in his time at school. Few of those had still ventured over to his house, but Hunter felt that finally he had the foundations of several long life relationships. It was comforting, like discovering something you never knew existed but realised you couldn't really do without it.

The boomerang managed to live on Hunter's small desk for roughly two weeks before it could do so no more. It, along with all the rest of his few possessions that were not already stored away in the rental house's garage, was to be placed in boxes and packed up.

"What are we doing that for?" Alex, as usual, asked the most obvious of questions.

"The new house is almost finished," their mother revealed. "All the rooms are nearly completed, we are just waiting on final touches like lights, and carpet and bathroom stuff to get done. We are going to go and see the builder about those things tomorrow. Then we will get ready to get the keys so we can start moving in."

There actually wasn't that much stuff to pack away in the room. The only things that the boys had were the double bunks they slept on, a tiny desk that they shared which held some small trinkets that both the boys owned, a bed side table each, and a large wardrobe that housed their combined clothes. It was more devastating to pack away the few videos that they owned, but even more so to pack away the old Nintendo. Hunter seemed to think that the absence of all these items could make a few short weeks seem like an everlasting eternity.

When the next day came both boys were about as excited as ever. In fact you had never seen someone who was told to put on their trashy clothes and old smelly shoes so happy before. They were going to be able to go and play. Hunter could tell that despite their new attire, and regardless of the change in weather into lovely spring time sun and warmth, that his mother had no faith in her sons. Extra towels were placed into the boot of the car just in case.

It was a Saturday morning, which Hunter knew from recent experience meant that his parents were prepared to have quite a lengthy conversation with the builders. This could last for hours, the only tell-tale sign that it would stop was that they had to have fish and chips for lunch which was locked in by their dad to be eaten no later than 1pm. The time frame for being able to play and explore was roughly about three hours then, more than enough.

The asphalt in the street, which was already worn from so much traffic from all the tradesmen attending the construction sites, was still wet from an early spring dew that had lingered after winter. The Sun was rising quickly sending steam from the enduring water up into the air, creating a low lying fog over the surroundings.

Hunter followed his parents onto the site with Alex close behind them. They didn't have keys for the house yet and it was still in lock up stage so his family had no access. Hunter thought that the word, 'complete', that his mother had used was a stretch. Sure the building looked almost finished but everything that surrounded it was still nothing more than mud, mess and puddles. The wooden border for the driveway was set in place, as was the wire mesh that lay beneath it, but there was nothing else that Hunter could see outside of the brick work walls of the house.

"The driveway and the paths aren't done," Hunter's dad said aloud to his mother. It seemed like an obvious observation but Hunter knew the undertones of his father's words which suggested that both of those things should have been completed already. It also meant that Hunter's dad was not starting this outing in the most positive light. He subconsciously locked that knowledge away as useful whenever he was talking or acting around his father. He knew that Alex wouldn't have, so Hunter also realised that he could either use that information to help his younger brother or to really put him in it. Hunter had not decided which yet, but considering they usually shared a consequence it was wise to use it for helpful purposes.

The family started the journey by orbiting around the south of the house, the side which was closest to the newly befriended neighbours. Hunter had discovered that their last name was Spigot, which was much easier than thinking of them as the neighbours all the time.

There was no fence erected around the boundaries or between the two households yet so Hunter and his family could see everything in their yard. There was a small swing set with monkey bars and a slippery dip, but apart from a small outdoor area with a rotting and seemingly abandoned wooden table on a concrete alfresco area there was sparsely more than dirt within the neighbours' yard.

Hunter was trying to see if they were home though, perhaps the boys would come and hang out with them whilst they were on site. He checked all the windows from a distance, and kept looking back to where they had left the garage behind just in case they walked out to join them from there. The curtains were pulled closed and not a single bit of light from within penetrated the outside world. Hunter decided they were probably not home, but also thought it may be too early for them and they might still be sleeping.

Hunter stepped over randomly strewn bricks and wooden planks but was amazed to see that the boot that had been swallowed by the mud still remained. It had been almost completely encased by hardened mud, and that was despite the damp colour of dark brown, which suggested sticky mud was still present, was still evident thanks to the morning dew. Hunter saw his father shake his head again and resisted the urge to laugh. Someone was going to get it.

Hunter imagined it would have been interesting to see his family at this moment. Both he and Alex were in the daggy clothes that they had been designated for playing in the muck, and they were not ashamed of just how ugly those clothes were. Their parents wore completely different attire. Hunter's mum walked around in jeans, a nice rugby style jumper she had bought from a shop, work style fancy black shoes, with her hair done up with a ridiculous amount of hairspray, a mountain of make-up and her most expensive jewellery. His dad had the usual sand shoes, sport socks pulled high up his shins, stone coloured shorts, Hunter assumed he had a belt but it was hidden under the overhang of his belly, and he had his thick black hair combed over.

They finished a lap around the outside where again his father shook his head with the lack of a path and concrete alfresco area. At least they had these pegged out in the backyard where they hadn't been on the neighbour's side of the house. These pegs revealed the possibility of a big retaining wall leading down to stairs into another large concrete area, as well as a second driveway leading out to the back paddock. By the time they rounded back to the front there was a four wheel drive ute parked on the front of the block with several people jumping out quickly.

"Sorry we are late," said an older balding man who Hunter suspected was in charge of the build. He also assumed that the man had seen the overly polite smile on his dad's face that suggested he was less happy than he appeared, as he quickly hurried along the rest of the occupants within his vehicle.

"It's probably best if you guys go and play now," Hunter's mum suggested quietly to the boys.

"Cool," replied Alex. "I saw some bricks and wood on the other side of the house. . ."

"Further away," their dad demanded with that same smile on his face.

"Can we go and see if the neighbours want to play too," Hunter attempted the request.

"Fine," his dad snorted with scorn. It was clear he just wanted the two boys gone. His smile grew ever wider as he started to swagger his large frame over to the new arrivals.

"That's fine," mum repeated. "Just be polite when you ask and only go where we can see you from the house." Hunter nodded and then elbowed Alex who also agreed. Both boys quickly fled the scene, making their way over to the completed maroon brick worked driveway of the Spigots'. They both waited until everyone else was safely inside the now unlocked garage before proceeding with the invitation.

"You knock," said Hunter.

"No you knock," argued Alex.

"Well you ask then," stated Hunter.

"No," debated Alex, "it was your idea. You can knock and ask." Hunter was prepared to fight, but realised that for once his brother was making some sense. Hunter didn't want to because it was not something he usually had to do. He had not had neighbours of the same age that he could play with before, and therefore he had never really had to go and knock on a door to ask if they could play. It was surprisingly terrifying. He knocked a couple of times and then stood back.

"That wasn't loud enough," Alex said negatively, which was what Hunter had been thinking. He stepped forward again and gave a much louder knock, hoping that he wasn't going to have the door ripped off its hinges and get yelled at for being impatient. Both boys waited silently. Hunter could hear his heart beating harder and could taste the chill in his spit as they waited in fresh shade of the front door awning. They both strained their ears for any clue that suggested Shane and James were active inside the dwelling. After what seemed like a lifetime of no response Hunter conceded that the neighbours probably weren't home. They walked away around the front of the house and over to the foot path which stood uselessly off to the side at the moment. If you wanted to access the back paddock you could do so from anywhere. There were no fences on any block and some blocks were not even being developed yet. Eventually it would be useful but it was now simply a small route in which your shoes could escape the complete wet provided by unkempt weeds and secret holes of sludge.

When they made it to the end of the path they walked along the border of the Spigot's property and then their own. The grass was just much shorter here underfoot, mostly yellow in colour or dead amongst patches of rock and dirt. Hunter noticed that the labyrinth of pasture was also prominently easier to navigate at the present. The long blades still reached high above both boys' heads but the weight from the morning dew dragged them down so they hung low. He could see even now though that the sun was evaporating the droplets and the grass was slowly starting to reshape back into its all spire like structure.

Hunter led Alex over to where he knew the dam was. They hadn't actually been to its side to see it yet and before they trod over previous paths Hunter felt that it should all be explored. He remembered Shane saying that if you weren't looking for the dam you would miss it and most likely fall in. He didn't have far to travel but even then the path was obstructed. Hunter pushed aside big walls of grass to traverse through their blockade and beyond towards his destination. He swore in his childish way as he realised that never before had he put much thought into why the long leafy part of grass was called a blade. Yes they somewhat appeared like a weapon resembling a sword, knife, dirk or dagger, but these were also razor sharp. Each blade bit into his flesh like a paper cut, opening up countless feather thin wounds in the process. This would have been manageable in the short term if not for the fact that there was a seemingly endless progression of the things.

"Sherbet," Hunter's low-level swearing got louder receiving laughter from Alex who so far had been avoiding the worst as he followed closely behind his bigger brother. Hunter clenched his hand into a fist as if it would help with the pain. He had just obtained a cut within another cut. He bit his lip and squished his eyes together to try and supress tears and a sound escaping him. He decided to take a different approach, wrapping his arms around his body and trapping his hands beneath his pits. He shouldered his way through the tall grass tussocks, battering his body this way and that, losing his balance countless times until finally he stumbled up a small incline onto the top of the dam wall.

"We finally made it," Hunter said a little too excitedly.

"Yeah," Alex said pushing past his brother, "but we still have to go back." Hunter shuddered. He simply stood for a moment looking at the dam in front of him as his brother skirted carefully around the outside. It sat in the shadow of the grass mound which hid the sun with its height at this time of the morning. It made the area colder, but Hunter imagined that when the Sun rose completely, and with it the mist from the evaporating dew and steam, that the temperature would rise quick enough. The dam was probably about twenty metres wide which meant it followed alongside most of the grass mound which towered above it on one side.

"There are rocks everywhere," shouted Alex as he reached the opposite side to Hunter. "Piles of them, and bundles of sticks too." Hunter glanced around at his feet where he too noticed that there were piles of objects on the ground. He picked up a small stone and rubbed its surface. The small folds of skin at the edge of his cuts grabbed at the rock sending tiny sensations of pain through his fingers. He slipped his hands into his long sleeved shirt before he continued, adding a small amount of security to his trembling fingers, while wondering why he hadn't considered to use his clothing as protection earlier. Hunter noticed that the rock, and all the others that were piled around him, was of a particular shape. It was long, wide, smooth and flat. Perfect for skimming. Hunter managed to get his fingers around the edge of the stone, with great difficulty from within his sleeve, and skim it close to the edge of the water. He counted. One, two, three, plop, gone.

"I can do more than that," Alex boasted before the rock had even sunk. He grabbed one of his own and quickly skimmed it back towards Hunter. He managed to skip it once before it spun away and then sunk on the next strike of the water. Hunter smiled knowing that Shane and James must have assembled these for this exact reason, and now Hunter and Alex were quickly reducing the pile. He looked at the sticks and saw some big sheets of bark there too.

"Hey I have an idea," Hunter called over to his brother.

"Yeah. What?"

"How about we play battleship?" Hunter suggested. He would use the bark as the ship and the stones could be the weapons to hit them.

"I don't want to play battleship," Alex whined.

"That's because you will lose," Hunter goaded his younger brother, knowing exactly how successful it would be.

"I am going to smash you at battleship," Alex said arrogantly, it hadn't taken much to persuade him. Hunter explained the rules quickly. They would take it in turns skimming rocks trying to hit the other person's bark. If your bark floated past the centre first then you won. If you had all your bark broken and sunk you would lose. Simple.

"I am going to go first," Alex demanded.

"Fine," Hunter agreed, "but this isn't a rock throwing game, it's a rock skimming game of battleship. You have to skim the rock off the water, and sound nautical at the same time."

"Nautical?" Alex queried.

"Yeah, like Pardy," Hunter replied. Pardy was the common name they called their grandfather. Alex seemed to understand, seeming to remember all of a sudden that their grandfather had been an officer in the Australian Navy, whilst still thinking for a moment about what to say.

"Whoop, whoop," he yelped out trying to sound like a ship's alarm. "Enemy sighted, commence evasive manoeuvres. Target locked on. Launch." He threw his rock at one of the five decent shaped battleships that Hunter had picked. The projectile missed but was actually pretty close, only just bouncing over the top, showering it with a small spray of water.

"Miss," Hunter shouted, "we are under attack. We must move quickly to take the advantage." Hunter threw his own rock in reply. He missed as well, but he noticed that the ripples that were created pushed back his brother's ships nearby.

"They have underestimated us crew. Let's show them what we are made of," Alex declared. He threw another rock but this one barely skimmed, it almost went straight at its target. He managed to hit it as his rock spun sideways, splintering the side and lodging into the top. The piece of bark which represented Hunter's ship sank. Hunter gritted his teeth, biting back the urge to suggest that his brother had cheated. Hunter looked on as some of Alex's ships started getting closer to the agreed halfway point, a stick protruded from the centre of the dam suggesting a log was probably hidden under there.

"You sunk my battleship," Hunter remarked sourly, still resolute in his belief that the game should still be played properly regardless if he was winning or not. With some force Hunter skimmed his own stone back in reply. Surprisingly to him it hit the target he was aiming for on its second bounce, but it also hit just underneath the piece of bark forcing the light object to flick up into the air and land on another of Alex's ships. They both sunk.

"Hey no fair, you cheated," he whinged. Ignoring his own efforts just before. Alex discarded the stone in his hand and picked up a whopping great rock that had been half buried in the muddy dam wall. "We have to change tactics commander, destroy them now." He heaved it with all his might and the rock managed to sail in the slightest of arcs before slamming heavily into the water, taking with it the second of Hunter's ships. The enormous splash that came as a result sent waves across the surface and pushed back the last two ships that each boy possessed. Hunter gritted his teeth. His brother had ignored the rules twice but Hunter was not going to do that. He picked up a super flat stone and thought long and hard about his shot. His aim was to skim it behind his own ship causing it to move forward again and towards the winning point, whilst bouncing over that ship and trying to hit his brother's. It somewhat worked, except his stone landed behind his brother's ship giving it a boost. Alex cheated again, throwing multiple rocks at the same time into the water behind his and a couple at Hunter's. The to and fro continued. The nautical language turned into something resembling pirate talk and it looked hopeless.

"It's over me hearty," Alex crowed with hands on his hips. His last remaining ship ventured closer to the winning zone. Hunter looked on and felt like he had only one shot left to end the game in his favour.

"Fire at will commander," Hunter said to his stone before bending down low. He had pulled his hand out from his sleeve for this throw, he knew it would hurt but he had to do it to stand any chance. He skimmed it. Once, twice, three times. Hit! His heart leapt, but the bark stayed afloat. It did not sink.

"Noooooo," he said as he slumped to his knees, holding his pulsing hands.

"Victory is mine," yelled Alex as he started to dance upon, and almost falling from, his side of the dam. Hunter looked down at his hands and then felt his short but scruffy hair fill with a cool slight breeze. He looked up and saw that the same cool breeze was causing ripples on the water. It stilled both ships for a moment. Hunter looked on with interest and Alex met his gaze with a concerned look. Then the breeze picked up and the whole game changed.

"Nooooo," Alex yelled this time, picking up an armful of rocks trying to force his ship to float back in the other direction.

"Avast," Hunter crooned now. Hands returned inside his sleeves he stood triumphant with hands on his hips. It was inevitable now that Hunter would win, and he did, but that only got Alex down for half a second.

"Well you won that game," Alex said, sounding almost congratulatory, but there was a reason for that. "But that is because you picked it. I'm picking the next one."

"Okay," Hunter seemed confused.

"First one to the top of the mound wins," Alex stated. "Ready? One, two, three, go."

"Whoa, wait," Hunter replied but it was too late. Alex was already stampeding his way towards that high wall which rose from the edge of the dam and became the side of the grass mound. Hunter ran around the edge of the damn to catch up, looking up at what his task had so quickly become. Above him resembled a cliff face with protruding grass clumps which were the only things to grab hold of and stand on. The rest of that wall was a mix of collapsing dirt and buried rocks.

Alex, although stumbling frequently, was already a quarter of the way up the part of the wall he had chosen to scale. Hunter started to follow and knew as soon as he started that it would be hopeless. He couldn't climb with his hands buried in his sleeves, but he couldn't grip anything with his severely cut fingers anyway.

"You're not going to beat me this time," Alex roared triumphantly. Hunter didn't argue. He didn't even contest. He simply walked around the base of the grass mound which was easier to traverse than the rest of the paddock and arrived at the base of the mound where he had first set foot upon with Shane the last time he was here.

"You lose," said Alex panting heavily, when Hunter arrived. It seemed despite Hunter's slow march of defeat Alex had still only just managed to have completely scaled that side in the same time. A mental note for another time that it wasn't the fastest nor safest route.

"I can't say that it was fair, but yep you beat me," Hunter acknowledged. "I am surprised you didn't fall back into the dam."

"I know," Alex nodded his agreement. "I did think that I would at one stage, I even fell down a little bit. Probably won't go up that way again." Again Alex put into words what Hunter had already surmised. The pair looked around them, each remembering what they had been shown the last time. They could see the tall eucalypt, which towered above them so it was hard to miss even when they were near the damn. They also saw the fallen trunk which had become a bridge over a rapidly flowing creek. Hunter had noticed last time that there was a small rock path across the creek which he had hoped to hop across to explore the other side, but that path was presently completely submerged.

"How about a race?" Alex said interrupting Hunter's thoughts. He was still panting.

"A race?" asked Hunter curiously.

"Yeah, from one end of the mound to the other," Alex continued presenting his idea. Hunter looked at the mound and remembered that there was a high path and a low path. He scanned both of them quickly and noticed that the top mound had more grass clumps but they were shorter and a path could easily be traversed between them. The lower path had less clumps of grass but the blades screened in several spots and were frequently random in their position. It looked like the bottom road would be quicker if it wasn't for those obstacles.

"Fine," Hunter agreed, "but I am running the high path and you are on the bottom." He watched as Alex's eyes lit up.

"Deal."

"And then there is no more competing, we are just going to check the rest of this place out," Hunter urged, thinking of his still aching hands and the pressure competing had put on them. He looked around at the things he could return to look at and investigate after, then he took his starting position. Hunter would have to run uphill at an angle for a few metres before his path flattened whereas Alex had a flat road straight from the start. His little brother had never beaten him in a race before, but that didn't mean he was any less eager to do so. Hunter let Alex call out the start and then the race began.

They both stumbled at the beginning. The ground was still damp there and flattened grass made the ground greasy. Hunter lost Alex to view almost immediately as he climbed the grass mound and a curtain of grass blades separated them both. Despite taking the easier path Hunter struggled to get speed. Almost every step he made fell on awkward ground which made him feel like he was going to roll or sprain his ankle, or worse. He maintained a fast yet cautious pace and despite not being able to see his brother he knew where he was the entire time. Alex was calling out sneers and insults from his path down below. He was like a beacon showing Hunter exactly where he was based off his voice. The mound wasn't that long in comparison to most things. The length of it should have had the space covered in seconds but Hunter almost immediately knew it was going to take him at least a minute to travel along his easier path. He managed to gain most of his ground and was making greater progress when he noticed he was about three quarters across its length. He also noticed that he could no longer hear his brother.

"Are you going to beat me now?" Hunter called out, eagerly awaiting the return call that would tell him where Alex was located. He was greeted with no sound. He had been smiling with the thought he had beaten the challenge that the path had given him, and he hadn't had to pull out his hurting hands from within his sleeves. He suddenly wasn't smiling now. He suspected his brother was ignoring him, trying to win or trying to trick him. "How far away are you?" Hunter called again. He managed to run to the side of the grass mound and look down to where the other path was. The difference in height was now several metres, but Alex could not be seen. The finish line could be seen on both levels and Alex was not there either. Hunter continued to probe the slowly swaying and rustling grass below with staring eyes and found nothing. With his senses suddenly heightened he started to hear splashing and then a gurgling sound. Hunter started rushing back along the top to where he heard the sound. It wasn't long until he found it.

"Alex," he called out as he found his brother. He was in a terrible predicament. He had fallen into a small inlet from the creek that been completely covered in grass and dropped vertically down for about a metre. The creek couldn't actually be seen as it was covered in a thick sheet of clover, but that same clover was keeping Alex from swimming and it looked like he was sinking. The edges of that pit resembled the cliff at the dam wall, and the fact that Alex was struggling and begging for help was enough for Hunter to know he was in trouble. A thought immediately smashed into him. If he jumped down onto that lower level he would be out of sight. He didn't care that he might get in trouble, particularly as his brother was in danger, but if he jumped down it meant that no one could see where he was, or possibly hear him, and that meant the possibility of getting no help at all was huge.

Hunter turned back towards the house which he could see more clearly now that the earlier fog and mist had finally lifted, and started jumping up and down waving his arms frantically. He called out for his parents but he knew they would still be inside, and there were no windows that pointed out from the house to face his location. He turned back and saw Alex grapple at reeds and grass before grasping some that wouldn't hold his weight. He went down again, Alex was struggling.

"Help!" Hunter yelled the loudest he could muster, jumping up and down for a moment longer, but then he knew he had to help regardless if he was out of view or not. He tried finding an easy way to get down but then just slid down wherever he could manage, tumbling painfully down to that second level. He rushed carefully to the edge of the pit ensuring he didn't fall in alongside his brother. He slid his shoes slowly through the grass until he found the hidden edge and brought himself towards it. Alex still splashed about with panic, only just managing to keep his head above water.

"Please help Hunter," Alex pleaded desperately. Despite his face being covered in water Hunter could see the fear filled tears of his little brother. Hunter grabbed hold of what he thought was a long and sturdy clump of grass, strong enough to take his weight for a small duration of time, and scaled his way down to his ailing brother. Pain immediately shot through his palms and body as fresh cuts were sawed into his already battered hands. He would not let go, even though he felt the grass become warmer as it was smeared with his constantly oozing blood. Hunter let his feet follow the flow of the pit wall until they were filled with water and he could no longer safely descend without submerging himself and losing his grip. He looked over and saw that his brother was almost within reach.

"Reach over and grab my hand," called Hunter. He hung on as tightly as he could with his left while stretching out with everything he had with his right hand towards Alex. He could feel the grass starting to snap and give way and clenched his fist tighter in an effort to give him more time. Alex floundered, spitting water as his mouth repeatedly slipped below the surface. Alex plunged a hand toward Hunter and missed, slapping it hard into the water, Hunter followed it with his right hand and found Alex there. He was shocked to see the murky water still become stained with the colour of his blood.

"Have you got me?" Alex squeaked, completely saturated and trembling.

"I have got you," Hunter confirmed trying to be reassuring, but he could feel the grass continue to slip out of his grasp. He tried to readjust his grip while dragging Alex over to the side but knew he was failing. He was making some progress when he heard the awful sound of grass ripping at the roots as it was separated from its base. Hunter started falling back towards the clover filled inlet, his hand scrambling to find something else to hang onto. If I can grab onto a clump with my feet, Hunter thought as he fell, I might be able to pull myself through the water with Alex. Then Alex could lift himself up the wall and Hunter would find it easier. The thought was cast aside as he was abruptly grabbed by something else.

Hunter was covered in broken grass and straw as Shane slid down the side of the pit and grabbed Hunter by the elbow. He was remarkable strong and instead of holding onto grass with his hand Shane had wrapped his whole arm around a clump which had a ball shaped base of about half a metre or more in height.

"Pull him over," Shane ordered Hunter who was doing nothing but looking dumbfounded. It was true that Shane had stopped him from falling in the water, but even the newly arrived saviour was struggling with the weight of both brothers. Hunter started pulling Alex in and despite help from Shane still found it hard as the clover had ensnared Alex in almost every possible way. He would have been moments away from being entirely captured by the foliage and consumed by the water as it dragged them down. He finally made it to the wall but there was no obvious way he would be able to climb out.

"Help has arrived," called out another voice as James popped his head over the top of the pit.

"Did you get it?" Shane asked urgently.

"Of course I did," James replied.

"Got what?" Hunter asked.

"The ladder we hid on the dam wall," James called back. "That thing is so steep a ladder will definitely help you."

"There was a ladder?" Alex roared still spluttering liquid as he breathed heavily amongst his temporary refuge.

"Sure is," confirmed James. "I have got it fastened off so when it comes down to you grab it Alex." Alex nodded but James would not have been able to see him. The simply made rope ladder was dangled down and Alex clung to it aggressively while still holding onto Hunter.

"Let Hunter go Alex," Shane ordered before urging Hunter to climb back up the side with Shane's help.

"Hang on Alex," Shane called out once Hunter had stumbled back across the top of the pit. "Here help me pull him up," he ordered Hunter, urging him to grab one side of the rope ladder. Hunter slipped as he pulled but then watched as Shane used the big bases of grass clumps to brace himself while sitting on the ground. Hunter did likewise and was astonished at how much easier it was. Between the two of them, and James yelling commands to Alex telling him where to put his feet, it wasn't long before Alex was slumped on the lower level of the grass mound. Everyone fell about panting and no one spoke for a while.

"Well?" asked Alex, finally breaking the silence and talking to Hunter. "Are you going to say anything?" Hunter nodded in reply.

"I win," he muttered, receiving outraged looks from Alex but Shane stopped him from putting them into words.

"What happened to your hand?" Shane asked Hunter. Hunter simply flicked the grass standing nearby with his elbow to deliver his answer.

"Razor grass?" James exclaimed. "You don't grab that stuff, didn't anyone tell you?" Hunter shook his head noticing the sarcasm in Shane's voice, realising that as he had calmed down a little both his hands were throbbing terribly.

"Well I know at least that I did tell you to never come out here by yourself," Shane sounded just like Hunter's mum. "But you are lucky

I look after peasants in my kingdom." He got up and urged everyone to follow. Hunter helped Alex up while James grabbed the ladder.

"I would say something about him claiming to be a king again," James started to say, "but then you just got called peasants. That's pretty funny."

All four walked over to the back of Shane's house where they slumped on that old wooden table outside. His parents were inside talking to Hunter's parents, which was probably going to take a while. Shane went in to grab a towel for everyone to get dry and brought out a small plastic shopping bag with some other stuff. James walked to the tap on the side of his house and told both the brothers to wash their hands so they didn't get infected. There was soap outside to help with the process. Shane came back allowing everyone to dry up and they all collapsed in separate chairs. The situation had been dire and no one had wanted to talk. Hunter finally broke the silence.

"Thank you," he said softly. James smiled at him as if getting ready to laugh, but Shane acknowledged differently.

"You're welcome," Shane said. "We should look out for each other if we are going to hang around more."

"I agree," Hunter said. "But that was more than looking out for one another, you really saved me and Alex back there." Shane thought about it for a moment then waved his hand away.

"Don't worry about it," Shane said, brushing it aside. "Let's just say that you owe me one." Hunter agreed and they returned to silence. The silence lasted for about two minutes before all four of them fell into hysterical laughter. When one stopped laughing another would set the rest off again and the cycle continued. Not one of them knew why they were laughing.

"So," Shane managed to talk again as he wiped a tear from his eye. "You guys are moving in soon." Alex nodded in agreeance this time which got Shane nodding as well. "Fantastic, I could get used to this. We are going to have some great fun. How are your hands Hunter?" Hunter looked down at his hands which looked like they had been attacked by someone with a red pen who had persuaded him to give high fives for the duration of the day. They were completely pink with small fissures all through the prints of his skin. They throbbed so much and were so sensitive to any brushing he was trying his best not to think about it.

"They hurt, bad, but they will be good in a few days," Hunter said trying to sound tough. Shane agreed that they would but then turned to retrieve something else he had brought from the house. He opened a big bag of chips in front of all the boys and said that he was willing to share. James and Alex quickly grabbed a handful each, as did Shane, who then showed them to Hunter.

"Do you want some chips Hunter?" Shane smiled.

"No thanks," Hunter said, noting the flavour as salt and vinegar. He loved salt and vinegar chips but his hands couldn't hold up to that. In fact he could feel them pulsing in fear. As he felt them on his tongue his hands clenched in an act of foreboding more pain.

"Come on mate, don't push away my hospitality," Shane continued to grin. "Don't you like salt and vinegar?"

"He does," Alex informed everyone. "They are his favourite." Hunter squirmed. His spit glands were firing, telling him he wanted to have them so bad, but his hands were almost literally screaming for him not to."

"Come on Hunter," Shane pleaded seeing the hesitation, "you owe me." The smile became bigger and broader. Hunter finally nodded. He closed his eyes, sweat beading at his brow. This would be one of the hardest things he would ever have to do, and it sounded silly, dumping your hand into a chip packet. Try and get it over and done with, he told himself. He bit his lip, braced himself and started a countdown. On the count of three get it in and out without thinking, he advised himself. His brain started a mental countdown, but also tried to reason with him at the same time.

One, you don't have to do this.

Two, you're going to kill your hands.

Three. Plunge into the chip packet.

"AAAAAAAAAAAAAaaaaaaaaaaaaarrrrgh!!!!!"

CHAPTER 4 – SECRET AGENT GRASS

The move was over and done with before anyone knew it. It was a roller coaster ride of emotions with constant bickering, tears, triumph and people generally just getting in the way of one another. While they continued to pack boxes away Hunter discovered that many of the small treasured items that he had collected, and had assumed were lost, were crammed into small nooks all around the house. The pile included comic books pulled from cereal boxes, small toys hidden inside chocolates, countless Tazos which he had accumulated from the odd chip packet, and supermarket magazines with much wanted toys on the pages. Clearly Alex was to blame, but when Hunter called him out on it his younger brother claimed that Hunter was stopping him from packing so the older sibling got given the move on from their parents.

When the moving truck came and quickly packed up everything from their short time rental the boys were left to clean quickly before abandoning the house to help unpack everything at their brand new house. Both boys refused the usual call from their mum to say goodbye to the house as they left, much to her dismay and only her dismay.

Hunter walked into the new house where boxes were dumped in non-important rooms all the way up to the roof while removalists quickly set about rebuilding furniture that they had taken apart earlier. Several of the box towers teetered dangerously, which made Hunter avoid those rooms all together; flashbacks of a poorly reinforced electronic clothes dryer tearing free from a wall and landing centimetres from a much younger version of himself was enough trauma to keep him away. It wasn't long before Hunter's room was finished and he was sent inside to unpack all of his belongings.

His double bunk bed had been set up so that the lower level hung out perpendicular to the top which gave him a small space to chill out underneath on his beanbag next to his bed and bedside table. There were several more box towers in his room but they sat neatly with little suspicion that they may collapse down upon him at a moment's notice. The only other thing that was set up in the room was a brand new addition which he hadn't had before. A large old banker's desk that the family had accumulated before moving back to Orange. Like most things, Hunter knew that his younger brother had exactly the same in his room, several of their items were a mirror so that neither appeared to get more or less than the other. The banker's desk took up a good portion of the room though. It had its own shelf, its own chair that Hunter immediately sat upon and started to spin, and it also had its own desk draws. Hunter pulled them out and noticed that either his dad had forgotten to remove the stationery that had existed there before, or he had added the equipment for his son's use.

As Hunter started to unpack his boxes of clothes he heard Alex get called into his own room. No sooner was he in there than he was back out again terrorising the house and getting growled at by their parents. Hunter took his time to some degree. His clothes were stored in no time, if it was on a hanger it was straight into the wardrobe and if it was folded than it was on a shelf of his very own, personal, built in clothing unit. He had never had one of those before. Hunter noted that the old wooden disintegrating one that had contained both his and his brother's clothing was nowhere in sight.

The next box contained everything else that Hunter possessed and, although nothing in there was of major financial value or particularly interesting, these had done the same trek that Hunter had done across the country and mattered greatly to him. First were things like his tyrannosaurus moneybox, followed by a desk lamp and an alarm clock. These were placed appropriately before the next items came forth. Dinosaur book ends and a small collection of books. Hunter had five that were his own. Four Goosebumps and a Where's Wally. He had read them numerous times but that didn't mean they would be discarded. He took each of them in his hands one at a time, feeling the creases in the front and back covers through repeated use and the raised deliberate lettering in the title. He looked hard at each book remembering the story within, but more importantly he remembered where he had read them and how he had gotten them in the first place. Mostly he had gotten them because he had been silent during one of the many trips to the supermarket which was a two hour round trip. That had been when he had lived at a previous house out near Hillston or Hay. Alex never got those books because he was anything but patient, the only thing he usually got from such a trip was yelled at.

The pair of them did have a joint collection of books which lived in the family bookcase, but these ones were Hunter's and they would stay with him. When he placed the books away he opened a small bag which contained comics he had obtained in a show bag when they attended the Royal Easter Show once. Alex had instead got a bag full of lollies which he had demolished in less than a day before wandering around the house verging towards and away from Death's door the entire time. But once he was finished he had nothing left to show for it, whereas Hunter did and he cherished them.

Finally he packed them away and dragged the empty boxes to the cardboard graveyard which was their new kitchen. He decided he would help out his little brother as well by retrieving the empty boxes from his room. No sooner had Hunter entered his sibling's was he furious. All the other things which Hunter had deemed lost were strewn about all over Alex's unmade bed. With one quick look to see that his brother wasn't there he grabbed at all of the things which were rightfully his and hid them away within the bedside draws of his own room which was right next door. He was not caught in the act, and he knew he wouldn't be either as Alex was in the middle of an argument with their father who was already on tilt and beyond his tipping point.

When Hunter arrived on the scene it was obvious what the matter was. In an attempt to distract Alex his mum had told him to go and connect all the cables from one of the old televisions into both the original Nintendo system that they owned and into the aerial port attached to the wall. In the process of doing so Alex had pushed the wall socket into the wall where it disappeared into the cavity behind it, leaving a non-existent socket, a hole in the wall, and, worse for their dad, the realisation that no television signal would be able to be picked up from the outlet for the foreseeable future until it was fixed.

"Out," their Dad puffed, his whole body seaming to inflate ten times over, which was a remarkable thing as he was already quite large, before releasing a loud and very audible breath.

"But you said," Alex tried to argue. Everyone in the room could see that he had committed one of the worst acts imaginable and that his dad was offering the solution which would enable him to not only escape work but also allow him to keep his life.

"Out!" the older man boomed. Everyone in the room cowered, visibly shaking with the noise. It was not often that Hunter's dad got really angry or loud, so when he was you listened and probably ran for your life. His eyes had become bloodshot, Hunter imagined that he had become the human form of what a dragon would be. Hunter could see that Alex was still going to argue the point and leaped forward into the fold. Despite his previous anger at his brother hoarding all of his stuff, Hunter jumped forward into the fold, cupped a hand over his brother's mouth before dragging him unceremoniously from the room. Usually that act would see him in trouble but it was the best course of action for all involved.

Hunter dragged Alex outside onto the relatively new concrete slab that now covered the proximity around the outside of the house. There were still no fences around the boundary so they could see everything nearby. They walked out the back because the removalists were still a bustle of activity dragging bigger items like armchairs and tables into the house, whilst also dumping outside furniture like the big heavy redwood tables and stools that their great grandfather had made. The garage opened out through to the back yard making it easier to move the items, but making it obvious that Hunter and Alex were still in the way. With it making sense to stay invisible for the time being, and from the increase in punishment that they would receive as a result, they headed around to the southern side of the house.

"You won't be allowed to play down there," Alex pointed out as they walked towards the back of the house and where the back paddock was placed. "You should have let me finish putting the Nintendo together so we could play it."

"I know we can't play out there today," Hunter replied. "But the way you were going you would have been lucky to play anywhere ever again. Dad was just about to come down hard on you."

"He wouldn't have done it in front of the removalist," argued Alex. The statement was true to Hunter. Their dad and mum were frequently telling them cliché's like 'a time and a place' and 'what goes around'. So usually that meant that disciplinary action would wait until they were home and out of view from other families. But Hunter thought again that there was something in the way their dad had looked which told him otherwise in this instance, that it wouldn't have mattered who was there Alex was going to get it.

His younger brother continued to test the boundaries, now stomping hard on the dark grey steps that led down to the back clothes line and a driveway finishing at a non-existent back gate, their dark colour revealing they had only recently been laid. Hunter just ignored him, half wishing that their dad's head would come flying out of the closest window and catch Alex in the act. Hunter suspected that a noose or guillotine would be the punishment dished out. He continued to follow the path away from his brother, all the while casting an eye over at the environment which had almost cost his younger brother his life. He was so focused that he did not see the soccer ball coming towards him until it was too late.

SLAP! The over pumped soccer ball bounced hard from his face before following the path away that Hunter had been following. He heard Alex's laugh, harsh and loud, followed by the footsteps of someone else on the path as well.

"I'm so sorry Hunter," Shane called out from next to him. "I called heads but you mustn't have heard me." Hunter didn't look at the boy immediately. Although it wasn't raining there was a chill wind surrounding them which had made the impact on his face hurt so much more. He rubbed at his instantaneously warm cheek which he knew was probably bright pink without him even seeing it. His nose twitched, pins and needles spreading from his nose tip up along the bridge before circling his right eye and meeting the pain that still throbbed at his cheek. He could feel that same eye start to water, he wasn't crying but he couldn't control it and he didn't want his new friend to see him. He sniffed loudly, finally managing to get his tears under control and looked away from Alex and towards Shane. It was clear that they were playing some form of soccer as there was a makeshift goal made from large orange witches' hats and a sheet of corrugated iron. Here he could see James rolling on the ground clutching his sides. Hunter hadn't heard him laugh because the boy had managed to give himself a stitch in the process. A vein pulsed on his forehead screaming for the oxygen that his laughter has suppressed.

"Can you breathe?" Shane roused on him. "Have you hurt yourself?"

"Totally worth it," James replied finally finding his feet and his breath. Shane walked back to Hunter and patted him on the back. Despite his concern a smile slowly filled his face.

"It was a good shot though right," he smirked. Hunter tried not to laugh but the act was futile. He released an ugly chuckle and the lone tear he had managed to hold back fell awkwardly to the ground. All of them erupted in an orchestra of laughter.

"Stop, it hurts," James cried out as he rolled over and returned to the ground, holding his sides. Alex fell clumsily down the stairs due to his laughter while Shane just leaned on Hunter. A few moments later the tears of pain had been replaced with tears of joy and all boys were hurriedly wiping them away.

"So, was that your old man going off earlier?" Shane enquired. Hunter was shocked but not overly surprised that his dad had been heard outside the walls of their new home.

"Yep, it was Alex's fault though," Hunter admitted and although his younger brother looked hurt and bristled at the focus he did not argue.

"What are you guys doing now?" Shane followed up.

"Well we are not allowed back in the house at the moment," Hunter said shooting another look over at Alex. He had been secretly waiting for the opportunity to play the old Nintendo as it had been in storage or unplayed for what seemed like an eternity, despite the fact that it had only been packed away recently.

"Why don't you come and play with us then?" Shane asked. "It is so out of the way you aren't even on the same block, and because there aren't any fences your parents could see you if they really wanted." Hunter didn't need any convincing, following Shane over to the makeshift field with his brother in tow.

The teams were sorted instantly, house against house, and the boundaries were outlined. It was basically free for all soccer with small goals at both ends of what was the yard. Hunter looked at the ground still rubbing his face slightly. There was not much grass, in fact there were more small rocks than there were green tinges. He thought back to the first time he had played rugby league. Hunter had played for a team called Coleambally Darlington Point Roosters, he had no idea where the place was because he hadn't lived there, and he just played for the team because his own town was too small to have one. He was somewhat lucky because one of his school friends played with him and that mate, Daniel, had been so confident and encouraging that Hunter felt like he was unstoppable. But as much as he liked that team, the players were not what he was having flashbacks about. Then, like now, he had been made to play on a field that consisted of more rocks than vegetation and despite winning the game by a lot Hunter hadn't finished it. That was entirely due to being tackled, which was not an unusual occurrence in a game of footy, but then in the process having a tiny sharp rock impale the very middle of his kneecap and be lodged quite hard there. Hunter's whole body shuddered as he grimaced with the memory.

"Already worried you will get smashed," James started shaking Hunter from his thoughts. The younger boy strutted around comically very sure of his ability. It hadn't been a question. "We play until we are told to stop, regardless if you are hurt or buggered." Everyone nodded and then the game started. James had the ball under his foot and beckoned with his hands for someone to attack him. Hunter waited. He assumed that Shane had some sort of skill because he had been witness on their first encounter to what he could do with a ball when he was focused. Therefore Hunter assumed that the younger brother would have a similar set of skills, especially as James seemed like the kid who would always try and one up his older brother. Hunter looked over at Alex who was carrying on as if he was a cage fighter, the thought instantly dawned on him that his assumption on skill being transferable through a family was not realistic of his own brother. A moment later, as if irony commanded him, Alex rushed forward at James who patiently and easily tapped the ball forward out of the reach of Alex. Hunter's younger brother tripped as he swung wildly for the ball he was never going to possess and he went down. James laughed at the sight and then turned his gaze on Hunter.

"What about you?" he sneered.

"If you want to know you will have to come and find out," Hunter replied defiantly. Hunter assumed a defensive position in front of his own tiny goal. It was obvious that it was going to be hard to score as Hunter could almost fill the space by simply standing stoically inside of its frame. Hunter watched as James started being tricky with his feet, dribbling the ball one way and then the other, before flicking it onto his toe, then onto his knee. Hunter rushed the younger boy just as his confidence couldn't have been any higher. He brushed off his tiny frame as James fought to regain control despite being off balance. James hit the ground as Hunter stole the ball and in the next instance struck it hard towards the other goal. It was an incredibly long shot, but Hunter hardly had time to breathe before Shane jumped forward, head butting the ball well away from danger.

"You will have to do better than that," Shane crowed.

"So it seems," Hunter replied. He had no doubt that Shane would have hurt his head in his defensive effort as Hunter had hit it with a fair bit of force. None of the boys moved to chase after the ball. Both Alex and James regained their feet while Shane and Hunter just stared at each other. Shane was the first to move, but it was simply a smile that spread across his face.

"This is going to be good," James indicated as he started fetching the ball. Hunter nodded at his younger brother who returned the motion by pursuing James across the yard.

"Oh yeah," Shane agreed, before the game started all over again with lifted intensity.

The game had continued for what could have been hours, or maybe many minutes that just seemed like hours. In that time the air had become chilly creating numerous occasions when players were so busted they couldn't move. After the one time that Alex had sat out, leaving an overwhelming two on one situation against Hunter, if someone wanted a break they would take it in goal while the rest ran around. There were not many goals scored but Hunter still hadn't remembered the score, and nor did he care. He was just happy to be playing with friends who were similar to him and were just happy for the experience. The two younger brothers clearly didn't feel that way, bickering constantly about what the score actually was, but neither Shane or Hunter stepped into correct them.

Eventually all the boys were called in by Shane's mum, but she made them wash down with an old towel at the outside tap first. It wasn't until this moment did any of the boys realise just how dirty and hurt they were. Mud was caked on and had dried, leaving the boys to scratch it off relentlessly with fingernails filled with mud to get it off. Underneath this there were gauges of skin that were missing and the early signs of scabs as their bodies tried to heal. When they finally scrubbed off all the muck their bright pink skin was revealed, the cold afternoon imposed unknowingly a ruthless and sharp effect upon them. All of them seemed shocked as the state of what had happened was revealed. It seemed to Hunter like the removal of the grime was an odd game of pass-the-parcel, where you never knew if the next layer would reveal dirt, mud, rock, blood, clothing or skin. There was definitely no reward in this game though.

When they had been cleaned satisfactorily, and it had taken quite some time to get to that level, they were all allowed inside to play. All the boys were exhausted and were shifted off into the front room with a couple of snack size chip packets each and a drink of lime cordial. The Super Nintendo caught Hunter's eye immediately and he propped himself into one of the seats where a controller could easily reach him. It was late afternoon though and Hunter's mind wandered to whether or not his parents would mind that he and Alex were inside someone else's house. Shane's mum seemed to read his mind as Hunter prepared to get up.

"Your parents have gone to get some pizza and some other stuff," she explained. "So you two can stay here with us for a little bit." Shane's dad returned shortly after and everyone became aware that he had been over helping with some of the moving of bigger items within Hunter's new house.

The television screen slowly crept into existence, as if each pixel had to be found and roused from their own beds to complete the task, and everything else was ignored immediately. If there was one thing that could drain Hunter's time like reading or playing outside, it was video games. He thought he was pretty good. Not like those who tried to make a living from playing such games, although there was a time when he considered that being a tester of new games would be an amazing occupation and living, but he was still decent. It was common for Alex, or even their parents, to ask Hunter for help getting through hard bits on the video games they played, but not so much the other way around. The same seemed to happen here.

"You ever played Star Wars?" Shane asked. Hunter had not, but the idea of Star Wars mixed with video games was enough to brighten his eyes even at their dullest. "There is a hard bit we haven't got through, did you want to have a crack?" Hunter nodded and whilst everyone was eating no one complained that he was playing a single player game with so many others in the room. Hunter played through the starting level once and died, but seemed to pick up what he needed straight away. The second play through he managed to pass the first level defeating the boss.

"Wow, we have never got this far before," James exclaimed in amazement.

"It's the first level," Hunter replied with astonishment, whilst also trying to hide the air of smugness that he felt he was portraying.

"Yeah but it is that hard," James shot back, still amazed at the apparent success. "You must be some sort of player." Hunter didn't answer, focusing his attention back towards the screen and playing the game. He offered several times to hand over the controls but the two brothers pleaded for him to continue playing so that they would know exactly what they had to do when Hunter was no longer present. They had only played through four levels when there came a knock at the door.

Hunter looked up with blurry eyes. There were no house lights on so the only way the room was illuminated was from the all-encompassing television screen. His view changed from neatly formed pixels to watery eyed smog. The front door light was turned on revealing again that the outside of the house had completely fallen black as the sun had long since set.

"Hey, hey," Shane's dad said as he greeted Hunter's at the door. "Looks like you've got the goods." He opened the door for Hunter's dad who strode through with a large pile of pizzas. His mum followed with a bag full of garlic bread and another weighed down by soft drink.

"I hope they weren't much trouble," Hunter's mum asked as she was led through to place her items on the dining table in the next room.

"No way," replied Shane's dad as he locked the front door and followed behind them. "They have been on that thing for hours." Hunter's puffy eyes opened wide. Hours? It had only seemed like minutes. He had effectively spent his entire afternoon and part of the night doing nothing but playing soccer and then video games with his new neighbours. It sounded fantastic.

"Hurry up kids or I will eat it all," Shane's dad called out. "I'm not joking, I am starving." All the boys could hear the boxes being opened and crust being torn from each other. As much as they all wanted to get up and stop their parents devouring the great food that is pizza the boys struggled. Each one was stiff from the apparent hours of just sitting and watching a television. Their spines had slumped down and compressed into their ribs, with their necks forced down on top of that. The squishy leather chair had all but formed a cocoon around them, a loud ripping sound could be heard as they managed to pry their exposed, and still somehow wet, skin on their arms and legs from the furniture. Getting up and walking wasn't any better. Hunter's whole body ached from slumping down and playing video games for so long, and that was after an already gruelling game of soccer which had hurt. Put that next to the fact that he hadn't been as active as usual because of the winter of rain and household chores and he was a mess. The only saving grace was the fact that the others appeared to feel the same and when they finally arrived in the kitchen they would get some pizza.

When they got there the usual excitement for a late night meal of pizza didn't show. Each of them sat down on the edge of an island bench with the pizza in front of them. They were the slowest form of ravenous in the history of the world. Each grabbed a piece from varieties including meatlovers, aussie, Hawaiian and supreme, and each appeared to drink the pizza down alongside a cup of soft drink which never touched the sides. The parents talked about how good it was to finally move in and looking forward to the coming weeks when everything was sorted and then they could work on other things. They looked over at their kids which now included the Spigot's daughter, May, and frequently laughed at them. The mums were sharing some sort of drink that Phil called lolly water, while both the dads drunk some beer. Another loud ripping sound was heard followed by an enormous groan.

"Aw man," James whined, but even that was half hearted. The pizza he had grabbed at tore a big chunk of cardboard up from the box as the cheese had attached firm to it.

"Eat it up, it's good for you," Phil tormented his son. Each of the boys knew they should have been laughing at James, it was after all the right thing to do, but each was too tired and simply forced in all they could devour. When they finished they weren't racing to go and play again, they just slumped on the bench, heads propped on hands that teetered dangerously on resting elbows.

"Come on," gestured Hunter's dad finally. Neither Alex nor Hunter protested, their bodies automatically walking to the front door. They waved goodbye as their new friends walked from the bench and disappeared towards what Hunter suspected were their bedrooms. It was far colder than Hunter had imagined, but night had fallen well and truly with the lingering breeze which had remained all day long. Both boys still only had shirts and shorts on rather than the far more desirable woollen track pants or even pyjamas. There was only one other light shining in the street and that was coming from above the door of their new house.

It was a trek of no more than twenty metres from front door to front door but it seemed to march on forever. The loud chirping of crickets on the absent grass irritated Hunter as he dragged his feet before jumping down a dirt mound and arriving at what was now his home.

"We got something else for you two," mum said as she turned the key in the heavy wooden front door. Both Alex and Hunter shook their heads. Whatever it was it could wait. They trudged through the door frame although Hunter's brain had already transitioned into shut down procedures he still took it all in with his senses. The heater had kicked on making a dusty gas smell, the smell you get when something is turned on for the first time in an age or even ever, but accompanied alongside that was the scent of freshly laid carpet and recently finished paint. It seemed more profound at this moment despite Hunter having already smelt these things earlier in the day. The boys kicked their shoes off in the hall before floating along to where they remembered their rooms were. Hunter's heart leapt as he turned the corner to his room and found that his bed had been freshly made. There was no better feeling, he thought, but then a moment later, no sooner had his head hit the pillow, all the lights were flicked off in his mind and he was fast asleep.

"A Nintendo 64!" exclaimed Shane as he stood in the dining room of Hunter's house. While the room and the furniture looked completely made for special occasions it had one blot. An overly large television, which dad had stolen from Hunter's grandparents place, sat on an undersized television unit which held a brand new games console and some games.

"You guys are so lucky," James agreed as he leaned on his brother. Both boys completely struck by the new piece of technology that sat before them.

"That's not even the best part," Hunter corrected them and reached into the double glass doors underneath. "We have four controllers." All the boys stood wide mouthed as they gaped at the news. No sooner had the realisation come that they could all play together then they were all crowding around and preparing to do just that. There were only three games to play. One was a single player, which effectively made the multiple controller reveal useless and redundant, and as such was ignored at the present time, another was a racing game and the third was a gun game.

The boys immediately set about playing the racing game and once again continued to do so until the neighbours were called home and both Hunter and Alex were told to stop.

While Hunter had expected the play to be mostly outside that hadn't been the case since they moved in. They saw their neighbours almost every day but most of that was just in passing or saying hello. Through the week Alex and Hunter were busy going to school and when they came home they were busy packing things away under instruction from their parents. Playing video games through the week was still a big no-no anyway.

When the weekend came they got to play with Shane and James but that had become mostly around playing the new video game console. They rotated between the kart racing game, and that of the shoot-em up style secret agent James Bond game 'Goldeneye'. That happened for about three weeks, in which time each boy had developed their own video game persona and style and had become very familiar with one another. Then it all came to an end.

"We want you outside," mum said to Hunter and Alex, which effectively meant that no one was going to be playing video games for a while. Alex, as usual, tried to argue the toss, but Hunter was already out the door with Shane and James.

"Well that sucks," James stated before they were joined by Alex who evidently had all but been thrown out behind them.

"Yeah, but we can do our own thing outside," Shane said to all of them, not once falling out of stride or ideas. He walked into his own back yard and started reaching for a whole bunch of discarded tennis balls that were strewn everywhere. Some were completely destroyed while others were mouldy and had an extra layer of sludge around them, very few would have been worthy of a game of tennis or handball. Shane didn't discriminate though, taking all of them and putting them in a bucket. He looked out at the back paddock which had been mown recently revealing an abundance of space to play in. Hunter thought to himself how hard it must have been to knock down all those large tufts of razor grass but he was glad all the same. The only area that wasn't touched was the grass mound which Shane had returned to calling Ayer's Rock every now and then. The image of a castle sitting proudly on an Uluru like monolith jumped in and out of Hunter's head as they hiked towards it. It couldn't happen in reality as Hunter knew it was a sacred site, but he supposed that was why the image appeared all the more odd to him. When they scaled the green rather than red coloured environment Shane stopped them all and gestured towards his bucket.

"We are going to continue playing the games we were playing inside, well one of them anyway," he announced. "I call this game Secret Agent Grass." All the others smiled at each other, knowing full well which game Shane was talking about and already hopeful of particular things that would be included, but continued listening to what they could do.

"We are going to play," Shane stopped to think through what he was actually going to say next. "Four games, I think, all based on levels we have been playing inside. In fact this game is going to be even better than what we have played before." He continued to explain that each of them had to start, or spawn, in different locations on the grass mound and would proceed to play from there. It seemed simple, using the tennis balls as weapons, once you were hit you were out.

The games were some of the best that Hunter had ever played. The first ones didn't matter so much if you 'died' by being hit by a ball. You would just go back to your starting spot, have a safe amount of time to get back in the game, and then start again. Each game went until someone whinged that they wanted to change the rules.

The first game was a free for all, where everyone started with five tennis balls but then after that the balls that were discarded were any ones to pick up and use, once hit start again. It was in this game that everyone started to really understand the strategy built into their playing environment. Using the still overly tall grass clumps as a barrier was key, but applying some deception tactics like sacrificing a ball to force a rustling sound in the grass thus luring someone to that area was also adapted.

Then a tag team style game was made, same as free for all but with a partner. The teams were changed every now and then just to keep it interesting. Shane and Hunter were ruthless when they teamed up forcing the two younger brothers to complain the entire time, during this Shane refused to change the game or the teams. When the teams did change again Hunter at one stage got annoyed with Alex and hit him with some friendly fire, making him go back to the start, before quickly requesting the game change so that Alex couldn't seek revenge upon him.

The third game was the most spy like. The tennis balls were taken away and it became one touch kills, inspired by a mode called slappers only. If you got touched you died and were sent back to your starting spot. The younger boys realised quickly that if they just ran up and tried to get Shane or Hunter they would get touched because they had longer arms, so from then on they would sneak along the ground, rarely standing, and try not to make a sound. Eventually that game came to an end too.

The sun started to set and when the boys looked up from atop their castle they could see pink and orange streaky clouds disappearing on the horizon, chasing the escaping sun.

"I think it is time to go home," Alex mentioned. The light was sure to vanish quickly now that the sun had disappeared and this time there was no doubt that they had been playing for hours. The rule on the weekend was that they couldn't play with the neighbours until after lunch. That morning time would enable chores and car trips could be completed quickly and easily before the boys were lost to play. The same chill that was thrown down in the twilight hours settled, and along with it came the familiar smell of dew as it floated down to rest on the grass. Hunter liked that smell, but it still spelled out to the group that time was up.

"I still have one more game," Shane revealed. It was the fourth game that he had suggested playing at the start but no one was convinced that he had actually known what it was at the time.

"Whatever it is it will take too long," James called him out. It was the first time that he also suggested that play stop completely.

"Not this one," Shane continued. "I am calling it 'King of the castle'."

"King of the castle?" James repeated confused. He stopped in his tracks all the same.

"Yeah," Shane stood this time as he revealed all. "There is one life only this time. Once you get hit you are out and you go straight home, no lives." The boys looked amongst each other, it would definitely make the game shorter if they were out straight away, or perhaps longer if they took more care. "If you are out you have to take it and yell out to everyone so we know who is left. We also already know where all the starting spots are, so you can start wherever you want. But I will only give you thirty seconds to get there before we start. Are we sweet?" Everyone nodded and then immediately sprinted to different locations, trying to be sneaky in the process.

Hunter knew where he was going to go. He was going to start at the far end of the grass mound where the top and bottom parts met and then he would wait until he heard or saw something. He would have full view of anyone who approached him regardless if they journeyed along the top path or that down below. Shane had counted to twenty and then left the last ten seconds unspoken so he could find his own spot without revealing his location. Hunter had a fair idea of where the other younger boys were as he watched the direction they travelled as they immediately ran away. But Shane, he had no idea. Hunter stood still, but crouched as low as his legs would allow him. He didn't want to be crawling or lying down because not only was he a bigger target but it was harder to throw a ball or evade quickly. The instinct was to lie down but he reminded himself that he carried a tennis ball, not a sniper rifle, despite whatever things he had thought during the previous games.

Hunter once more found himself scanning for any signs of life. He had taken on the role of spy and every movement he made, and even those he didn't, was cold, precise and calculated. He could sense everything. His eyes saw the tiniest of movements, either a bird fluttering far away in the distance coming into his periphery as it ventured home for the night, or the wind gently bending a nearby reed which rubbed harshly on its partner nearby. He was so aware he even saw the arrival of a small group of beetles which jumped between grass clumps trying to remain unseen. He heard the tiniest of rustles in the grass, the croaking of frogs and even the bubbles they made which popped on the creek's surface, which also had its own rolling sound of a nearby yet unseen waterfall.

Hunter heard the movement of one of the other boys but he could tell that it was far away and he didn't need to be alarmed, yet. The smell of damp mulch was becoming more potent as the light continued to fade and the moist dew continued to settle. He tasted the ever growing chill which settled on his lungs and made his breathing harsher to manage, on the verge of hurting. He could taste the dry saliva which he rolled around on his tongue as a glob of spit, if he got rid of it he felt like the sound would reveal his location immediately. Hunter felt like his whole body was trying to give him away. His heart thumped like an iron pipe hitting a metal pole, his breathing heaved like a giant closing massive bellows on an intense inferno, his ear drums could have gotten a Grammy for their performance, and even his brain was belting a gong as it tried to betray him from within.

There was a sudden movement, different to all the others Hunter had identified. Almost automatically he cocked an arm and threw one of his balls into what seemed like a dry bunch of brush. The hollow thump that echoed in the dwindling light revealed that Hunter had hit his mark. A moment later an unimpressed Alex walked forward making as much sound as he possibly could. His brother didn't reveal to the others he was hit until he was standing right beside Hunter.

"I've been hit," he yelled out so the others could hear. "Alex is gone." He had done it on purpose so that the two neighbours knew exactly where Hunter was. Alex motioned to hand over his now useless tennis balls, with a huge smile spreading across his face. He tossed them back over his shoulder where they fell hidden in the shadowed undergrowth, out of reach and not worth searching for in the fading light. "Good luck," he whispered before running at a trot away from the fight. Hunter watched him go, but then remembered that it wasn't a wise thing to be doing. He refocused on his surroundings. His concern of now having two others preparing to take him down was a short lived fear as a scream reverberated under the darkening sky. Hunter instinctively ducked lest he be seen by either of the brothers.

"No fair," James yelled, his stomping purposefully crushing grass in his anguish. Hunter saw the younger boy pop up from cover and settled himself further behind a grass clump. The look upon James's face was one of disgust. His eyes were shooting laser beams and his bottom lip hung with contempt. Hunter saw him throw the remaining balls in his hand towards an unknown source, but Hunter knew that must have been Shane's location. He continued to watch as James continued his tantrum down the side of the grass mound, creating yet more ruckus, and off towards his house. Hunter swore he saw his brother still standing there at the boundary, but he couldn't be sure as he returned to the game.

It was now one on one. Winner takes all. The darkness was settling faster. Anything that was not within ten metres of Hunter had merged into one solid silhouette that surrounded him. Hunter resumed his statue like trance as he refocused on his surroundings. It seemed like he didn't move for some time and had fully blended in with his environment. He now heard the sounds of small lizards that were comfortable enough to move around him where they hadn't before. He could hear the scratching of birds atop the nearby eucalypt trees and at one stage he had to resist slapping at his own neck as a particularly annoying group of mosquitos admired the meal he laid out for them. Their high pitched whining buzz swooping frequently at his ears.

The light was all but gone and the game had not progressed at all. Reluctantly and with heavier breathing Hunter decided he would have to take the fight to Shane. He calculated the best path from his hidden spot, which would enable him to advance through the scrub and remain concealed.

The sound of his own body was instantly replaced with tunes of stealth from all his favourite spy movies and cartoons. The music that played in his mind was so loud that he had to subconsciously turn the volume down in his head as it drowned out the sounds he was actually making. But he didn't turn it off. It seemed to enhance his senses a further tenfold and pumped adrenaline into every muscle of his body as he prepared to vault at any moment to either unleash his fury or disappear once more.

It was lucky the moon was full as it was now the only thing casting light as it rose steadily behind Hunter. He saw it as a positive thing, the light was behind him showing him what lay ahead whilst never actually being in his line of sight. An unnatural ruffling and movement was heard from in front of him. Hunter's eyes flicked from side to side as he tried to pin point its origin. Once it disappeared he reanalysed his route, changing his bearing so as to put himself into a position to be able to surprise his adversary where he assumed he lay hidden. Hunter continued to creep his way along the top of the grass mound. A bird overhead would have been able to see him, and there were several of those like ibis and heron taking flight to return to safety nearby, but Hunter was convinced that he was like a chameleon to all others.

The rustling continued and Hunter knew he grew closer to his quarry. There were other sounds coming from elsewhere now. Hunter assumed that a Kangaroo had wandered down for a drink from an adjoining paddock and largely ignored them. He moved into a crouching position now, remaining as low as he could while lifting his torso as high as he dared. He took one last breath, prepared his throwing arm to launch his tennis ball immediately while preparing another one to reload from his other hand with a flick, and then he leapt.

Hunter flew through the air. His eyes adapted to the lack of light on the mound but squinted against the floodlights which had been turned on at the back of both houses that the boys lived in. He launched the ball hard and hit his mark, but instead of a thud or the similar slap that he heard when he struck Alex he heard crunching. The crunching of dry leaves. A fallen eucalypt branch lay there and the limb was long enough to effect sounds from a decent distance away from its holder. Hunter's heart fell, he had been duped and he had foolishly allowed the ruse to lead him straight into a trap in his hastiness. And as Hunter lay flat on the ground after his heavy landing, and was laid out for all to see, the trap was sprung.

"Got you," Shane yelled as he bounded forth from his cover with a ball held aloft in his hand. His face was a twisted snarl of aggression and glee. The ball didn't leave his hand though. The reason why Hunter saw his face so well was because as soon as he had broken cover a torch had shone bright on his previously unlit features. Shane cowered away from the light, shielding his eyes with his throwing arms. The crunching sound that Hunter had heard earlier becoming more apparent.

"Boys you are in a whole heap of trouble," the voice of Hunter's dad spoke from the void behind the glaring lights.

"You should have been home ages ago," added the voice of Mr Spigot. "So you had better get there quick smart." Shane lowered his head, never actually getting the opportunity to throw his ball and seal his win. Hunter followed on behind him. When they finally passed by the shroud of the torchlights both boys' feelings of despair turned to rage. For there, hidden from view by their parents, stood the sniggering forms of Alex and James. They had been ratted out by their younger brothers just because they had been eliminated earlier. Neither Shane nor Hunter would forget it, but right now they were led away from one of the most enjoyable games they had ever played, like convicts on a chain line, to receive the punishment that lay before them.

CHAPTER 5 – THE PLATINUM AXE

Hunter leaned forward in a chair looking down at those below him. He sat on an upper level suspended walkway of a squash centre, glancing down at the multiple games being played across a number of courts. He sat next to a lady that he didn't know, but his mum seemed to. The lady was paying particularly close attention to the game that Hunter's mum was involved in, taking note of the score and which side of the court the serve should be taken from.

While Hunter sat Alex was laying down on his stomach next to him, hands propping up his head as he watched. Occasionally, frequently, Alex would lose all interest in the game and go about becoming a massive pain in the neck. He would try to untie Hunter's shoelaces or try to pull his chair back when he was swaying, threatening to tip him over and for his older brother to hit the deck which echoed loudly due to the suspension of the platform. Alex pressed his face against the wire mesh barricade which he observed the game through, then proceeded to harass Hunter as he tried to make him look at his face. Thick indented lines covered his cheeks making it look like he was attacked by a potato masher. When Hunter didn't respond how Alex wanted him to he would roll around on the ground before repeating everything all over again.

The game finally finished and both boys had to follow the scorer down to the court, as per their mum's instruction. The action itself seemed easy but it was fraught with danger, or fun, depending on how you looked at it. There were two ways to access that overhanging platform. The first was at the far end, opposite to the way they were going. The boys weren't allowed to go that way. The outside door was just below the stairs and whenever their mum couldn't see the boys she would worry. It wasn't that they couldn't be trusted to stay within the facility; Hunter rarely did the wrong thing and usually followed instruction, whereas Alex was immature but despite his whining he always hung around. No. It was more the case that mum thought that both boys would be abducted by the next person who walked in regardless of who they were or their intentions, so most situations like that were non-negotiable instances of 'stay where I can see you'. Hunter volunteered a suggestion once that there was a room near those stairs which was full to the brim with huge gym equipment and bigger guys using them, and if anything was to happen then those huge guys who all but lived within, who did not do much else but look at themselves in the mirrors, would be able to run out and help them. These guys rather than forming a solution in his mum's mind became the second reason not to go down there.

The end that they travelled towards though was accessible from the top of a grand stand which stood in the middle of two courts. The seats which resembled a pyramid between the courts stretched up about five metres so everyone could see all the action, and at the very top you could see two games if your head was on a swivel. The problem was that the seats were also the stairs and each chair was about half a metre in height. Hunter had had fun playing up and down the grandstand until inevitably someone fell down. It hadn't been Hunter, or even Alex in this instance, but another boy and ever since that time there was a cloud of fear that hung around when ascending and descending the frame.

When they carefully reached the bottom they waited beyond the closed door for their mum to come outside. She was playing in a group with three other ladies in a round robin format. Two played while the other scored and then they rotated with a small five minute break to allow the player backing up to have a short rest before they recommenced play, which was entirely filled by the ladies gossiping. It was their mum's turn to score next, which meant it was also time for the usual request for money to spend at the centre's canteen.

"Mum can we . . ." Alex began to ask but was stopped abruptly as his mum raised her hand in front of his face. She didn't say no, in fact she didn't answer at all. She simply reached into her small sport bag, grabbed the purse she used for such occasions, and gave each of the boys a two dollar coin each. They both looked down at the money in their hand.

"Two bucks!" Alex exclaimed before tearing off towards the canteen area. "Thanks mum." He yelled his thanks from halfway down the corridor, directly beneath where the boys had waited upstairs before. His mum simply yelled back at him to stop running. Hunter followed along behind, walking though as he was in no hurry. There was never a line and he would only have to wait for Alex.

The centre was old and almost derelict, which was mirrored in what hung from the walls or what was on display in its faded and dusty timber trophy cabinets. Multiple grand awards and trophies were contained within the cases but all the notices and pictures were only in black and white. Some were so old that the normally white paper had turned yellow with damp brown stains splotched and smeared all along them. One of the newspaper articles spoke of a local player who went to the Olympics representing Australia. That fascinated Hunter, but again because of the age of the claim he doubted whether he, or anyone else, actually knew that player or even whether he existed anymore.

When Hunter rounded the corner he saw what he expected to see. Alex was deliberating with the salesperson about how many of each lolly he could get with the money he possessed, and trying to haggle so that he could get more than he could afford for the same amount of money. Hunter waited patiently, looking around the room to notice that there was a television showing heavy static buzzing in one corner. A single man watched the show, which was clearly an old video recording as he kept pausing and rewinding the image on the screen. As Hunter looked on he noticed the resemblance between the man in the video and the pictures on the wall. The gentleman who watched the video suddenly spied Hunter looking on and gave him an odd expression. Hunter, now feeling like he had interrupted something, and still waiting for his brother to make a decision, quickly said whatever came to mind.

"That guy was an Olympian," Hunter blurted out quickly, hoping that his assumption was correct. "I heard he was one of the best." He had heard no such thing, but who wasn't a good athlete that ever made it into the Olympics? The man watching the video twisted a grubby coin in his fingers and simply nodded in Hunter's direction before

67

returning his focus to the screen. Alex finally finished with several large white bags seemingly filled with lollies.

"Three lollies for five cents, and I spent it all," he stated with astonishment and then proceeded to do the math in his head. He failed. "I don't even know how many lollies that is." Hunter wasn't surprised.

"What can I get for you young master?" the older man behind the counter asked. Hunter knew what he was going to get.

"Could I get a bag of skittles please, and a packet of chips," he said to the man. Hunter watched as the bag of candy was quickly grabbed and placed on the counter, and then took particular focus on which chips the salesman picked.

"Not those ones," Hunter blurted out, grabbing the man's attention quickly and slightly embarrassed at how rude he sounded. "The one beside it please."

"They are the same chips boss," the man called back apparently unphased by the abrupt request.

"The flavour is," Hunter agreed, "but what is inside isn't." The man simply nodded and told Hunter what the price for both was. It was cheaper than the two dollars that was held in his hand, and when the man asked if Hunter wanted anything else he simply shook his head.

"Trying to save your money are you?" he said. "Admirable. I'm going to give you something else for that. Just because I am a nice guy." The man whistled through his teeth as he spoke, but as another packet of chips came to Hunter for free he was happy to ignore any odd characteristics.

"Thanks," Hunter said as he dragged the skittles straight into his pocket and took both chips in his hands and walked away. He was halfway down the corridor which passed his mum's playing court when a voice called out from behind him. It was the man who had been watching television.

"Hey kid," the man called out. Hunter noticed that despite the man's apparent old age he still wore an entire sporting get up like a professional. Perfectly clean white shoes, socks, and shorts with a striking sport polo covering a thick gold chain. Alex, who had been waiting for Hunter beside the grandstand pyramid, while he smashed a packet of lollies already, ran to Hunter's side to see what was going on. No doubt he suspected that his older brother was in trouble, but Hunter himself didn't even know what was going on.

"Did you actually know who was in that video?" the man asked. Hunter shook his head revealing he didn't. "That guy is called Wayne and he used to be a fairly formidable player. He played right here. He still plays here in fact."

"Who plays here?" Alex asked through a mouthful of strawberries and cream lollies.

"An Olympian," Hunter confirmed. The man nodded before pointing towards a door.

"That was his room there," the man stated. "Did you want to have a look?" Hunter nodded. There wasn't much else to do while they waited, but he was nonetheless intrigued. The thick padlock was undone and the old light flickered to life inside. Hunter felt like the room hadn't been used in some time. His eyes darted from one side of the still dark room to the other. On one side there was fitness equipment, boxing bags hanging on chains from wooden beams in the roof as well as old mounted bicycles, many of which contained cobwebs or had a thick layer of dust living upon and within them. On the other side there were more cabinets holding yet more trophies and awards, and at the back of the room there were things that caught his eye immediately. Hunter ignored those as he didn't want to be rude once again and followed the man who led them towards a display case. It had its own special light that was flicked on. Once the gases in the long light tube were fully heated Hunter had to hold back a gasp.

"What is that?" Alex asked. Hunter knew what it was but he was too busy looking at all the other pictures that surrounded the outside of it.

"That my boy, is an Olympic gold medal," the man beamed.

"Is it yours?" Hunter asked rather curtly, seeming to recognise the face that was in all the photos that surrounded the award. The man didn't answer immediately but a smile appeared on his face after a short moment. "It is, isn't it?"

"Yes," the man admitted finally, "it is mine. From a long time ago. I don't usually show people this. I don't let people know. But I figured that you kids have shown an interest so I will show you." The room fell silent as no one had anything else to say, the silence eventually broken by a knock on the door.

"Wayne," the salesman called to him. "There is a guy on the phone who wants to talk to you." Hunter thought they were going to get ushered out but to his surprise Wayne left them alone with his prized possession. Perhaps he really wanted the boys to soak in the importance of what was in front of them.

"What are these?" Alex asked with growing enthusiasm after Wayne had gone. Hunter turned to what he had seen before. There, on the far wall, stood a pinball machine and an old arcade game. Before Hunter could stop him Alex had found the power cord and plugged it into the socket on the wall. It still worked. Hunter glanced back at the doorway expecting to be sprung any moment but no one appeared there. It took a long time for the picture to emerge but when it did Hunter was captivated.

Platinum Axe.

The title appeared blazing across the screen as snippets of the game blurred in and out of focus through various cut scenes.

"Aww it takes money to play," Alex groaned as Hunter continued to stare at it. "Do you have any left?" Hunter remembered that he did, but he hadn't really envisioned using his remaining cash on an old video game hidden in a side room. Alex moaned and groaned some more. Hunter knew it was a complete waste if Wayne or the salesman just happened to re-emerge in the doorway and scare them off, but he relented all the same. He pulled the coin from his pocket and slipped it into the appropriate slot and then watched as it buzzed to life and the game begun.

"You first and then me," Alex stated. That was what usually happened, so that Hunter could show his younger brother how it worked and then Alex could use that information to get a higher score. There honestly wasn't that much to the game. There was a joy stick and two other buttons. Move, strike, jump on a seemingly three dimensional map. It was still exciting to Hunter, but what was more exciting is how the environment within the game took on the form of the back paddock and the surrounding features behind his house. Trees became the eucalypt, hills became the grass mound, and waterways became the dam and the creek. Even during a night time bit where the characters were ambushed the area took on the appearance of the so far unexplored bog turned swamp area. The battle axe that Hunter's avatar wielded was glamorous as it swept dazzling across the screen despite the damage it was wreaking on the bad guys, who seemed to swarm towards the blade like bugs to the zapper. Just as Hunter continued to progress towards the levels final boss, and just as Alex started to demand that he was allowed to play, the game went blank. A single line fading across the centre of the screen as the power and the accompanying audio and visuals were cut ruthlessly from the game.

Hunter searched nearby to try and discover what had happened as Alex was left with a besmirched look on his face as if he had been robbed. Hunter pulled the cord out and proceeded to look around to see where the cord from the wall socket actually ran to. Alex did the same thing which led him towards the boxing equipment, whereas Hunter was brought back to the gold medal.

"Well you guys seem like you had fun in here," Wayne arrived back in the room. Both boys nodded trying to show an enhanced level of excitement at the medal, while trying to hide the fact they were more interested and now disappointed by what else they had found. "I am really sorry though, I have to duck off," Wayne continued and gestured them back towards the door and beyond it. Before he left he stated that he was happy to talk about the history of squash another time, including the gold medal, to which Hunter politely nodded and agreed that the offer was splendid.

Hunter felt bad as he resumed his seat overlooking the game of squash which was still being played down below him. Wayne was so excited at being an Olympian and Hunter knew it was a tremendous achievement, but it was number three on his list of amazing things that he was thinking about at that moment. It should have been number one, but it wasn't. Number two played out in front of him. The two ladies who were squaring off in their squash match now held the formidable platinum axe which had been on display during the arcade game he had been playing. The court around them likewise transformed into a brutal jungle environment with enemies popping their heads above the red lines which followed the walls. They were in a battle no longer of sport but of survival and should they lose they would die.

Hunter enjoyed imagining it all unfold in front of him, but as his brother continued to stuff his face with another bag of lollies Hunter turned to what was the number one thing that excited him this afternoon. He opened the first of his chip packets and let his hand jump inside. He imagined his fingers grew eyes as he felt his way around the packet, searching for something that didn't belong, before finding a silver foil item and hauling it out. Within the foil contained one of the most cherished items in Hunter's young life, as well as all those that he knew at school. Within was a popular Tazo, based on any number of films or movies which were out at the moment. They were in demand, they were rare, and they were more exciting than a battlefield come to life and even a gold medal. Hunter let his fingers rip the slippery foil before holding his breath to peer inside.

The ban had been lifted for Shane and Hunter to venture out towards the paddock once more. They had been forbidden from playing out there for two weeks for staying out too late. Although initially it had sounded terrible there always seemed to be a silver lining in Hunter's consequences. Usually it was metaphorical, and an implied moral that Hunter would have to understand and learn from for the next time.

The moral in this sense was that he couldn't trust his brother. But there was also a literal note which had brought Hunter much amusement, and Hunter imagined also to Shane. There was a massive thunderstorm which came and went for most of that fortnight. Creating rain which made your bedroom windows look like waterfalls, or like you were about to sink below the ocean, as well as thunder which made you question just how sturdy the foundations of the house actually were. There was no chance that they could play outside throughout it, even his mum hid below blankets every time the house shook with a massive thunderclap and sonic boom. Hunter's grounding therefore wasn't that bad, and the regret of playing for too long and getting in trouble left him.

But then it got better.

Both sets of parents decreed that neither James nor Alex could go and play in the back paddock without the accompaniment of either a parent or their older brother. The parents definitely wouldn't go down there, and both Shane and Hunter couldn't. Hunter just laughed.

Once they finally met up again Hunter couldn't stop telling Shane about his new Tazos and then the old arcade game that he had found in the back room of the squash court. He mentioned the fact that the guy, Wayne, was an Olympian but Shane showed as little interest in that fact as Hunter imagined he would. It was not spoken about again.

"Platinum axe," Shane repeated the name. "Never heard of it. Sounds cool though." The boys all stepped carefully as they ventured further south than they had ever done before. The back paddock was in Hunter's estimation five hundred metres long. The middle was all space filled with grass, skirted by the creek on one side and the boundary of all the houses on the other. At one end was the grass mound which Hunter was growing to love even more and found something new every time he visited, but at the other there was just mystery. Reeds and long grass usually stood as tall as the juvenile eucalypt, wattle and other native trees which poked out from beyond, but the thunderstorm had provided such an abundance of water that the creek had flowed like a river and flattened all but the trees which still lingered on its bank. The surge of water had revealed that the creek turned and formed its own boundary to the paddock, which was skirted by a small path which went along the construction sites and into an area which was out of bounds.

The boys followed the creek back and marvelled at how quickly it was flowing despite the fact it hadn't rained in days.

"Our part of the creek is like the furthest away from the source," Shane stated answering the questions Hunter held in his mind. "It keeps flowing hard for days, all the way through town and down from the nearby mountains, but it doesn't usually stay up this high for this long." Shane proceeded to dare his younger brother to jump the creek. When James refused Shane said that he was scared, but Hunter doubted that Shane could have managed the task himself, even in the thinnest of sections. They instead simply followed along its side until they finally appeared back in a familiar spot; the start of the incline up the mound just ahead, with the large eucalypt tree towering above as it hung over from the other side of the water. There was a small ford like bridge which sat underneath the water here made entirely of neatly assembled and accumulated rocks, allowing some sort of access to the other side. Shane gestured with his head that the small group should cross here and without hesitation put one foot into the water and vaulted across to the other side. He made it look so easy.

"Come on guys," he encouraged them by making them seem weak. "Don't be soft, it's easy." Hunter was the first to step forward, knowing his brother would push him to go first anyway. He looked at the small stream that hurriedly flowed along, finding a way between the rocks and surrounding vegetation to form a small waterfall. Water bubbled and splashed lazily, along with small particles of foam and soaked debris. The sound was soft and soothing to Hunter, and usually it would have been quite calming and welcome if it didn't invite pain on this occasion.

The large stone that Shane had used to launch himself from in the creek's centre was wet. It rocked slightly under the influence of the cascade which flowed softly around it which pronounced warning signals in Hunter's head in regard to its stability and therefore safety. There were also signs of sludge resting just underneath the surface, which was partially hidden by the moss which had grown there. Small strands of algae hung loosely from the rock, dragged out as it stretched with the pull of the water. It was wet, insecure, and slippery, with still a decent sized step needed to cross the divide. Hunter breathed deep. He conjured up an image of an archaeologist he enjoyed watching at the movies who had also been asked to take a leap of faith. Then Hunter took the step.

Hunter exhaled.

"Well done mate," Shane said slapping a hand on his shoulder. "You made that look easy." They both turned to see that Alex was the next to take the trek, Hunter was relieved that he had made it across with no consequences. Alex rolled his tongue along his lip as he focused on his job, analysing what he would have to do just like his older brother before him. Branches rustled above them from the tree but no one took any notice. He took a quick planned step onto that one rock which showed the most promise. He made it easily but the rock swayed under his foot. Alex's shoe slipped into the water slightly but he regathered, managing to keep his balance with a fine display of waving his arms around like a windmill in distress. He breathed a sigh of relief, gathered himself, and then threw himself forward with all his might. No sooner had he arrived safely on the worn down bank, where it seemed countless others had either taken the plunge or had travelled across the makeshift bridge at a lower tide, then his smile disappeared and turned into a mask of fear.

Alex yelped and threw himself down to the ground before scrambling up the bank towards the supposed safety of his brother's location. Hunter didn't feel safe and didn't rush to help his brother. The rustling they had ignored before should have been the first clue that there was a resident nearby that wasn't happy at their presence. A black and white devil bird swooped down low, snapping and cracking its long sharp beak as Alex escaped in panic. The call of the magpie, the screech and warble as it dove again at the retreating young man, mixed with the heavy gust it was causing by the erratic flapping of its wings was terrifying to all who heard and observed what was happening.

"He is done for," Shane whispered to Hunter, and although Hunter felt a small bit of guilt for not running to the aid of his younger brother, and despite the fact that they were talking about a bird, he had to agree.

"Yep," Hunter said, "there is nothing we can do for him." The magpie struck once or twice more before sailing back up towards where its nest was hidden up in the heights of the tree.

"Made it," Alex blurted out breathlessly as he arrived at his brothers side. He sucked in deep breaths as he bent over his knees for a couple of seconds, then he gave Hunter an accusing glance. "Why didn't you help me?"

"It's a magpie," Hunter answered simply. Alex looked at his brother for a moment and then nodded his understanding, accepting the few words as reasonable justification of his inaction.

"Fair enough," Alex accepted finally without argument. There was, after all, very few things in a person's life more scary than a magpie. They all looked at James who seemed both annoyed that he was the last one left and concerned by all the variables that surrounded him. He was already shorter than the rest of them so his longest stride would be even more difficult if not unachievable. Now with the magpie added and that the rock was visibly rolling after Alex had driven it backwards when he had jumped, the difficulty level had increased dramatically.

"Watch this," Shane said behind a hand, seemingly unashamed that he had little faith in his brother's ability. James took a run-up which was something none of the others had to do. He ran and leapt, launching earlier than Hunter imagined would have been useful or successful.

SPLASH! James had landed well short of the safe rock but had still stretched out to reach it. He plunged sideways, slipping on the shale beneath the surface and landed into the thick mucky silt like soil which existed there. His arm dug into it in an effort to push himself out of the dirt. That same arm had wet streaky blood running down its length, no doubt from a rock it scraped along as he either landed or pushed himself up. James was crying and this time Hunter did take a few steps forward to help the younger boy. He was pulled back by Shane, not in spite of his younger brother this time but because the scream from the birds had called out once again, and there was more than one that dove down to attack.

"Run!" screamed Alex and Shane at the same time. Hunter followed behind them as they all ran beyond the eucalypt tree and up the far hill towards the fenced off farmland. The cows located there were unconcerned by the sudden appearance of the boys as they continued to eat the long pasture at their feet. James was lost from view as he found his feet and slowly but noisily rushed from the creek, now weighed down from all the water his clothes had soaked up like a sponge. Alex, Shane and Hunter stopped when they arrived on the hill just above the fallen log, the one which reached back over the other side of the creek to the lower part of the grass mound. They weren't puffing too hard as they had only run about thirty metres. It had been enough to give them adequate separation from the eucalypt trees and the crying magpies as they continued to harass James nearby.

Finally, after nearly a minute, James had cleared the creek and come running to join them, tears streaming down his face mixed with muck and blood. He ran straight at Shane, teeth clenched and spitting fluid from between his fangs. He ran with an angry fury straight at his brother and jumped towards him. Shane simply brushed his younger brother aside, who landed awkwardly on his shoulder and started sobbing some more, screaming insults in between hiccups caused by his blubbering.

Shane showed little concern and grabbed a couple of long sticks which lazed on the ground nearby. He handed them to Alex and

Hunter, throwing one on the ground near James who grumbled at the action.

"Want to ride a boat down the rapids?" Shane said and moved towards the fallen log. Hunter had seen it before from the other side, and while you could cross it from there it didn't fall flat to the ground, instead it stood about a metre above the very edge of the creek which was somewhat treacherous. Hunter could have reached up and climbed onto it but he knew Alex could not so they had never done so. He and Shane walked into the trunk which had been ripped apart as it glanced up at the sky. The trunk was hollow with old rotten bark, dirt and termite ridden wood crumbling inside it. There were small holes that you could look through to see the flowing creek below. It was also wide enough for all of them to sit inside. Hunter could see what Shane had meant straight away as his neighbour took a seat near the front of the tree and started dipping his long stick into the flowing stream below. He followed suit jumping in next to him with Alex slumping down behind his older brother. They each dipped their makeshift oar blades into the creek looking over at the mound but not beyond it.

"Follow what I do," Shane said and Hunter obeyed. To make it easy Shane called out each command as he initiated the action so both Alex and Hunter could follow quickly.

"Lean forward," he called out. "Now back it off. Dig your oars down low, that's it, slow it down. Nice and steady, good." They followed the river which appeared in Hunter's mind calmly for a few minutes. Tall pine trees which didn't exist grew up on both sides of them. The tree upon which they sat stayed grey in colour but became a larger rubber dingy which bumped along the tranquil crystal clear water which existed within a mighty gorge. Hunter marvelled at what now surrounded him and was entirely ready to buy into this adventure. This also gave James enough time to get over his injuries, and the fact that everyone was ignoring him, before grabbing his stick and coming to re-join the group.

"Watch out now," Shane called out again. "We are heading into a rough patch ahead, rolling waterfalls and hidden rocks. We must be careful. Hold on tight to your oars. Here we go." It happened as Shane had said. Hunter lurched forward as the dingy took a bump and then returned to the water. He heard Alex follow behind him, falling hard enough to break part of the trunk on which they all actually sat upon. Shane swung to one side causing everyone else to do the same. Their oars were pulled up out of the water to avoid losing them before being plunged down again but with a deeper strike. Shane, no doubt on purpose, dug down to the bottom of the creek and dragged up broken sticks, reeds and water, spraying them all over his younger brother who roared with contempt. James dragged the muck off him, appalled at what his brother had done and turned his stick around to use it like a weapon on Shane rather than an oar.

"Mutiny is it," Shane called out as he responded in kind, snapping his stick and wielding it like a rapier. "I will deal with you." He leaned over towards Hunter and Alex and issued another order. Shane was playfully parrying his younger brother's blows which Hunter suspected were actually intended to do damage. "Stay the course lads, we are almost out of this." Both Hunter and Alex obeyed, neither wanting to get involved with the fight that was proceeding at their side. Both were aware they could get struck at any moment but were quite happy to go along with the fantasy. As Shane and James twisted and lunged in their epic battle, Hunter and Alex proceeded to ride the waves. Both sets of brothers deep in conflict with their current situations. After following Hunter's lead for quite some time Alex finally called out from his spot at Hunter's rear.

"We are almost there," he called out. "You have to dig your blade deeper."

"Alright, I am on it," Hunter answered the call.

"Me too," Shane said as well, referring to his own very different blade. Hunter dug down once, twice and three times and felt his brother keep the pace. Then finally, on the fourth strike of the water, Hunter's stick shattered.

"We made it," Alex said as he collapsed exhausted back into the hollow of the tree. Hunter wasn't sure if the timing was in response to the destruction of his stick or purely a coincidence. The handle remained in Hunter's hand, along with many small splinters and a tiny jarring sensation he had received when his stick broke.

"Yield, traitor," Shane snarled. He had his brother on his knees, somehow in their battle he had disarmed James and had triumphed over him. James still had vengeance in his eyes, but seeing as how he was beaten he put his hands up and retreated towards the back of the log. Hunter instead looked over the side of the boat and into the water behind. He knew he hadn't hit the bank, and he suspected that the creek bed was mostly sand and mud, so what had broken his stick? He watched the ripples cease as no more activity disrupted the water's surface, and the fog created from his stick impacting on the sand shifted away. Then he gasped in surprise.

"What? What do you see?" Shane enquired as he clambered over to Hunter's side, breathless as his eyes found what Hunter had revealed. "Is that what I think it is?"

"I think so," replied Hunter.

"Is that an axe?" asked Alex.

"No way," said James.

"Alright then," Shane said finally, "James go in and get it."

"Me, why me?" James responded in a low whine.

"Because you are already wet," Alex answered the obvious reason.

"I am not going in," James refused. "There are leeches and yabbies in there, plus it's freezing, thanks so much for your concern. I am not doing it."

"Fine, I will do it," Shane replied quickly. "But then it is mine." He pulled off his shirt and kicked off his shoes. He wasn't wearing any socks as he had told the boys on a previous occasion that they just picked up seeds from the grass which stabbed at your skin.

Then Shane jumped in. Hunter was probably about to say something about being careful but there hadn't even been time for that. With a gigantic splash Shane was lost to view. Amidst the murk Hunter could see bubbles rising to the surface and some sort of movement but he couldn't see Shane at all.

"Gee it's heavy," Shane called out amidst gulping for air as he broke the surface. He disappeared out of sight a second later. It seemed like minutes had passed when finally the water was broken again. This time it was the axe and only the axe. Shane must have been standing flat on the bottom of the creek. His arms wavered as the axe was held aloft, Hunter understood immediately that Shane needed help. He reached over as far as he dared, anchored down from behind by Alex who was stretching Hunter's slim shirt as he held on tightly. Hunter grabbed it just, fumbling several times with the slippery and rusted handle, and pulled it to safety on the grassy bank a metre above the water. Shane resurfaced again and sucked in a massive amount of air before swimming over to the side. He looked up at the others and after several attempts of trying to pull himself out from underneath the grass clumps on the bank he gave up. Instead he allowed himself to float downstream with the flow and came to an easier spot to crawl out just before the swamp area.

While they waited for his return, ideas started flowing; about what it was, where it had come from and what it had been used for. It was indeed an axe as they had thought. It was about metre in length and the entire object was made of metal. That metal was old. It was rusted so much in some parts that there were bulges of metal running all along its handle. There was no shine to the blade which was not of battle axe design, instead it was a shallow blade which resembled a flag more than an axe. It clearly had not been used for some time. But although that description was literally what existed in front of their eyes, it was not what each of the boys saw.

Hunter saw the platinum axe that he had seen in the video game. As he looked upon it he imagined a story where that character who had possessed it in the game had somehow lost it or had been beaten in battle and it fell into the creek which was before them. That train of thought allowed the environment to once again transform into something magical. Alex was convinced it was a knight's blade as well and despite it still laying on the grass he was brandishing the imaginary version, sweeping it around and around him laying waste to scores of bad guys. James was doing a similar sort of action.

"It's a farmer's axe," Shane stated as he arrived. Water dripping down his lean body as he spat out bits of dirt that had entered his mouth. "It looks so old you can't even use it."

"Yeah, so that's why it is mine," James stated moving forward to pick it up.

"No way," said Alex. "If anything it is Hunter's because he found it. Or even mine because I told him to."

"You didn't tell me to find an axe," Hunter said back. "And what would I want with a rusty axe anyway?"

"It could be worth a bit," Shane told his neighbour and both nodded in agreement. Alex and James heated up their claims for the item, starting to not only abuse each other but to start a push and shove contest. Shane looked at Hunter, asking by pointing whether or not he wanted it, to which Hunter simply shook his head saying no.

"It is pretty cool," Shane said as he picked it up. Hunter agreed. The younger brothers still argued. "I know just who to give it to." Both James and Alex stopped their disagreement. They stood tall and straight just like at school when a teacher says they are going to pick someone for a task. Shane stood looking at both boys, appearing to be choosing which one deserved the axe. Then, without warning, he ran off with it. Both James and Alex assumed that Shane was stealing it away from them and took off after him. Shane didn't run far, but he was pursued all the way.

He approached the edge of the swamp like area which was still swollen from the recent storms. Shane swung the axe a few times, using all the strength he could muster as it was ridiculously heavy. Then with an almighty grunt he released it, launching it into the middle of the swamp. The axe spun dangerously and seemed to fall in slow motion before finally it struck. Hunter had expected it to simply splash and sink into the water but surprisingly that had not been the case. It landed blade first into a solitary island of grass and stuck hard with a mighty squelch. It protruded from the swamp and stood there without collapsing under its own weight.

Hunter laughed. It would have been cool to own such a thing, but not at the expense of his new friends, and the temptation to sell it was too much. The memory contained within the item would be sold along with it. It was for the best and he entirely agreed with Shane's decision.

"You ever heard of the sword in the stone," Hunter asked the two younger boys. "If you can pull it out from there you can have it." Shane walked past to retrieve his shirt and shoes and high fived Hunter as he walked away. Hunter could see both Alex and James analysing if they could retrieve the rusted axe. The swamp was almost impossible to traverse while it was flowing so high. When the water lowered it became a bog which was filled with mud that would suck you down. Plus the axe was heavy. Shane had managed to wield it with great effort and both boys knew that they could not haul it out or carry it back by themselves. Hunter laughed again as they both realised that it was useless and with a huff they each walked back to the log before jumping off its far end and heading back towards home.

"This isn't the end of this," Shane said to Hunter alone as he pulled on a single shoe, watching the young boys leave.

"They can't possibly get it," Hunter declared to his friend.

"No, you are right," Shane agreed. "But they definitely will not be happy about it." Hunter nodded in agreement. Then he sighed. Then he groaned. Then Hunter and Shane followed after them.

CHAPTER 6 – THE TURF WAR

Shane was right, it was the start of a month from hell. Initially James and Alex only hated their respective siblings and acted out towards them considerably more than usual. Alex hated Hunter for the part his brother played in rejecting his claim for the axe, and James had a similar complaint about Shane. Both boys protested and sniped insults towards their older brothers but it didn't end up doing them any good.

James had initially tried to pass blame for the huge gash on his arm from where he fell into the creek, and he had also tried to claim his brother had been irresponsible and wasn't looking after him when they went out playing together. They had both gotten in trouble from swimming in the creek and chances were their parents were going to be getting some sort of old clothes so they could get dirtier in the future. Neither their mum nor dad cared if they got dirty, just the clothes that they got dirty in. When their dad had delved deeper into the whole responsibility issue he came out laughing.

"Magpies are so dangerous," he had lectured. "Especially around spring. The only thing you can do is run away from their area. If you are too slow that's your own fault." James had continued to whine despite the fact that he had well and truly lost the fight. This continued although everyone was ignoring him or giving him a sharp response, if there was any at all. James was undeterred by his family's response to him and his behaviour generally got worse, until finally it went too far.

James was moaning and groaning one morning when his younger sister came in. She pointed towards the television asking him to change the channel, which James refused to do, before he then proceeded to take the small bowl she carried which contained her morning tea of chicken crimpy biscuits and sultanas. May burst into tears and ran away. His dad returned seeking a response as to why James had stolen the food, to which James simply responded that it didn't matter what he took because everyone was ignoring him and May was a brat.

James had a long time to contemplate his actions in the solitude of his room for a couple of days, where he realised that his current course of action hadn't and wouldn't work. He still wanted to blame someone but it wasn't going to happen within his own home.

Alex had gone down a similar route. The difference was that he hadn't been ignored. His complaints against Hunter were unfounded and so unreasonable that they didn't make sense. Branded untrustworthy for the time being Alex had also been sent to his room for isolation. Any attempt at trying to convince his parents otherwise had been met with sterner judgement and eventually he planned to simply get Hunter back his own way rather than trying to manipulate his parents to do the work for him.

There came a day when both Hunter and Alex were left at home alone as their parents were only ducking out to get some curtains that had been made at a local retailer. It meant despite the fact Alex's mum said they were going for ten minutes they would actually be gone for the best part of an hour if not longer. Hunter was fine with this and stayed in his own room reading a new book he had received for his birthday a few weeks prior. Alex was told to remain in his room as part of his own punishment but Alex was not going to be following that order. Alex strode out of his prison and deliberately walked slowly past his brother's chambers.

"Shouldn't you be in your room?" the question came immediately from his older brother.

"Yep, but you can't make me stay there," Alex called out. He was met with a groan but Hunter did not move to chase him. Alex had progressed to the pantry in the kitchen, taken out a large packet of cheese twists and proceeded to chomp down on handfuls of the snack. He walked into Hunter's doorway, not yet venturing past the invisible boundary which existed beyond its timber frame.

"You shouldn't be eating those either," Hunter looked over from above the rim of his book. "You will just get in more trouble."

"I won't," snapped back Alex, "besides, I will just say that you did it and then you will get in trouble."

"You are being punished for being dishonest," Hunter laughed back, returning his gaze to the pages he was reading. "Who do you think they are going to believe?" Alex smiled in reply and proceeded to drop a handful of chips onto the floor.

"Oops," he said as they bounced noiselessly on the carpet despite their light mass. Some pieces were big enough to pick up easily enough while others hid amongst the grooves. Alex stepped across the precipice of the boundary to his brother's room. Hunter snarled at him to get out but Alex ignored the call, instead deciding to grind the snacks into the greenish carpet, altering the colour in the process.

"Get out of my room," Hunter yelled again, visibly becoming angry and distressed.

"You can't make me," Alex continued to be belligerent. He danced around the room dropping more cheese flavoured treats on the ground while gnashing wildly with his teeth causing spittle to sail everywhere. He could see that his brother was fighting himself back from causing harm to his younger brother, but Alex was still going to push it as far as he could. Hunter jumped up suddenly and made his way over towards Alex. Alex didn't see him coming and despite Hunter not touching him Alex threw one of his hands with cheese stained fingers out to defend himself. Alex accidently struck out at Hunter in the motion, but he didn't connect with his body. He had connected with his book. Cheese stains were wiped onto the new book with the fresh smelling pages right before Hunter's very eyes. Alex knew he had gone too far, and even the most skilled bullfighter would not have been able to stop Hunter's charge for what Alex had done. He gulped and allowed his face to remove the overconfident bravado he had been parading and replaced it with a sunken look of fear. You never damaged Hunter's stuff and especially not one of his books.

Alex had his face crushed into the carpet under Hunter's immense strength in an attempt to remove the stains and crumbs from the surface. He also had his whole body flung towards one of the walls where his head struck first and left a giant bend in the plasterboard. Alex had never seen a wall get a bruise before but that was exactly what it looked like. Alex was made to clean his mess and never informed their parents as to what had happened despite thinking that he had almost received a concussion, he knew if he did he would only be met with a harsher punishment.

Alex, just like James, had decided that his family were not going to take the blame for the loss of the axe. Therefore it was the neighbour's fault, and in particular the younger sibling, James.

The next few weeks consisted of both families coming together as their parents worked out some landscaping ideas between the houses. They were working towards a number of things that they were going to get done together to reduce the amount of money it would cost. Those things were fixing the concrete paths that were mostly complete but didn't connect in certain areas, as well as sorting out the fences, building some retaining walls and then laying some grass.

Shane and Hunter would continue to talk about anything, their friendship was becoming pretty solid. They would talk about different brands of bikes, new video games that were coming out that they wanted to play, going to the video store and renting some new movies because they had heard somewhere it was good, and more recently Pokémon. In the last instance it was more about Shane getting a copy from a relative that was entirely Japanese and Shane having no idea what was going on. The pair would make up the words as they had no clue how to speak the language and would fall about in fits of laughter.

Alex and James would just stare at each other. One day when the fence tradesman arrived Hunter and Shane had gone to play on the trampoline together while Alex and James had stayed with their dads. Each just sneered at each other, neither saying a word to the other. They got so caught up in their supposed hatred of each other that when asked a question from one of the grown-ups they simply answered with a growl. They didn't look at anything else apart from one another, nor did they actually voice why they disliked each other. They got laughed at by both Hunter and Shane but they were undeterred in their loathing.

Over the next few weekends their parents had organised all the trades required to come and do what they needed. The first weekend would consist of an excavator coming and digging a trench for a retaining wall at the front of Hunter's house, as well as clearing all the weeds and unwanted grass from the front and back yards of both houses and digging postholes for the fences. The following weekend would consist of fences being put up as well as other builders coming to brick a wall out the front of Hunter's house. Then finally the last weekend consisted of turf getting dumped at the houses and laid out. To reduce costs even further both families had agreed to do everything they could to help in regards to labour, which involved all the children as well.

An excavator came on the first weekend to scrape all the grass, rocks and garbage from both blocks. Hunter's house took longer as a big trench had to be dug across the front of the veranda to place a small retaining wall there. It was also the case that the back yard sloped along a medium sized decline whereas the Spigot's property was fairly flat. Once these were scraped the excavator attached a big posthole digger and started digging spots for fence posts to be placed in. This was a long task which took up most of the time. While this was happening the boys had been given another job.

"You have to move all the dirt piles that the bobcat has made and go and place them on the vacant corner block," Phil said to all four boys. He showed them a couple of wheelbarrows and shovels that could be used for the task. "I don't care how you do it but it has to be done today, work together or we won't feed you." Phil smiled as he thought his joke was funny, but then his smile vanished as he walked over to assist with Hunter's dad, leaving the boys unsure of their fate should they fail to complete the job.

There was already a big pile of dirt on the vacant corner block that had been put there when earth movers originally built Hunter's house, and this had been added onto by the excavator as it dug out the trench for the retaining wall. Four medium sized piles of dirt, each no taller than either Shane or Hunter, stood on both properties. One pile in each of the front yards, relatively close to each other and only separated by a driveway, and one more pile was in each of the back yards. The older boys decided that they would divide and conquer, each pair of siblings working on their own pile of dirt and then if one group needed help they would jump in and do so until everything was moved. They both started in the front yard as the piles of dirt were smaller and less spread out than those in the backyards. It was a choice which grated at both Hunter and Shane, not because of the work itself which they were happy to do due to the promise their mums had made of treats and relaxation afterwards, but because of the immediate show of disdain between the younger brothers.

Both Alex and James renewed their disgruntled looks at each other. This was mostly fine as each person had a shovel and they were managing to fill burrow loads pretty quickly. Due to how they started it meant that Alex and James were never in the same place for long. James took a burrow while Alex waited for the next load, driving his shovel into harder bits of dirt to break it up while he waited, and vice versa. Each of them decided eventually that the impact of their animosity was either largely being ignored or lost. With this train of thought instead of glowering at each other they decided to try and one up each other.

"I was voted the best player in my soccer team." Started James as he slammed his spade head down into the dirt.

"Well I was the players' player in my league team this year," countered Alex, thrusting his own tool just as hard into his own mound. Hunter and Shane exchanged glances, both deciding that they would stay out of this, while bringing down their respective brothers as the opportunity presented itself.

"Well soccer requires more skill."

"League requires physical toughness."

"You have to be smarter to play soccer."

"Footy requires strength."

"You have neither size nor strength," added Hunter as he reprimanded his brother.

"And you have never been considered smart," Shane discouraged the argument, "and we were in the same team this year and you were not the best player."

Knowing full well that their boasts were going to be disregarded or mocked by their brothers both younger siblings were smart enough to only argue when they were left alone together, or when they were pushing the barrow away at the same time. Hunter and Shane shook their heads at the pair, the annoyance of it driving them to dig faster so that they would be separated when they reached the back yards.

When the front was clear of both piles of dirt and they trudged out the back there was only sparse separation from their verbal tirades. Alex and James volunteered to keep running the wheelbarrows and Hunter and Shane let them. They were volunteering to do more work and the distance between the dumping spot and the shrinking dirt piles was longer than it had been in the front yard. Shane and Hunter did start piling up the barrows with more dirt though, making them heavier and harder to manoeuvre than previously. Alex and James didn't seem to care. They actually secretly relished it. They had started a new competition as they could no longer reprimand each other as effective as before. Each had started their own pile of dirt next to the much larger pile that already existed. Each would comment in passing how one was becoming bigger than the other, and it continued all afternoon until all boys were completely exhausted. There was no winner as the piles were relatively the same in size and the parents called it a draw to avoid a fight. This only encouraged their youngest sons to detest each other even more, as they had both failed in their task of beating the other.

The following weekend saw the installation of the fences around both properties. Shane and James had the promise of a brand new Nintendo 64 sitting on their kitchen bench the moment they finished the fences and the retaining wall. Again the group split the work. Hunter and Alex ran bricks for the front retaining walls for the quick and efficient brickies which toiled there; James and Shane kept running metal fence panels for the at least half a dozen workers, including their parents, who were building them as they went. The verbal garbage started all over again. This time it consisted of Alex and James boasting about how much extra work they had achieved over the other, regardless of how true, accurate or even plausible those claims actually were.

"One hundred bricks at least," bragged Alex.

"I've moved at least sixty panels all by myself," opposed James.

"I'm close to finishing this whole pallet of bricks," Alex continued.

"A whole boundary fence has been finished because of me," James confirmed.

Hunter and Shane, while initially bagging out their younger siblings, had moved onto being keepers of the peace as their brothers were as frustrating when they were annoying someone else rather than them.

"Apples and oranges," Hunter began.

"Yeah, you can't compare these things," added Shane, "we are all working bloody hard."

"I don't care who is doing what," Hunter continued the next time they were altogether. "Our common goal is to get this stuff done so we can go and relax and start playing those new games on that brand new console." Shane whole heartedly agreed with him, and the younger boys did too, but the conflict started up again. The tradesmen had been enjoying the toing and froing of the younger brothers and when it stopped they felt like they had lost a small trace of entertainment.

"I think that the kid who is taking the fence panels is working harder at the moment," joked one.

"No way," mocked another, "bricks are way harder to move. This young fella's doing a far better job." They only dropped the comments within earshot of each boy, but it lit the spark between them anew and the clash continued.

Eventually after a full day of torment and torture the retaining wall was built and the fences surrounding both properties were in place. After a long shower at their own houses all the boys converged in the Spigot's front lounge room to assemble the long sought after game console, before collapsing with a couple of packets of chips each and the promise of a lazy afternoon and night. They started playing some new games that they had received which could be played by everyone. Once these were tried and tested they fell back on previous games that they already knew well. It was here where James and Alex started their rivalry again, boasting about how good they were. Once more it was short lived. Too concerned with beating one another they were oblivious to the fact that Hunter and Shane had formed a united front to them and quickly dismantled their limited strategies within the games, making them lose without ever seeing it coming. This continued until both younger brothers were evicted from playing the games and, surprisingly, this expulsion from the new console was supported whole heartedly by their parents.

"You are both being twits," Phil had said. "Give it a rest." He was greatly perturbed from being dragged away from his small, but well earned, drinking session with his neighbour. Hunter's dad agreed completely.

Finally the last week of massive labour arrived with the dumping of several pallets of grass. They were placed upon the road in the cul-de-sac, which was an inconvenience to no one as they were the only ones who lived there and the builders from nearby sites had gone home for the weekend. The task that was laid before them was simple enough. Get all the grass from the pallets and into both yards. The parents would start to make sure that it was all exactly where they wanted it and then they would dictate where the next roll of turf would be placed as they arrived. Both dads would be running with the wheelbarrow, taking multiple rolls at a time, whereas both mums would be the generals of the operation, directing everyone where to place their incoming loads. The boys all looked on as the proceedings commenced but before they started they were abruptly halted.

"We told you that you would all have to wear the same thing," Shane's mum walked over to them. "So we made sure that we got cheap clothing for all of you to wear, and ruin." She laughed slightly and started dishing out what she had obtained. They were just plain white shirts, probably no more than a dollar for each of them at the local department store. The boys were not embarrassed of each other getting changed right then in front of one another, the white shirts were enough to make them ashamed by themselves. "Try not to get them too dirty though," she laughed as she went to coordinate her own yard. Shane laughed at the comment. There was a moderate amount of rain falling on that Saturday morning. It wasn't heavy enough to abandon the upcoming task, nor was there thunder and lightning heard or seen to stop them for safety reasons. But it was wet enough to completely drench the boys, as well as smear mud as they carried the thick rolls of grass pressed to their chests.

"How about a competition?" Hunter suggested.

"Really?" Shane looked at him quizzically. They had done everything they could to dissuade contests for the last few weeks between their brothers, it seemed odd that Hunter would suggest one.

"Yep," Hunter answered cheerily, "We are going to get absolutely drenched today, and it is going to be a bit of a slog moving all those things. I suggest we have a competition to see who gets through the most rolls to keep us going, so we can focus on something else apart from how much this is going to hurt."

Shane nodded in agreement, noticing the look that James and Alex instantly shared. "Yeah sounds good, but just so you know I could do this all day long. You lot don't stand a chance." No sooner had he made his declaration of intent to win did he step out into the deluge and towards the first placement of rolled turf. Shane lifted it up with the smallest of grunts and disappeared towards where his mum was standing ready to give instructions. Hunter followed suit, and then finally the two younger boys jumped into action.

It took moments to realise that the tallying of the grass would be more of a mental competition against oneself than against the others. The grass was heavy and awkward to carry as it was, but the scraped ground had left slippery slurry underneath which formed puddles in the boys footprints and ridges where they slid. They were instantly on guard as to where their feet would have to be placed and the best path to get there and back without sliding and falling over. Shane and Hunter had figured it out early, each identifying the safest path to their destination and a conservative route back. They also had both started in Shane's backyard. Alex and James took this as permission to take on each other within Alex's own yard, to keep their rivalry going. The fact was that it was a shorter route and Hunter and Shane were being smart about conserving energy and increasing their turf totals.

"Twenty one," Shane yelled out stupidly as he returned to the stacks of grass.

"Same," yelled out Hunter right on his tail. Alex heard the claims but didn't have that amount and instead asked what James had accrued so far.

"I'm not telling you," James snapped back. "I'm keeping a tally in my head so you can't cheat." Alex powered on beside James, both pushing each other to finally get that elusive victory over the other. It mattered so much and so little at the same time.

Every boy felt the squelch each time their feet hit the ground. They were avoiding stepping in puddles and getting mud and small sticks stuck in their socks, but the rain was still pooling in the base of their soles so every step provided a weird pressure sensation around their socks. This was manageable for some time, but Hunter could feel the onset of blisters. His mind wandered away from the competition and onto what he remembered from all the war stories he had been told.

Trudging around in the mud gave him what he thought was a familiar sensation and feeling to what the diggers felt when they travelled around the Gallipoli peninsula. Rain was bucketing down, he was against others to try and win, and his socks were sticking to his feet. Is this trench foot? He thought to himself. He grabbed another roll of turf, imagining that it was a sandbag that he was having to place to provide cover for his mates.

"Keep moving," Hunter finally called out, receiving odd looks from those around him. Their effort did increase in response. He imagined the unwanted tools that were being used to cut and shape some of the grass were discarded guns and bayonets, thrown down in the struggle to survive. Their parents, the commanding officers, kept giving them encouragement every time they came back. The boys looked a mess now. Mud was clumped all over their shirts as a result of constantly holding the heavy rolls to their chests. Their damp fibres clinging to their skin and revealing the skin beneath like windows. Their hands were covered in mud, which was manageable as long as they didn't dry, but it meant that every time they wiped dirt, rain or sweat from their faces they smeared gunk from their chins and up through their hair. Hunter noticed his dad taking a break for a moment. Hand on hips as he watched what was happening around him.

"Keep moving soldier," Hunter called out again, disregarding the difference between fiction and reality. His dad simply nodded, panting to regain his breath, and returned to stacking his wheelbarrow. "Good lad," Hunter cheered him on as he flung another roll onto his shoulder. He found that he too was beginning to tire. He didn't mind so much that his shoulder was covered in mud as long as his chest and arms were receiving some sort of relief.

"Fifty," Shane called out as he headed back in the opposite direction.

"Fantastic," Hunter replied enthusiastically. "We may just survive this." His shirt was starting to dangle from his shoulders and his waist as it was weighed down by the constant stream of rain. As he threw down his next delivery he looked around and saw that the back of Shane's house was almost finished. It had taken the best part of two hours and they had done about half of the work but there was no time to stop now. Hunter noticed that everyone looked as bad as he did but despite taking big deep breaths they all powered on.

Both back yards were finished leaving only the fronts to do. Hunter flicked back from his trench warfare scenario that he had been envisioning and stepped up his own assault.

"I'm about to hit a hundred," he bellowed, "None of you are going to beat me." Surprisingly, even to Hunter, he started to jog. The boys all matched his enthusiasm whether they felt the same or not. They started trotting around, managing to grab more than just one roll in every minute and increasing the pace. The clouds cleared above them and everyone groaned. It was not that they had enjoyed marching around in the mud which now covered most of their legs, because they very much didn't. It was because as soon as the sun hit the mud on their hands and arms it turned it from a slime and then into a hardening crust. It made their hands feel gritty and irritable. It made the rest of the muck on them harden and snap painfully as they moved, clinging to skin or hair and inflicting harm as they persevered. The competition subsided for the time being and everyone looked to the finish line which was coming along fast. The space which had been brown before was now diminishing, being overtaken by the most vibrant green colour. Hunter washed his hands with the moist blades of grass as he made what was about his millionth trip back to load up again. His body was becoming prickly with the same motions. His knees weren't liking him turning the same way, his arms weren't amused by holding themselves up for long periods of time, his neck and back were sick of taking the load.

Then finally it ended. There were no rolls of turf left and no spaces remaining to be filled. All the boys collapsed in close proximity to each other. Their breaths heaved and even though Hunter wanted to call out a random number to see who bested him he didn't. He had no idea what number he was up to, anything he said would have been a lie, and he imagined the other boys were the same.

"Well done boys," Hunter's dad said walking over to them. His old ripped rugby jersey hanging off him at odd angles, interesting splotches appearing all over his clothing. "You have done so well, we are all proud of you," he continued. "We are all going to go inside and get cleaned up, then we will start getting a barbecue ready for later on and everyone can chill out." He looked at all of them and smiled as Shane's mum walked over carrying some items. "You can't go inside yet, you are way too muddy, and we don't want you waiting around out here or inside. Judy has got some pump packs for you to go and play with."

Hunter realised that pump packs were actually water pistols, but as he looked up with limited interest he noticed that these were not just any ordinary water guns. They were huge, and each had a massive backpack filled with some sort of liquid which he didn't think was water.

"I don't think you are wet enough, nor your clothes dirty enough, so I figured you can go out the back and play with these while you all wait," she said. Hunter's body screamed no way, but his brain made his limbs move automatically countermanding the instruction to stop. He thanked Shane's mum as he grabbed hold of one and strapped the backpack over his shoulders. The others followed suit.

They all begrudgingly for the moment traversed out towards the waterlogged back paddock. For the first time ever since they had been together they had to access the space by using the path thanks to the newly erected fences. They got to the end of the path and looked over at the grass mound which seemed so far away now, due to their bodies straining with fatigue and their new approach from the path.

"Okay, quick game," Shane finally said. "Game's over when you run out of water. Whoever is the cleanest, wins. Alex and James, we will give you a head start to reach the mound. Go." No one waited on agreeing to the terms or even argued over them. James and Alex somehow found it within them to start sprinting towards the grass mound. Seeking the highest ground, which was supposedly essential in the next stage of their fight. Hunter just groaned knowing he had to make the same journey.

"Hey this isn't water," Shane stated as he tested out how his weapon worked, it was best to know those sort of things before entering a melee. "It's dye."

"That will make it easier to see who is the cleanest," Hunter suggested, "there are very few spots on our once white shirts to actually get dirty now anyway." As he watched the two younger boys approach their destination he started to walk in the same direction, flicking off clumps of loose mud as he went.

"I don't really want to climb Ayer's Rock right now," Shane groaned.

"Don't worry about it too much," Hunter responded weakly. "By the time we get there those two would have wasted all their ammunition on each other. Then we drench them and go home for a nice hot shower."

"Great plan," Shane agreed.

Hunter wasn't wrong. James and Alex had taken off at a sprint for exactly that reason. This was the next and hopefully final time that they would get to show that they were greater than the other. What started as placing blame for not possessing a rusty old axe had become a competition for a higher place in their hierarchy of friends, and neither wanted to be on the bottom. They each sprinted into different spots amongst the grass mound and started stalking one another, previous games creating the groundwork for how they should proceed. Each snuck around as if totting a sniper rifle rather than the tennis balls they were used to. Both seemingly attuned to any sudden movements.

A shot was not fired for a long time.

Alex finally saw James slip down to the lower level of the grass mound and watched him in secret. He noticed that after his fall James was constantly looking up at the top ramparts of the grass castle, expecting Alex to ambush him from above. Alex, seeing this, slid quietly down to the lower level as well. This would be an attempt to surprise him from a location he wasn't expecting. He was too eager and ruffled some grass as he made it to the lower landing. James turned and saw him, before ducking instinctively in behind a large tuft of grass, pressing himself up against the mound wall. They each snuck forward when they deemed it safe until they were only a few metres apart, definitely close enough to strike the other with a burst from their water guns.

"You're going down," Alex called out.

"Don't make promises you can't keep," James replied. "Just give up, you know I am better than you."

"I know that if you step out from there you are going to get wet," Alex sneered again.

"I'm already wet, loser," James countered.

"Then why are you afraid to show yourself?" The question lingered in the air. Both boys could hear the other breathing they were so close.

"You are both losers," came another voice from nearby. James and Alex stepped out from their hiding places instinctively and looked up.

"Well that was dumb," called out Hunter.

"Fire!" yelled Shane. Both Shane and Hunter launched a full attack from their pump packs. In the walk over they had figured out how to use them almost expertly, including reloading and aiming. Their younger brothers had been so loud and so focused on getting each other that they were easy to find and never saw their brothers coming. James and Alex discovered too late that the pistols were full of dye. After emptying their barrels Shane and Hunter reloaded but James and Alex ducked down into the grass where they couldn't be seen from above.

"No fun," Shane groaned, "now we have to go down to get them."

"Yeah, but I am not sliding down," Hunter moaned. "I will walk around to get them." Both boys shuffled off leaving Alex and James alone. Finally, when Alex was sure the older boys had gone, he stepped out with his hands raised in surrender.

"Why are we fighting each other?" he asked James, who saw him and held his soaker up to point directly at Alex's head. Both boys had few spots left on their clothes that were white anymore. "We should be fighting them." James was still reluctant to accept that Alex was surrendering.

"They are stronger and faster than either of us," James answered, shaking as he aimed his weapon at Alex and clearly reluctant to make the admission. "They always get us in trouble."

"Yeah, I know," agreed Alex. "When we are inside, when we are alone." He gestured between himself and James. "But if we work together, then just one of them can't contain both of us, and we would be a handful when they are united. When we are fighting each other we are easier targets for them." James dropped his water pistol's sights, finally seeing the sense in his neighbour's words. He nodded once.

"So what were we fighting about?" James asked with a smile. Their month long feud almost instantly forgotten.

"We were fighting about who the better brothers were," reiterated Alex, "the youngest or the oldest. I have an idea follow me." James no longer needed any reason to follow Alex. Their hatred dissipated and they were finally united in their quest to get out of the shadows of their bigger brothers. No sooner had they disappeared and formulated their makeshift plan, Shane and Hunter re-emerged on the lower level of the grass mound.

"Where have they gone?" Shane asked, immediately realising that Alex and James were no longer where they had left them.

"I'm not chasing them," Hunter shrugged with weariness. "They are probably just off somewhere beating each other up."

"Not my problem, or yours," Shane replied. "I don't have much dye left anyway. I don't know what I was going to do. I am very happy to go home." Hunter and Shane turned to head back to the very distant path. The idea of a steaming hot shower gleaming in their minds, especially as the drizzly rain had returned. A hot shower, hot food, warm clothes, and an afternoon of video games was an amazing draw card. So focused on their goal were they that Shane and Hunter were completely oblivious to the return of their younger siblings.

A roar echoed through the air as both boys jumped from their hiding spots nearby, commando rolled along the ground as they regained their feet, and pumped their guns with all their might. Shane and Hunter had been taken completely by surprise and as a result they had completely disregarded where they had positioned themselves. They stood on a higher grass platform, which overhung the creek, so they could initially get a better view of where James and Alex had been. In the act they had completely surrounded themselves with water and an impossible leap to safety across it. They had managed to corner themselves and could do nothing to defend themselves against the onslaught they received. After a long time of getting pulverised the flow eventually stopped.

Hunter and Shane shook off the dye which covered their arms and hands, the only defence they could muster to stop the bullets of water getting into their eyes. James and Alex high fived and congratulated each other, completely content in the fact that they had not only worked well together but they had done so by defeating their brothers. Shane, after finally clearing his face, managed to open his eyes and extended a hand forward.

"Well done, you got us." He congratulated the pair as Hunter extended his own tired hand in recognition. It was more than James and Alex could have hoped for. They were friends now, their troubles vanishing, they had beaten their older brothers and they had done so by battering them down with a tank full of dye. After smiling at each other they shouldered their guns on the loose straps that were attached and walked forward to accept the congratulatory handshake that was being offered.

Hunter and Shane smiled as they shook the boys' hands, acknowledging that in this case they had been bested. They took one look at each other, nodded once, and as everyone shared a smile together Hunter and Shane struck. With one mighty tug each they pulled their younger brothers forward, lurching them headlong unprepared, and hurled them into the cold creek below. Shane and Hunter didn't laugh at the pair as they floundered about, trying to comprehend what had just happened to them. Instead they forged their own unspoken bond that stated that they would be united against the endeavours of their upstart siblings.

"Hot shower?" Hunter questioned, not even caring at what they had just done to Alex and James.

"Hot food, warm clothes and video games," Shane answered showing just as much fatigue. "Sounds good." With no idea of helping either James or Alex, they then left. Shoulder to shoulder.

CHAPTER 7 – STUNT BIKE KINGS

Life wasn't always restricted to the house or to the creek. Hunter loved those places and the more he explored and played the more they became imprinted in his brain. But the world also expanded out the front of their house and onto the road.

They were restricted to what they could do within their own backyards as the new turf was strictly off limits, as shown by the star posts and fluorescent tape, to allow the grass to establish its roots and become stronger. Even the family pet Buster, who had been confined to the house for most of his childhood, was still not allowed onto the grass. The fear of their mum, dad, or one of the kids stepping on the now green slope and dislodging a mat of turf was too great so they would not risk nor allow anyone to set foot upon them. Buster would still have to go for predetermined walks, which was hard for such a young pup and accidents still occurred, which was frequently changing the new house smell within their home. These consisted of walks out towards the back paddock to do his business, but only along the boundary fence. This also resulted in a towel being used to clean his low lying coat on every single occasion.

Shane and Hunter found that they were spending more time riding their bikes and talking all about them. They were still restricted as to where they were allowed to ride to, but the more they showed how trustworthy they were the further they were allowed to travel. James and Alex were constantly restricted to a speed hump which existed up the street maybe five hundred metres away, unless their brothers were with them. This gave the older boys a little bit more power, but it also meant that they were annoyed by Alex and James to travel further up the road almost every time they were out. In truth Shane and Hunter were only allowed about another hundred metres beyond that speed hump to the next corner, as beyond that point the road left the safety of Northstoke Way and entered the extremely busy highway of Molong Road. That hundred metres however, consisted of a hill that went straight up and provided a ramp of sorts that delivered a stunt opportunity or moment to shine in front of the other boys.

Shane and James were better at simple stunts, whereas Hunter and Alex had not massively been into that aspect of riding but were still eager to try. Some of these stunts consisted of trying to pop a wheelie by dragging back the front wheel, doing bunny hops down the road by bouncing on both tyres while going slow, or doing small jumps off the curb. All of their bikes were small BMX style bikes which allowed them to attempt such stunts with less confusion than a geared bike would provide.

Hunter was amazed as the conversation would move from simple bikes to new accessories that would make them cooler. Stunt pegs added to the front and back wheels allowing someone to be piggy backed on either the front or back of the bike. They were also supposedly used for grinding along things but as the area only consisted of concrete edges they marked them rather easily. Shane also added a front brake to his bike to allow him to 'walk his bike' as he called it, which consisted of hitting the brakes and allowing the bike's momentum to shift on the front wheel lifting up the back, and then rotating the whole frame around the handle bars to land the rear wheel back on the ground in front and carrying on. Hunter couldn't do it, and admitted it, simply marvelling at the new ideas that they would come up with. Shane never put down his friend knowing full well it was not something that everyone could do, but he didn't mind sledging both James and Alex.

The younger siblings had formed a tight bond after their month of hatred, but all that seemed to unite them was their desire to be the most annoying combination in history. James would try to do whatever Shane did, claiming the older brother was stealing his ideas, where Alex would solely dish out unpleasant comments towards Shane, not even attempting the trick he gave so much grief over.

It seemingly came to a head one day when Shane had decided to try and do jumps off of that speed hump part way up the road. The ride up the slope consisted almost entirely of the younger boys bagging out the older ones as they progressed to the top. They would each go one at a time, three would wait at the bottom to see what occurred while one rode up to show off their skills. Everyone got a free ride at first to see how fast they would come down, the control they would need, and the impact of the speed bump on the tyres.

Then it started.

Each of them managed to find some sort of air in their first attempt. Whether that was the ruler high gap that Shane managed or the jump over a small ant that Hunter delivered it didn't matter. But it was clear that they would all have to step up. Shane led the charge for the next run, providing a wheelie into a jump which he managed to land. James did the same trick but almost fell off as he hit the speed hump. Alex went before his brother for the first time ever, trying to knock him down before he went and managed to pull off a small wheelie, basically just lifting his tyre up off the ground the smallest bit before rolling slowly over the top of the speed trap. Hunter fluked the second round win as he lost complete control. He came down fast managing to pull a wheelie just before he hit the bump. His momentum was still turning as he leant back and made impact, the front wheel lifting higher with the hit along with the rest of the bike. He landed it safely, although extremely awkwardly with his teeth firmly squeezed together preparing for a stack, and received a cheer from Shane and a shake of the head from James.

"One more," Shane declared as he set back off to the top of the hill. They all yelled out the presence of an approaching car and moved well to the side of the road. Once clear Shane shot down for the last time. He came down faster, but not in a straight line like he had done before. He swerved slightly then approached the speed hump at an almost forty-five degree angle. He came up off his chair and shifted his weight completely. It resulted in the back tyre of his bike swinging completely around as he managed to find big air. The bike landed safely, going straight down the road as if nothing happened. Hunter cheered while the younger boys clapped, sharing a look of contempt between them.

"My turn," James called out, and managed to ride his bike as close to Shane as he could manage without hitting him. It was a mute act, there was no point in trying to intimidate Shane after he had already landed a pretty amazing trick. James turned at the top of the hill and dug his feet down hard into the pedals, driving his bike forward at an immense pace. It was clear that he was going to attempt the same trick as his brother by the way he approached. He found air as he connected with the centre of the road, though not as much as Shane, and his bike lurched around in reply to his actions. James landed safely, with all boys clapping as a result, but he wobbled about awkwardly as he landed facing backwards. He hadn't achieved the full rotation that Shane had. James knew he hadn't done as well, but Hunter cheered him on hard anyway as the attempt had still looked spectacular and was better than anything he could come up with. In fact Hunter thought it looked more spectacular than Shane's as the difficulty in landing backwards safely was multiplied tenfold.

Next up was Hunter. He had no desire to even attempt to do what his neighbours had tried. Instead he was going to roll down and try a small hop with the intention of landing safely. He came down the hill easily but with a bit more pace then he originally desired. The idea changing slightly so he could land safely on the other side of the wide speed hump rather than jarringly on top of it. He leaned forward into the handlebars, envisioning that he was more aerodynamic this way. He could hear and feel the air as it whistled past his ears and grabbed at his flapping shirt behind him. He squinted his eyes so his eyelids stopped flustering and he could see better. Hunter tucked his arms to his sides as he tried to stop the fluttering of his loose fitting shirt as the wind filled it causing unwanted drag behind him. As he advanced towards the jump his mindset changed from bike rider to Winter Olympic snow skier. In his head he imagined that as soon as he hit the ramp he would complete a thousand flips and tumbles up in the air before landing safely back on the ground. That idea was one of his more ridiculous, even for Hunter, and he flipped it from his mind as he refocused on what was real. Just as he prepared to make his jump Alex ran out into the ramp.

"Ooga-di-booga-di," Alex yelled, waving his arms frantically. No doubt he was trying to put off his brother, but at that speed Hunter could not stop or even slow down, a sudden turn would definitely cause him to topple sideways and crash hard into the asphalt. Hunter didn't want to think about how much that would hurt, but he didn't have enough time to think.

He acted.

Hunter turned his handlebars slightly so he avoided collision with his stupid younger brother. He still hit the speed hump at pace but his trajectory changed from open road to small tree. Hunter yelped as he found more air than he had desired and flew towards a small silver birch which lined the curb side nearby. He ducked his head out of instinct, avoiding major limbs which jutted out towards him and allowing his helmet to take all of the slaps from smaller twigs that hung there. As he made contact with the ground he was relieved that he hadn't hit anything or come off his bike, his feet bounced off the peddles and extended out in front of him as if acting like another buffer to anything he might come into contact with. Hunter still had to pull back towards the road quickly to avoid hitting a parked car in the driveway positioned there. The motion sent him back off the curb at speed and once more he sailed through the air. Hunter finally managed to apply enough pressure on the brakes to stop in the middle of the road as he landed. James and Shane both looked at him dumbfounded before leaping into a mighty cheer.

"That was so cool," James congratulated him, the competition seeming to disappear with the desperation of Hunter's flight. The outcome had been favourable, but that didn't stop Hunter sucking in air deeply as his body recovered from the adrenaline buzzing around inside, contemplating what his fate very nearly could have been. Hunter shot a look at his brother.

"Geez you are an idiot," he said calmly despite the quiver in every breath he inhaled.

"Whatever," Alex replied, shrugging off the accusation. "You're just jealous because I am going to beat you." He rode off to the summit and the starting position to begin his run, completely oblivious of the stare he was transfixed with by his older brother. What made matters worse was that Alex was apparently going to do his own commentary.

"Now for the moment you have all been waiting for," he declared to the three boys at the far end of his run, and anybody else who was nearby the top to listen. "You are about to see the amazing Alex as he steals the spotlight from those who have come before him." His arms were spread wide, appealing to nobody in particular but continuing with his small show. He finally gripped his handlebars and pushed off the ground to start his roll down the hill. "How will he do that you ask? Simple. The amazing Alex is going to do a jump over the speed hump." The others were not impressed and just watched on with folded arms as Alex continued. "But if that wasn't enough he is also going to do it with no arms on the handlebars." Alex struggled to keep himself steady, but after applying a decent amount of brake he allowed his arms to slump down at his sides. They momentarily came forward to correct his direction. The road appeared more curved from the centre to its side than other roads, with Alex's bike continuing to make its way towards the driveways and gutters which followed him down. Alex appeared to have less control than he felt as the bike constantly wavered backwards and forwards.

"Not enough you say," Alex persisted with his speech, an obvious touch of fear had entered his voice. "The amazing Alex will also do all of this with his eyes closed." Hunter and Shane looked horrified with the suggestion, having no faith in Alex's ability to pull off what he claimed. James was grinning from ear to ear, but Hunter couldn't decide whether it was in support of his comrade or the knowledge that Alex would most likely fail. Alex kept his eyes open even after his claim. Closing one at a time as he tried to fix his motion. They didn't close entirely until only a couple of metres before the speed hump.

"How is he going to control the bike without his hands on the bars, or with only a little speed?" Shane asked not expecting an answer.

"Oh no," Hunter said, unable to turn away but semi covering his mouth and eyes with one hand.

"Oh yes," whispered James, clenched fists as he watched on with delight.

"The amazing Alex," Alex called out as he closed his eyes shut tight, throwing his arms up in the air. As soon as he hit the bump everyone, even Alex, knew he had made a mistake. He had rolled onto it with his tyre shaking, his direction not going in a straight line down the road. His front tyre had turned and jack-knifed the entire bike frame. His hands flung out to correct the action but with his eyes shut his hands shot off in the direction that Alex thought the bars were when they had already long since turned. He flung over the top of his handlebars as the bike collapsed but Alex's motion stayed straight on. The rest of the boys could do nothing but watch on as Alex sailed through the air and dove towards the consequence of his actions. Time seemed to slow but that would only make the pain even more disastrous.

Alex landed with a thump. His arms had been flailing wildly to cling onto anything that existed within reach during his plight. His legs still pumped comically like they were striking the pedals which had disappeared behind him. He felt the full force on his chest. Alex groaned and the wind was punched from his lungs. He tried standing, groaning as he searched for the missing air that escaped from within his body. He couldn't speak nor groan because of his pain until several moments later when it all rushed back into him. He coughed several times. When he turned to face the boys who had rushed over to help him he was met with looks of anguish. They stared down at Alex's chest. He first clutched at his chin which had been grazed as he slid along the black bitumen. He was greeted with skin clinging to his face and the warm touch of blood on his fingers. Then he looked down at his shirt, or rather where his shirt had been. His clothing had been completely torn away from the impact, whatever was left now completely coated with blood or dirty tar follicles and stone.

"Come on mate," Hunter came over to his brother and quickly threw an arm under his shoulder, guiding him back towards the path that led home. Hunter had abandoned both his own bike and that of his brother as he assisted. He knew that he could come back and get them, but secretly was aware that his neighbours would bring them back for him. All rivalries were gone, and despite Hunter wanting to jeer his brother or tell him how uncoordinated his brother was it was all left unsaid.

"How funny was that," James said with a low volume cackle as the pair trudged slowly away. Shane pointed over to where Alex's crippled bike still lay in the middle of the road, insisting silently that James retrieve it, before going to recover Hunter's.

"It was not that funny," Shane replied. He wasn't reprimanding James because he himself was holding back the urge to smile. "You know what this means don't you?" James looked puzzled as he made his way back to his brother, pushing one bike with each hand.

"No, unless you mean we can bag him out about it for ages," James smiled again.

"You can do that anyway," confirmed Shane. "But because he got injured up here trying to jump over the speed hump you can say goodbye to doing that again anytime soon." It suddenly dawned on

James what that would mean, the smile he had carried before completely vanishing from his face.

"Aww man," James groaned, his smile lost in an instant.

Shane's prediction was correct. Alex was harmed under the watch of the older boys so all had been restricted to only playing within the cul-de-sac for the foreseeable future. Hunter and Shane knew that the constraints would be eased eventually so tried to make the most of it. James was the only one who seemed to argue against the outcome.

"You were responsible, and Alex got hurt," he stamped around thrashing his arms. "This has nothing to do with me. You lot should be stuck here, not me. I should be allowed to ride off and up and down this street as much as I want." His complaint fell on deaf ears as both Hunter and Shane continued to ignore him. They had all been restricted from going down to the back paddock as well, for the simple reason that Alex would want to go and it wasn't fair to him. Alex had torn great gauges out of his chest and the fear was that with so many open wounds and weeping scabs that he could get infected and really sick. Alex then had to stay within the house at all times. Eventually, after he had become tired from having his voice ignored, James went inside and joined him. They simply played with the Nintendo together without the in game abuse from their older brothers, which meant they were more evenly matched and had a fantastic time.

Hunter and Shane loved the fact that their little brothers were absent as it enabled them to do something else with their time. As their bikes were as grounded as they were and they couldn't ride for long distances anymore they turned their attention towards short distance endeavours instead. Using wheelbarrows and shovels along with discarded building equipment they set about making jumps.

The process was simple enough to the boys. They would use the vacant corner block which already had a huge mound of dirt stacked at its rear. They would get mounds of dirt and pile them in various locations. Initially they got about ten wheelbarrows full and formed the same amount of tiny jumps within the block's boundaries. They were hardly jumps, but they provided an obstacle course in which they rolled around and slowly turned into a track. These small jumps were added to slow them down, as well as extra lumps of dirt used to assist with turning corners easier. Apart from the shovels they also used their own bike tyres to mould each small dirt jump as they grew, providing tread marks in the disturbed soil to pat it down and make it denser, making it less likely that it was going to give way under the weight of the bike or if they rolled over it the wrong way.

This lasted for several weeks and the entire time the younger brothers stayed inside playing video games until Alex healed, and whilst they played they plotted on how they could annoy their older siblings once they returned to the outside world. Their decided target was to influence and take over the small stunt bike course that Shane and Hunter had created on the vacant block.

Hunter and Shane were busy working on their newest build when the younger boys eventually returned. A tall half metre high jump which had a flat table top like surface at its summit, so you could not only jump over it but you could jump onto it before vaulting your bike back off from the top. Despite its relatively small size it had been a formidable accomplishment to build it up so quickly into a shape they were proud of. Before they could test it for themselves and see how well it fitted in with the rest of the course they were disrupted by James and Alex on their own bikes.

"Cool course," James crowed as he rode his bike around the two boys with Alex close behind him.

"Too cool for you," Alex added. It was clear that his injuries had not helped to build up some humility or make him show more care towards his actions. "We have to thank you for making this for us to use though."

"You aren't going over this jump," Shane interrupted them, "not before we do."

"Fair enough," James agreed. "But we will use the rest of the course while you aren't using it."

"Fine," grunted Hunter. "Just get lost." James and Alex started riding their bikes around the course, taking it all in as they rode. Both boys were impressed, but they weren't going to tell their brothers that, and it was quite fun to go over it, especially when they didn't have to help make any of it.

After the first few times around though they decided that they could have even more fun by tormenting their older brothers. James made the first suggestion and implemented his ideas quickly. Every time he rolled over a jump he was going to stop with his back tyre resting on it, or at least resting partially on it. Then he was going to spin his wheel and destroy it from one side. Alex on the other hand would hit his brakes as his back tyre swept over it and drag big gaping holes in the jumps that had been painstakingly made.

"When I get hold of you," Shane threatened holding a long stick that he picked up from nearby. He didn't chase after either of them, instead turning back to the task in front of him. James was happy with the response but it was clear that neither Hunter nor Shane really cared what happened to their creation as long as the jump they were working on wasn't disturbed. James then called Alex over to one part of the vacant block, formulating another plan.

"Here is a good one for you," started James, immediately sucking Alex into his new scheme. "They are only caring about that jump they are working on. It is too big to destroy, at least not while they are here, so we have to do something else." Alex nodded as he followed the train of thought. "I reckon we continue riding around like we don't care about them anymore, like we have given up, and then when they finally go and get their bikes we go over it before they do. That will really annoy them."

"Yeah," agreed Alex eagerly. "But don't you reckon your brother will try and get us?"

"Maybe," James said with a tinge of despair.

"Don't worry," Alex said, coming up with another suggestion. "How about I just do it. Hunter wouldn't dare come after me, not while I am hurt."

"Good plan," James approved, it seemed like the result of Alex riding over it was his plan all along. "I will stay on the lookout as we ride around and as soon as Shane goes to get his bike I will let you know. Then you can take the first jump." They nodded at the prospect of their mischievous plan.

Around and around they went, actually starting to enjoy the jumps as they focused on using them properly rather than destroying them. Hunter and Shane almost completely ignored them now as they toiled, which was precisely what was needed. James rolled around the course for what must have been the tenth time before finally he saw their opening. Shane and Hunter had stood back to admire their handy work before finally Shane went to get his bike, while Hunter stood guard. It was clear that the two older boys had no trust for the younger brothers to be left alone with their masterpiece. James didn't care about that and gave Alex the signal that told him it was time. No sooner had he given it had Alex made his intentions clear. But Hunter was alert, spotting them immediately.

"Don't you dare," Hunter called out from behind the jump. He would not be fast enough to step in front to stop his little brother.

"What are you going to do about it?" Alex laughed as he gained speed, preparing to launch himself over the new hurdle. He was already calculating where he would land and flexing his leg muscles expecting to have to take off quickly as soon as he landed so Hunter didn't grab him. Alex watched as a surge of anger spread over Hunter's face. There was nothing he could do. Alex rolled up the ramp and onto the top at increasing speed as he continued to pump his legs.

Alex had hardly made it to the top of the ramp when Hunter reacted quicker than Alex had ever seen him do so. Hunter grabbed out and reached the stick that Shane had threatened James with. In no time at all he turned sharp on his heel and stabbed it forward at Alex's bike. Hunter found his mark, lodging the fallen tree limb firmly in between the spokes of Alex's front wheel. The stick hardly made it through one rotation before it jammed up against the fork in the front of the bike's wheel holding frame. The bike stopped dead but the frame rotated up towards the sky because the bike could no longer move. Alex was flung through the air like a rock from a catapult, but this time for a much longer distance and speed than he had done previously over the speed hump. He hit the dirt hard and dug in with his shoulder, creating a small trench with his body from the impact. Alex slowly got to his feet and revealed that something must have made contact with his head as he landed.

There was no blood. Alex, despite his obvious dumb actions, was not silly enough to ride without a helmet. That same green helmet though had disintegrated upon his head and crumbled to his feet. Hunter knew he was in trouble, but that wouldn't change regardless of what his next actions were. He held his ground with fists clenched and looked over at James who was visibly cowering from the action.

"I don't know how many times we have to tell you," Hunter blasted the pair, regardless if Alex was hurt or not. "If you want to muck around and act like jerks you will be treated like jerks and face the consequences." He was spitting through his teeth as he breathed in heavily. Alex had no courage left within him. He ran. Straight past Hunter at a distance where he couldn't be struck, and bolted straight into the open garage and into the house.

"What's going on?" asked Shane as he rolled over with his bike, completely unaware to what just happened. Hunter let out a tremendous sigh as he continued to eye off James who hadn't moved at all since Hunter had flipped his brother.

"Let's just say I probably won't be able to come out and play for a little while," Hunter said simply, ignoring Shane's look of confusion. Knowing what was to come he patted Shane on the arm, shot James a look that could have killed, and slowly walked off towards his house.

"Wait, where are you going?" Shane asked.

"HUNTER!" the voice of Hunter's dad boomed out from within his home.

"Oh," Shane said with eyes wide open in shock and sudden understanding.

"Fine you can come out," dad said as he walked through the open garage. It had been two weeks since Hunter had flipped his brother off his bike. He had lost basically all privileges for that time, but so had Alex. Alex couldn't see how it was his fault and as to why he got punished. Hunter did, which is why his mum had given him the 'you should have known better' talk.

"But when you come out you can't leave the cul-de-sac, you can't use your bikes and you can't take anything else out either," continued dad as he shuffled beyond the roller door and up towards the mailbox. He had the demands laid out simply, clearly trying to dissuade both boys from coming outside at all or as a reminder to not get into trouble. Alex had that train of thought, the one where he looked as if he was going to argue, but Hunter accepted it knowing full well you could do many other things without ever needing equipment.

"Sounds good, thanks," Hunter said pushing past his brother, who slid back inside to mope about and possibly try to convince mum of a different solution. He had seen Shane and James outside as well through one of the front windows and hurried out to see them. They had not been let outside either because of what had happened and this was the first time they had spoken since then. Phil was walking over towards Hunter's dad with Shane and James just behind him. There was a new car parked in the cul-de-sac, one that neither belonged there nor had they ever seen before. A man stood beside it with dark hair and a neat goatee, his wife standing a little bit further away from him.

Hunter jumped in beside Shane immediately as they walked towards the newcomers, and followed his gaze as he gestured towards the vacant corner block. Hunter understood instantly what Shane was getting at. The block looked like it had been attacked. An excavator had visited the site through the week and dragged most of the dirt from the surface and made a huge pile near where the other one had been previously. There was a level spot in the centre where a slab would probably be laid for the commencement of another build. But what that actually meant was that all their work, their jumps, obstacles and BMX track, they were all gone.

"Hi there," Hunter's dad said offering his hand to the man near his car, before offering his name, "James."

"Hi James, I'm Michael," the new man said.

"Phil," Shane's dad said also shaking the man's hand and pulsing it roughly. Phil turned to Shane.

"Go and play," he said. Hunter looked at his dad who nodded his head saying it was okay. "Not you," Phil added as James tried to follow. It seemed that James was dealing with consequences as well.

Once they were out of earshot and skirting around the foundations of the once vacant block Shane started talking.

"So what did it cost you?" he asked.

"Apart from not being able to do anything I had to buy him a new helmet," Hunter revealed, allowing a secret smile to creep forward. "Worth it though, I would do it again." Shane laughed.

"Do you think Alex will ever learn?" he asked, to which Hunter just shook his head, dismissing the memories of what had gotten him in trouble. They were both walking towards the large pile of dirt. Hunter was thinking of what to do, but the answer was so obvious.

"Bike jump?" he asked Shane.

"Sure," Shane replied with confusion, "but we don't have any bikes."

"We don't need them," Hunter said back and walked back a little bit. He looked up at the dirt mound, taking a few sideways steps as he analysed the easiest way to make it to the top. When Hunter decided

112

his route he opened his mouth to make a sound. It wasn't a screech or any identifiable words. It was the sound that Hunter imagined a dirt bike sounded like.

"Rrrrrinnnn, rrrrriiiiinnn, rrriin," he yelled as he pretended to kick start his imaginary dirt bike to life. His brother was not going to stop him from having fun, regardless if he had any equipment or not. Then Hunter lurched forward as if he had accidently hit the accelerator too hard. He flicked his wrist as he clicked over gears and dragged his back tyre through the mud. Then just before he attacked the dirt hill which would be his jump he got louder as if stating the exact amount of energy he needed to make it to the top.

"RRRRRRIIIIIIIIIIIIIIIIIINNNNNNNNNNNN," Hunter bellowed as he took off. He sprinted up the slope as he held aloft his invisible handlebars. Keeping that image was hard as he started slipping back down the dirt mountain as soon as he set foot upon it. Hunter realised that as he made the top he would have to jump over the other side, or lose all speed and slide back the way he came. He hadn't looked to see how to do that but Shane was following closely from behind. There was nothing for it.

"RRRRIIINNNNIIINNNN, IINNNN IIINNN NNIINN, NIN," Hunter choked out as he leapt. He abandoned his bike as he understood how badly he had judged the jump. He landed hard on his back, which wasn't too bad as he still ended up landing on relatively soft dirt that had been placed there. Hunter stood up in surprise. In front of him stood a boy and a girl.

"Hey," Hunter said stepping forward. He was slightly embarrassed that someone else had seen how he played without actually knowing him.

"Hi," the boy said in reply. The girl stood behind him near a small tree that still stood on the property. Before Hunter could say anything else, he ushered the boy away to the side.

"It might be for the best if you stand away from the mound," Hunter suggested. The boy didn't have to ask why as Shane came flying over the top in a similar yet more graceful manner to Hunter. Shane stopped his motorbike next to Hunter.

"Hi," said Shane offering his hand, "I'm Shane. Who are you?" The boy seemed to look through Shane for a moment as he took his hand.

"My name is Raul," the boy said making weird signals with his face and eyebrows.

"Your name isn't Raul," the girl called out behind him.

"Quiet Alana," Raul snapped back.

"So," Shane started slowly, shooting glances between Hunter, Alana and Raul. "What are you guys doing back here?"

"This is our new house," Raul said.

"Well, it will be," added Alana.

"Cool, so you are our new neighbours," Shane said to both of them. He wasn't really keen on making short talk yet so he jumped to the next important question. "Do you guys have dirt bikes?"

"No," replied Alana in disgust. She looked like she was about the same age as Alex whereas Raul was probably closer to James.

"Yes," said Raul. "I will show you how to do this properly." Raul immediately pulled back the clutch of his bike and took off back up the hill. Shane and Hunter didn't move, waiting to see how well the new boy would buy into the game. They were already impressed that he had jumped into accepting the manner of the game so quickly. The thought did dart through Hunter's mind that the boy had just run away, not really wanting to join in their game at all. The familiar sound of a motorbike climbing the hill returned, revealing that Hunter's fears were unfounded.

"Rin, din, din, din, din," Raul called out as his dirt bike found more air than Hunter's had. He landed in about the same spot as Shane, but then appeared to lose control. "Watch out," he screamed as he drove his imaginary bike towards the small tree and crashed into it.

"Phew," he said wiping a hand across a supposedly sweaty brow. "I think I am going to need to get a new bike." He walked a couple steps towards the others who took a giant step back. Raul looked hurt as the others pulled away from him. "Hey guys I was thinking that this might be the start of something, but if you are going to act like that . . ." Hunter turned tail and ran. Shane followed straight after him. Raul turned to say something snide to his sister but she disappeared along behind Shane and Hunter.

"What was that about?" Raul asked himself. "Alana needs to learn something about loyalty." He twisted around to see if there was something that he missed, and discovered that he did. When he crashed his bike into the tree he had dislodged a massive wasp nest.

"It's only a wasp nest," he said aloud, trying to convince himself that the others were cowards. He didn't even manage to convince himself. A small horde cleared the grass and rose in the air in front of him.

Raul turned and ran. He didn't even care if anyone heard his high pitched scream.

CHAPTER 8 – THE NEXT SCHOOL

Hunter and Shane collapsed on a huge grass cushion atop the parapet of his castle. They had spent weeks over the Christmas school holidays playing outside and imagining almost every possible scenario of game. They weren't always playing. There were days when both families travelled abroad and escaped from Orange. There were other days when it was just too hot and neither family left their house, choosing to stay as close to the small fans and water coolers as they were able. They had to manage what they were doing with great care. A day used which resulted in sunburn or injury would result in being incapacitated and being forced to stay indoors for several days after. They also had to manage their parents. For the most part they stayed home with the boys, but when they returned to work the expectation of chores completed and other tasks at least part attempted had to be followed otherwise there would be penalties.

Most of the time though, the parents were only too happy to send the kids on their way and out of their hair while they either relaxed or continued to potter around the house. The side gates had been completed on Hunter's house resulting in Buster the dog finally being let loose and owning his territory for the first time. Buster was conveniently watching the boys on the grass mound from his perch on the back patio. The first days of Buster's freedom had mostly consisted of chasing after him as he was immediately drawn to holes in the fence and without hesitation scurrying through. Hunter's dad would make a temporary fix by barricading the holes with left over bricks or drilling hard black plastic into the fence metal. That was repeated at least a dozen times on the first day.

The heat had been so extraordinary, compared to the months of rain they had received only a short time ago, that most of their play time had consisted of simply avoiding the heat or relaxing. They created their own small grass huts by digging into the small gap between huge tufts and moulding the blades of grass into vast canopies that acted like a shelter and a shield from the Sun's rays. The shade from the intense sunlight sending the boys to sleep on multiple occasions. There were other days where they were told to go and have a swim in the dam or the creek to cool off, and on those days it was amazing how much difference there was in temperature between the arid air outside and the much cooler liquid within. You could be called out of the water and by the time you returned home you were bone dry without the use of a towel.

On some other days the boys were joined by Raul and his younger sister Alana as their housing block continued to be developed. This also drew the attention of May as there was finally another girl in the street. There was about two year's difference between them but they hit it off without any trouble. The boys would ensure that they could see the younger girls at all times, but that didn't mean they looked after them. Frequently the girls were dismissed from Shane's castle as they tried to enter and play with the boys, or they were sent on a fool's errand to only get stuck somewhere else, fall down the trapdoor or try to cross the creek. The boys weren't always affectionately mean, sometimes, like on this particular afternoon, the girls had been given access to the top of the grass mound and relaxed alongside the others. The girls had been given the name Damsels. The name was devised by James who thought it was clever to use dam in their title as there was a dam nearby, and a play on word for female characters in distress from countless old tales that involved a kingdom, like the one Shane had thrust upon them. The girls didn't like the title, but as the boys thought more about it they realised that at the moment they fitted the name pretty well, therefore it stuck hard and remained. James had also proclaimed that James, Shane, Hunter, Alex, and now Raul were to be known as the Creek Crew.

"That name is so lame," Shane reprimanded his brother. "It will never stick."

"It already has," said James in revolt, smiling at his brother as he marvelled at his own brilliance. "It is better idea than 'Shane's kingdom," he mocked. "And unless you have another name Creek Crew will remain."

"He is right," Hunter reluctantly agreed. "There is no other collective word for our group. Each time we get bigger it makes it more difficult to say each of our names in a row. I just say guys but Creek Crew is cooler." Shane ignored the logical conclusion and continued to look over at the houses which continued to be constructed. Raul's house had come along a fair way in the last few months. The slab was down and the frame had started to be raised during the week. It would take some time, as unlike the others it was a two storey house and towered over the dwellings nearby. His kingdom was starting to be enveloped by buildings which took away a small part of the charm, but it made him appreciate what they had a whole lot more.

"So back to school next week guys," Hunter changed the topic and onto one that was no doubt resting somewhat on their minds. He heard the others rustle from within their grass beds and hammocks but no one really moved.

"That sucks," James proclaimed and received agreement from Alex and Raul. "That means we won't be able to play every day anymore."

"We don't do that anyway," Shane shot back, always looking for an opportunity to knock his brother back down a few pegs.

"Yeah I know," James stabbed back quickly. "But we won't be *able* to anymore. We won't have the option to do it."

"We will still play a bit," Shane set the idea aside. "There are still a couple of months of summer before autumn hits. Besides going back to school is not nearly as bad as going to a new school." He looked at Raul and Alana who lay nearby before setting his gaze firmly on Hunter.

"School is fine," Raul stated firmly. "I am going to own that place."

"Me too," squeaked Alana.

"Yeah, but you two aren't going to high school yet. Hunter is," Shane made his point finally. "That can be a big deal for a whole heap of reasons."

"Any tips?" Hunter asked the question enthusiastically, but the response was not so positive.

"Keep your head down," Shane said turning away once more. "You will be fine but there will be some kids who will be out to get you."

"Why? What did I do?" Hunter sounded concerned.

"Nothing," Shane informed him. "But you didn't have to do anything in the first place. Some people just like to pick on others for no reason." Silence followed that comment. Hunter didn't know what else to say and just let his own mind try and come up with solutions to the problem he had been presented with. He felt like Shane had wanted to say more, but couldn't bring himself to say anything. Nothing that would help Hunter out at least. Lost in an instant gloom Hunter resigned himself to the fact that he would just have to wait and see what happened when school finally came back around.

Hunter thought that the group of four boys all looked like a mob as they walked towards the bus stop that would enable them to get to school on the first day. Alex was busy trying to make himself look scruffy, while James and Shane were trying their best to look like they didn't care, when clearly they did.

Hunter and Alex were used to being dropped off at school soon after their mum dropped off their dad at his work. They would get to school early, too early as they were notified by most teachers, arriving when the frost still made everything dangerous to step on or no doors were open to hide from the elements. Not anymore though. They were left at home as both of their parents left for work and Hunter and Alex would walk to the bus stop. As they stepped out the front door they were joined by Shane and James and made the hike all the way to the top of Northstoke Way, where the bus would pick them up from the highway. The bus wouldn't come down the road as it was too hard to turn around, especially considering the rest of the road had not been finished yet.

As one of the first stops on the way into town the bus was relatively unoccupied. The only others there were students who lived out of town and had to get on the bus from Molong or somewhere in between. All four boys sat down in close proximity to each other. Despite the high school being the closest location from their bus stop it would be one of the last spots to deliver the passengers. After a scenic route around the north of the town it would head towards Orange Public to drop off Alex before going to Calare for James to disembark.

Despite sitting with Shane for the duration Hunter found he was having more of a conversation with another passenger. It was a girl that he knew from his time at OPS, but as Hunter was not the best at talking to girls (let alone anyone else) he had usually been too shy to engage in conversation. Hunter reluctantly welcomed her attention though, if not but for the simple reason that she was someone familiar and she was giving Hunter a whole bunch of kind attention. Her name was Hannah, she was the cousin of one of Hunter's friends at school which made it a little easier, and after a quick re-introduction to Shane she engaged in a conversation where she was the primary participant. They discussed holidays, who had left town, who was still going to be at school with them, as well as a range of other topics like school subjects and timetables. Shane moved to sit next to one of his friends who also caught the bus, allowing Hannah an unspoken invitation to come and sit next to Hunter.

When the bus finally arrived at the high school Hunter jumped off just like all the others, but he was one of the first. He was virtually dragged off by Hannah as surprisingly there was no one else he knew on the bus except Shane, so he had no reason to wait. Shane was one of those who waited to the end, but he didn't miss an opportunity to try and embarrass his neighbour.

"Only just arrived at high school and you already have yourself a girlfriend," he called out through the small gap at the top of one of the bus windows. Hunter felt his face flush red. It was obvious that Hannah had heard Shane as she turned back with a look of disgust, but Hunter was also sure he saw her hide a smile as she turned away. Hunter told himself it wasn't true and that it couldn't happen for a few reasons. One was that this was the longest he had ever spoken to Hannah, or any other girl for that matter, and another was that he had no idea what he would have to do in that situation. Hunter still followed Hannah with embarrassment as he looked around for someone else that he recognised. He wished there was, even someone he sort of knew, just so he could escape into another less awkward situation. He didn't see anyone, but that didn't mean he wasn't spotted.

"Hey newbies," a boy called out from nearby. He had been hiding behind a nearby pine tree which stretched high up into the sky within the arrival area. It was immediately clear to Hunter that he should be on his guard. There was more than one student who stood behind him. Hunter could see a congregation further away in the main quadrangle, suggesting that these boys were loitering out of bounds. Hunter was sure that he and Hannah weren't the only new students on that bus, but he didn't know any other kids. There were one or two who slowed their pace and stayed behind Hunter and took a wider route to avoid detection, hoping that he would draw the attention, whereas several older students just walked by as if nothing was happening. Hunter could see that Hannah, who still walked a couple of paces in front of him, shirked at the new attention, her bag clutched closer to her shoulder and arms folded across her waist.

"You're pretty," said another boy from behind the first. This one was the biggest of the group despite having a lanky and wiry frame. "It's your first day in high school and you are in luck. You are the first that could have me as your boyfriend."

"Ew," she said sickened by the comment, taking a few steps back as the big kid strode towards her. "That is the last thing I would want. Besides I already have a boyfriend." She stepped backwards again until she hid behind Hunter, who simply stood there waiting for what happened next. Hunter knew the comment had been a lie, but he was also smart enough to realise that instead of it being a proposition it was a subtle cry for help.

"Him," the kid seemed offended. "You think he is better than me?"

"I know it," Hannah responded, apparently gaining some courage while standing behind Hunter. Hunter didn't want a fight, especially not on his first day, and he didn't want to get involved with bullies or relationships with girls. He was less than mediocre in all regards, but he saw that unwanted confrontation was probably the road he was heading down.

"Well, let's see about that," the boy said as he jumped over and attempted to stand over Hunter. Despite his more senior position in the school the boy was hardly a centimetre taller than Hunter would have been. Without feeling smug Hunter felt that he could probably hold his own against him if he had to, but he really didn't want to. He could also see the small group of half a dozen other boys that supported this bully start gathering closer. Some of them were looking out for a teacher while the others egged on some sort of physical assault. Hunter eyed down the main kid, he was good at math but you didn't have to be to know that his odds were not looking great.

He was thinking about telling Hannah to run as soon as it started but he didn't want to turn his head.

"Back off Reece," Shane's voice echoed from behind Hunter. Hunter still refused to look away from the other boy, but Reece directed his attention towards Shane instead. Hunter pretended to follow his gaze but took small steps backwards instead, keeping Hannah behind him at all times. It appeared that the reason Shane had taken so long to get off the bus was because he had been meeting up with some of his other mates at the school gate.

"Aw come on Shane," Reece whinged as he left Hunter behind. "I was just having some fun with the newbies. Remember, just like we said." It was clear that Shane was not just intervening to help Hunter. He knew the other student, which became evident as several of Shane's mates walked over to the rest of the group sharing high fives, fist bumps and handshakes. Shane still stared down Reece as this happened.

"I know," Shane responded. He looked at Hunter in silent dispair, and Hunter swore he saw shame spread sadly across his face. The image of Shane being a great friend and the coolest of kids was being damaged somewhat. Hunter realised that Shane wasn't the cool kid, he was the too cool kid.

"But not this one," Shane continued giving Hunter a firm slap on the back.

"Not any of them," the voice of one of the teachers boomed out from an overhead window, who appeared there watching with arms crossed as he waited for the students to disperse.

"Of course sir," Reece called back to the teacher high above, acting out a decent show of remorse and respect. "Sorry sir." It was clear that the teacher would wait until they moved into the correct area. Shane ignored Hunter's gaze as he lead the rest of the group away amongst a joining crowd of arriving students. Reece hesitated for a moment and then walked close to Hunter, whispering so only he could hear him.

"Not this one," Reece hissed, "not yet at least." He smiled as he retreated back to his gang. Hunter heard his voice being called but refused to turn to it. When finally Reece was gone Hannah moved from behind Hunter.

"Thanks Hunter," Hannah thanked him. A slight tremor showed in the ringlets of her curled hair. She was either still rattled by what had happened, or scared at showing Hunter gratitude. Perhaps it was both. "That was really nice of you."

"No worries," Hunter gestured that it was no big deal with a shrug of his shoulders. "Forget about it." Hannah smiled at him warmly, before turning and walking away.

"Hunter," the voice called again from Hunter's side as it arrived.

"Hey Mark," Hunter replied, finally acknowledging the presence of his friend.

"It's great to see you mate," Mark said with a huge smile that pinched in all of his face. He had deliberately lowered his voice. "How have you been? Tell me what happened in your holidays." Hunter waited a moment, watching as Shane disappeared with this other group. Then, finally when he was out of sight, Hunter gave all of his attention towards Mark, who it seemed like was his only friend now.

The morning of that first day was confusing. All of the year seven students, those newly arriving in the first year of their high schooling career, were forced to gather within the gigantic gymnasium which occupied a good portion of the onsite buildings. Every student had sat on the floor as they were informed of where their home room or roll call class would be, where they were to attend first up every morning, and how to use the timetable that they were getting for the first time. Hunter had shared pleasantries with a whole bunch of his returned friends, said hello to those he knew but didn't really get along with, and acknowledged a few others. At least half of the cohort were new to him so he stuck close to his friends, knowing he was safe there for the moment. He marvelled at how he now had so many subjects on one day, and then on each day after that. He had Maths, Science, English, Physical Education, History and Art. It was an eye opener to say the least.

They finally emerged into lunch after a waste of the entire morning and were charged with trying to find a spot to eat their lunch and hang out. A spot that could be their own spot without upsetting any of the other students. Doing that just the once on the first day was more than enough.

The task was harder than they thought. It seemed like every location was occupied by another group, and in most situations those students weren't happy to see Hunter or Mark, let alone deal with having them sit nearby.

"We could ask your brother," Hunter suggested to Mark as they crossed the concrete quadrangle and headed towards the large enclosed canteen area. They finally found a bunch of chairs around a circular steel table sitting in the sun, but close enough to cover should it ever rain, that was not being occupied by anyone else. They hurriedly sat down, relieved that they could finally have a break after walking around for so long. Mark was telling one of the other kids who had followed them that this was the twentieth school that Hunter had been to, which was clearly a lie but Mark liked to embellish stories involving his friends some times. He then told them that the reason why there had been so many was because Hunter loved the smell of a new school and it was a weird behaviour for someone to have. The lie was reinforced, but at least Mark was making new friends at Hunter's expense.

"Hey newbies," a voice yelled out. "That's our spot." Hunter turned to see that Reece had appeared yet again. There were fewer boys hanging around him now but they still outnumbered Hunter, Mark and the couple of extra friends who hung around. Hunter noticed that Reece suddenly recognised him, suggesting that this was a random occurrence and Hunter was not actually being targeted. It seemed that he was just unlucky, but his bad luck had enabled Reece another opportunity to hassle him. Hunter gazed amongst the group, searching forlornly for Shane to be amongst them, hoping that he would step forward and stop this from happening again. His neighbour, however, was not there.

"Split," Mark yelled. The others who had been with Hunter all ran away in various directions, though Mark stayed next to Hunter deciding not to leave. Hunter thought on whether or not he had actually been targeted as he divulged the information that was present before him. Hunter was facing down the same bully he had previously, for the second time in a day. None of those who followed Reece had taken off to pursue Hunter's friends who had fled, all remaining to further outnumber Hunter and Mark. Plus Shane was conveniently not there amongst them. Whether that had been planned or not Hunter still couldn't decide.

"It looks like a good spot," Mark admitted. "I think we will keep it." Hunter had to laugh at the confidence of his friend.

"You think that's funny?" Reece snarled as he took another step towards him.

"Yep," Hunter replied. His friend's confidence had given him courage. It wouldn't help him with the overwhelming numbers against them, but at least it allowed Hunter to stand firm and resolute in the face of a bully.

"Well I don't think it's funny," Reece hissed. "We, don't think it's funny." He waved at the rest of his group whom all smiled along with the comment. Hunter knew that this sort of thing had most likely occurred before with this group. "And there is more of us than you, so that means majority rules. You have to leave now. But not before you pay us a toll for using our spot."

"Ha, Ha, Ha," Mark laughed slowly, loud, and deliberately. "No way." Mark crossed his arms in front of him as a sign of defiance. Reece thought it was funny as well, laughing just as boisterously as his small gang slowly walked to surround Hunter and Mark. There were others nearby who could see what was going on. None stopped to intervene despite having the power to do just that. Some even quickened the stride or headed in completely the other way to avoid the upcoming confrontation, and amongst those were students who were most likely part of the school football team due to their immense size and height. As Hunter looked around, pleading silently for anyone to interfere with what was happening, he noticed the presence of Shane. His neighbour had slunk off to one side, leaning against a dirty brick wall. He hadn't abandoned Hunter but nor was he helping him. He also wasn't helping Reece though, which offered some small comfort. Hunter gulped down the desire to call out for him seeking help and refocused on Reece. The wiry looking boy had also noticed Shane and laughed loudly in Hunter's face.

"See, you have no friends here," he crowed as he paced around the pair, like a lion teasing its prey. "It would have been best for you to mind your manners and do what you were told but you chose a different road, one that will make you pay. Every day, for as long as you are here. And no one is going to help you. Call out, do it, no one will come." Mark continued to smile in the face of the bully while Hunter was less confident. Out of those who surrounded them some seemed a bit skittish at the idea that they were bullying two year seven students, but more than enough of them were too busy licking their lips at what they saw in front of them to care.

"No?" Reece seemed perplexed by the response he was receiving, "I will do it for you. Help, help, somebody help these kids. Anyone." He smiled back at Mark trying to match his smirk.

"You are in so much trouble," Mark said, seemingly amused at what was going down. "Me and Hunter could take you by ourselves, but, we won't have to." Reece had seemingly had enough of Mark's show of boldness in the face of overwhelming odds and intimidating tactics that usually worked. What was originally supposed to be just standing over the pair so they cried, had turned into an embarrassing show for the tormenter, so he chose to act. He took one big angry step forward and pulled his arm back in a clenched fist. He started his swing, Mark still had his arms crossed, still laughing despite Reece's approach.

Hunter was amazed as Reece didn't make contact with his friends face. It was not because he did not desire to do so, but entirely due to the fact he had been lifted a metre in the air by a much larger student who had appeared almost out of thin air. Reece was raised off his feet and pinned to a nearby wall, hard.

"Are you picking on my little brother?" the new participant growled into the bully's face.

"He sure was Jono," Mark answered because Reece could not. Jono was a senior student, in his last year of schooling, and he was a farm strong, enormous, blonde haired, well-built tank of a young man that would not see a family member harmed. He had arrived with all the power, presence and look of a rampaging and hungry polar bear. Jono's own friends had accompanied him though he didn't need them. In the first instance of him picking up the now crumpled heap of Reece all of the other boys fled in fear. Reece was visibly shaking in terror. Jono not only had him hanging half way up the wall but he had also managed to pin one of his arms behind his back. Hunter had had something similar happen to him when he had been around to Mark's house before, albeit in a more friendly fashion.

"If I ever see you or any of your mates hanging around my brother, any of his friends, or picking on anyone else, I will find you and what is happening now is only a taste of what you will receive then. Am I clear?" Jono alerted Reece to what would happen. He hadn't yelled but he had scarcely raised his voice above a hoarse whisper as he informed the bully of what would happen. Reece nodded and Jono dumped him hard into a heap on the ground. "Get out of here." Reece bolted with tears streaming down his face from the pain and shame that he had been dealt. Hunter doubted that Reece would be a presence at school anymore, not until the next year at least when Jono was gone, which only meant that Hunter and Mark could enjoy it more now.

"It's a good school," Jono said with a thumb poking up into the sky, a large smile spread across his face as if nothing happened. Jono's strong frame easing into a carefree hunch as the fight within him subsided. "If he comes back let me know, otherwise, have a fantastic day." Mark waved after him as if nothing major had happened and then turned to his bag.

"Lunch," he suggested.

"Sounds great," replied Hunter, slightly bewildered, but entirely satisfied.

The return bus ride at the end of the day was more interesting than the one at the start. James and Alex were already present in the vehicle before Hunter and Shane jumped on. They sat together, no doubt conjuring up some other sort of mischief to play on their brothers later that afternoon or on the weekend. Shane had waited way down the line, almost as far away from Hunter as he could manage, but Hunter didn't really mind. Some of his friends jumped on with him, as well as some new ones he had made that very day. Many of these skipped off relatively early in the trip, which left Hannah to return to a nearby chair and resume their earlier conversation. It started off awkwardly as she thanked Hunter for helping her for events prior, and also for saying that they were boyfriend and girlfriend. Although Hannah suggested almost too quickly that it actually wouldn't have been the worst idea in the world. Hunter had no clue as to what to say to that and found no words, luckily she ignored that fact and started talking about something else, much to his relief.

Hannah was pretty in a tall and sporty sort of way, which Hunter actually really liked. He made no show of that though as he could already see in his peripheral vision the forms of James and Alex playacting to make out with each other, or turning to face the other way while wrapping their arms around their waists, pretending that someone else was kissing them.

Hunter and the rest jumped off the bus eventually, leaving Hannah on the bus by herself for a long drive back to wherever it was she lived, and no sooner had they departed had the two younger brothers continued their torrent of nonsense. One threateningly swift step forward that suggested pain was about to be inflicted was more than enough to send the two terrors on their way. Their flight in fear forgotten nearly five steps later as they turned their retreat into a race between themselves all the way home.

Shane was the last to get off the bus and made sure he was always a few metres behind Hunter when they walked. Hunter imagined that usually that walk home would have been one full of chat but both boys walked back in silence. Hunter thought it would end sooner rather than later, but it lasted all the way back to the corner of their cul-de-sac of Angus Place.

"Hey Hunter," Shane finally called out as he crossed the road towards his driveway. Hunter stopped and turned in the middle of the road, no concern as to whether a car would come as the chances were quite low. Shane took a deep breath before speaking again. "I wanted to say that I am sorry."

"What for?" asked Hunter as surprised as he could manage. It was clear that Shane had waited this long to apologise so that he could retreat quickly inside his house if he needed to.

"You know what for," Shane replied back. He looked really hurt, no longer the confident boy or royal leader he had come to be known as. "I didn't help you at lunch today, and I absolutely had to."

"Yes you should have," Hunter stated frankly. "That, guy, is a bully, why do you hang out with him?"

"Because he is my friend," Shane blurted out. "Or at least he was. I used to watch him do that stuff all the time to kids. I thought it was funny, and it never happened to me. I never had any second thoughts about it until I saw it happen to you today. Not until you looked at me like that, and I realised I had let down a real friend." Hunter thought for a moment.

"No harm done, besides, you helped out when I really needed it, at the start of the day," Hunter said calmly. He half believed the compromised acceptance he offered to Shane.

"It won't be the end of it," Shane seemed convinced of the fact. "But don't worry I won't let anything happen from now on." Shane looked hard at Hunter showing just how serious he was by making the comment. "Are we cool?" he shot out a hand hoping that Hunter would accept it. Hunter ignored the hand and moved in closer to Shane. He wrapped his arms around the boy in a warm embrace.

"Never better," Hunter responded to his friend, wanting to believe that nothing had changed.

"Thanks," replied Shane with deep relief.

"No worries," Hunter replied. He let the hug linger a moment longer until finally it turned uncomfortable. "It's still cool for friends to hug each other right? People are allowed to cuddle Kings like this?"

"No that is not cool," Shane responded with a smile. "And don't call it cuddling."

"Oh," Hunter said with some confusion. "That's too bad, suck it up your majesty." Hunter refused to let go and smiled some more.

CHAPTER 9 – CONSTRUCTION SITE CHAOS

Hunter held the notion that he had forgiven Shane, but not forgotten the deeds, by anyone. He didn't know if you could do such a thing but that was how he felt. The threat of bullying from school was there, but he was pretty confident that nothing would happen to him. It was like looking at a lion at the zoo. If it wasn't for the clear strong perplex or glass window the beast would probably devour you, but that same glass gave you courage that let you know that everything would be okay. That glass enveloped Hunter.

Every now and then, and only for the first few weeks, Hunter would find himself face to face with Reece. They were either right next to each other, where Hunter could deal with glowers or an attempted arm bump, or an awareness that across the playground Reece was there watching him. Noticing Reece wasn't the weird bit though, it was the fact that Shane walked close by as part of the same group.

Hunter had told the truth when he said that he forgave Shane for his inaction, but despite this the smile they shared was still forced. It was, in Hunter's mind, entirely due to the fact that Shane hadn't proved or put into action what he had promised. Hunter's previous school had the moto of 'Deeds Not Words', and as odd as it might sound it was a moto that stuck with him. Words hung around doing nothing but irritate you until acted upon.

Apart from those small inconveniences, life stayed more or less the same. The boys continued to play in the back paddock. The days were still long but the heat started to wear off towards the end of summer. Every now and then Raul would come and join them as he frequented his new development in the same fashion that Hunter did, although without the daily routine of avoiding torrential rain. It was also during these times when May and Alana made their presence known. Where May had hardly been seen for the first six months of Hunter living next door it was now rare if she wasn't around. Unfortunately, for Shane and James rather Hunter or Alex, May had brought along the same stubborn attitude to play that James had done before her. There was almost a routine as to how they greeted each other.

"We are playing too," May would demand with the slightly older Alana beside her.

"No way, get lost," James would disagree, usually barring their route to whatever game the boys were playing. "You are just going to ruin things."

"I'm going to tell mum then," May countered with a heartbroken look, which quickly changed into a vindictive smile.

"Urgh. Fine," James would give in almost immediately, every time. "But we aren't looking after you, and you better not get in our way." Both girls would smile with delight. Hunter really didn't mind because the younger girls only spoke to each other anyway, and with their relationship being very new there wasn't much chatting between them.

Whenever Raul was around they would go to repeating some of the things they did or played before he arrived. They revisited games like the tennis ball shoot out, and they would ride bikes when his parents brought his along. Hunter was happy with one of his quirks as well. For the most part he partook in the activities with about as much enthusiasm as all the other boys did, which was fantastic, but where Hunter bought into a game by altering his environment around him and relying heavily on his imagination Raul did so differently. He would do one of two things.

Raul would either say that he was someone within the role he was playing. Once when they were riding bikes he would change his name to Dave Mirra and pretend to do stunts just like the famous rider despite the fact they were only clearing gutters like they had done before. There was another day when he called himself James Bond, replicating all the mannerisms within the game. The boys would usually let him live if he quoted a famous line, then they would eliminate him. Raul, despite Raul not being his name, would always revert back to being Raul though.

Then, sometimes, he would just change his name to some other name, just to suit himself. They were playing soccer together in the backyard on one occasion, when the extra plush fresh green lawn was finally made usable, when Raul changed his name to Tex. Hunter, who knew very little about famous names in soccer, asked Shane if he knew who Raul was trying to be, but even he had no idea.

It made it more fun anyway, and there were times when the other boys would play along or take on other personalities as it suited.

One afternoon, when Raul had come around after school to allow his parents to check on the continuing construction, all the boys were passing a soccer ball on the vacant cul-de-sac road. All the parents had gathered to admire and talk about the development of the two story structure. It had slowed down somewhat, with tools and resources laying discarded all over the site. Shane claimed he had found an interesting magazine along with some drinks left abandoned inside but they were quickly taken by Phil and promptly thrown in the bin. Not really caring what they were or what the parents were talking about the discussion changed to sport.

"So do you play sport?" Shane asked Raul as he passed the pumped up black and white soccer ball towards him.

"Yeah," Raul, admitted. "I play soccer."

"We do too," reported James with far more excitement than was usual.

"I know," Raul said with little interest. "I have seen you play before. You play for Waratahs, I play for Ex-services." The boys went silent for a few moments. Both of those teams were rival clubs, and at that age it was an unspoken law that you were not only rivals with those from other clubs, in some instances you were enemies.

"Do you play Hunter?" Raul asked the other boy. Hunter wasn't sure if Raul hoped that Hunter would play for his team, or that if he played another sport then there would be a change in the topic altogether.

"I've played a few sports," Hunter finally answered. "I played soccer in Canberra, and then played rugby league when I was out west. I play cricket now in summer but apart from playing tennis, squash or something else I don't play sport much in winter."

"You should play for Ex-services," Raul said almost immediately, but Shane wasn't going to let him have that discussion too easily.

"That makes no sense," Shane interrupted. "You guys wouldn't be in the same team because you are younger and he isn't going to know anyone. But if Hunter plays with us he will have both me and James on the same team. No brainer." Despite the fact that he hadn't been asked whether or not he actually wanted to play, Hunter was happy to have people fighting over him, even if it was only to get one over the rival team. Hunter imagined he would be an okay player, he was pretty athletic and a solid, bigger guy in most age groups, but he hadn't played soccer in a very long time. As the conversation changed to something else Hunter made sure that he was extra focused on how he passed the ball to the others. He would hate to have them change their minds before he even got to play, or ask his parents in the first place.

The signups were one afternoon after school. It had seemed that Hunter's parents were as keen to get back into a sporting environment as Shane had been to lure Hunter there in the first place. Hunter would be playing and so would Alex, although Alex would play for a younger age group. Alex had been playing footy but he hadn't been enjoying it, so despite all his bravado about how good he was he would also be playing for the Waratahs as well. Hunter suspected that this was more so that with only one car in the family that they would be in the same place.

As Hunter rode the bus after school he sat with Shane and James, all of them excited about the signups that were later that afternoon. The discussion had gone between who else was playing for the same club and would be in the same team, as well as what people's positions were. Hunter had no idea who any of the names were that they rattled off in quick succession, and despite Shane's claim of knowing people on the team his two neighbours were the only ones he knew. In a slight touch of irony if he had played for Ex-services, whilst it was true that he would not have been on Raul's team, Hunter would have been on the same team of several of his current and even newfound friends from school. Mark was on that team, as were Seb, Robbie, Joey and several others, most of the team in fact was made out of people he knew. Hunter let out a small sigh but was quite happy to be playing with Shane and James, if only for the fact that his lack of ability would only be shared within the street.

The boys waited as they got off the bus. A few younger kids had started taking the bus to and from school from the same bus stop. One kid had a car waiting for them to be picked up, which Hunter thought defeated the purpose of a bus in the first place, whilst there were also a handful of other parents who waited to walk their children home. The boy in front of Hunter jumped from three steps up and landed hard on the ground. His dad was waiting with a smile for his arrival and the young boy got swept up in his arms as he went in for a hug. The man was huge, Hunter pegged him as being one of the first grade players for one of the local football clubs, and he easily threw the boy around effortlessly before planting him safely on the ground and seeking answers of his day as they walked down the road in the same direction as Hunter.

"Well, well, well," a voice called out from behind the bus. The sun was starting to set in that direction so Hunter found it hard to see. By the time the rest got off the bus he could see clearly who it was. Reece was sitting on his bike along with two others. Hunter had no idea why they were there, but suspected that one if not all of them lived somewhere nearby. He couldn't remember seeing them around but then he had never really been looking for them. Hunter had the numbers this time, though he still didn't want to fight. He was pretty sure that he could handle one, Shane could handle another and between Alex and James they could hold their own.

"Just ignore them," Shane said turning away, leading the rest down the street. Hunter found that he quickly caught up to the huge dad as he led his son, who was either doing cartwheels or generally just ambling by, but he was also aware that they were being followed. The three bullies on bikes shadowed them. Hunter didn't have to see them although there were visible clues everywhere. The setting sun created giant shadows that stretched in front of their slow pursuers, even casting them in front of Hunter who was in the lead. The sound of the iron chain cranking on spikes and the spokes as they rubbed against brakes and loose wire continued to remind Hunter of their presence. He started breathing heavier despite his earlier confidence in his own defence.

While Reece followed he made snide remarks under his breath. The other two who were with him merely shadowed along behind. They didn't say anything apart from urging Reece to turn around and go back the other way, it was clear that they weren't overly keen to be there. It wasn't long before Hunter had had enough.

"Rack off would you," Hunter said raising his voice. He could see that Reece was about to laugh at him when the bully's face suddenly went white and he quickly flicked his frame around and rode away, fighting to go back up the hill he had come down with little to no momentum. Hunter half expected Shane to be there next to him as he heard footsteps on the grass but it wasn't his voice that he heard.

"You alright?" came the deep voice of the huge dad, with the twinge of a New Zealander accent. Hunter just nodded, embarrassed that a stranger got involved, especially as his neighbours and brother stood uselessly nearby.

"Yes, thank you," Hunter replied trying to sound grateful.

"All good," the man said with a smile and then turned towards his son who sat patiently on a brick mailbox. "Just mind your language in front of my boy." Hunter was thankful for the man's intervention, but was instantly threatened by him despite the dad never once raising his voice. Hunter took a deep breath, once more putting the thought of the bullies out of his mind. He told himself that he had to be more careful though. He was no longer in school, so that thin veil of protection he had before probably didn't stretch this far into home life. He was also finding that he had a temper which was becoming more noticeable, regardless if Hunter thought it was justified to surface or not.

The next afternoon started without event. Hunter had signed up alongside Shane and James and was now part of the team. Training was going to start the following week, and there would also be a game. Hunter was surprised how quickly that had occurred but was later informed that despite his parents always being on time they were actually late to sign up, due to Hunter's late decision to play. It didn't matter to Hunter, the sooner they played the less time the other players had to prepare for how bad he would be.

The boys, with May, had all met up on Hunter's driveway. His parents were not home yet as they were still working but Phil was home for the day. He said he would watch them from the comfort of his front veranda but they couldn't leave the cul-de-sac. If you hadn't known he was there you never would have noticed him, he was almost entirely hidden by one of the wooden pillars that held up the short overhanging roof. The presence of Phil's blue and white locksmith van parked in the driveway was still a reassuring sight to Hunter though.

Hunter had opened up his garage door which was void of cars. He placed several old brown cushions against the far wall and fetched a couple of skateboards. Shane and James brought their own over, but unlike Hunter's and Alex's theirs looked like they had been well used. Hunter and his brother were not kids who would or could skate, but they had received the toys as presents and tried to use them where possible. The driveway was level with the road at the top, then dipped into a sharp decline over ten or so metres before entering the garage. Today Hunter was bringing out his inner bobsledder, skeleton or luge rider, as he and the others rode the boards from the top at speed before slamming into the protective cushions at the back of the garage.

Hunter lay down upon the board on his back with his feet pointing towards his target, which was the padding not too far below. On the count of three one of the others pushed him for a couple of steps, usually the start of the slope was the moment of release, or he was kicked forward into his journey. Hunter accelerated quickly towards the target and he held on tight to the board until almost the very end. He lifted his hands and braced them against his chest, avoiding the lip at the edge of the slab which the garage sat upon, so as to avoid mangling his appendages. The wheels moved from rolling down rough concrete and onto smooth flooring before Hunter jolted with the inevitable hit.

Alex discovered for the rest of the group that you had to line up your board first, before you vaulted at the decline. If a correction was needed during the course of the trip it would greatly affect your fun. If you used your feet to correct your line to the target you would slow your descent considerably, and although it was frightening it was also less fun to go slow, therefore the boys always wanted to go fast. If you corrected with your fingers there was a massive risk that you would graze them on the hard concrete, get them stuck beneath a wheel, or pinched between the board and the ground. Alex's entire right hand was more than enough reminder to do it right the first time and to focus on the task beforehand, and that was despite the fact that his entire palm was constantly hidden within his mouth as he tried to soothe his pain.

They didn't just roll down on their backs either. Part of the fun in maintaining any of their games was to diversify and modify it. For a solid hour all of them tried new ways to ride. Sitting down was successful and less frightening, but that was only when you travelled forward, when they tried going backwards it was an utter disaster. The cunning of lying down was that by simply rolling over it made it more interesting and more dangerous. Rolling onto your front while facing away meant you couldn't see what was happening, having to judge by the look on the others' faces or identify small landmarks next to you to gauge your decision. Going down head first was a hair brained idea, they all wore helmets and the cushions helped soften the blow but any wrong move resulted in pain. Sometimes a simple stone in their path was enough for catastrophe to claim them.

At one point they tried to see if they could get more than one person on a board as it rolled away. They could, and they continued to stack more and more of them on, but there was no occasion where it was successful. They rolled off the sides, slumping into big piles there as whoever was left had to deal with an out of control jack-knifing board that shot off in the wrong direction. Riding down the slope standing up was immediately abandoned but every other attempt was simply fun.

"That looks fun," came a voice from the roadside, "fun for babies." Hunter groaned and shook his head as he recognised who it belonged too. "I knew I would find you."

"Why were you looking for us Reece?" Shane fired back as he returned to his feet.

"Stay out of this Shane, or you will get some too, I don't care who you think you are friends with," Reece snapped at him. Hunter noticed that the two boys that were sitting on bikes behind the bully exchanged glances of concern. Hunter was the one in trouble here but he felt that it was only from Reece. Hunter could feel his brother slink back down towards the garage as James made his way slowly over to the safety of his own yard.

"This is our place," Hunter said, sounding braver than he felt. "You guys need to get lost."

"Our place?" Reece repeated. "Are you married? That's so cute."

"Watch it," Shane said again, but he was entirely ignored as Reece continued.

"Why didn't I get an invite to the wedding? That is mean of you, you have really hurt my feelings. Hey, which one of you is the girl?" Shane finally had enough and stepped forward into breathing space next to the bully. "Watch it Shane, I don't care if I take you down too," Reece added leaning in close. "Don't pretend that I am not going to let everyone know about your kiddie play here, and how you are sticking up for nerds." Shane held his gaze for a moment longer and stepped away, apparently ashamed of the comment. Hunter took a deep breath, holding his skateboard over his shoulder ready to wield it as a weapon if required. Reece turned his attention back to Hunter revealing an ugly smirk.

"It's just you and me now nerd," Reece bellowed with his arms held wide.

"Oi, loud mouth," Phil had stepped out of the shadows giving everyone a fright, including Hunter who knew he had been there all along. "Beat it."

"Or what old man," Reece slunk backwards, not prepared for the intervention of anyone else. Phil stepped away for the briefest of seconds before returning to walk down the driveway, with a cricket bat being tossed from one hand to another. Reece looked shocked, Hunter was equally as stunned but it was more because a kid had threatened an adult. "You won't do anything," Reece stammered, "I'm a kid, you can't hit me."

"I don't know what you are talking about," said Phil never breaking stride. "I am mostly blind, and I just decided to do some cricket practice. If anyone gets hit as I swing it is their own fault." The other boys who had accompanied Reece had fled at the first sight of Shane's dad and were out of view already. Reece turned tail quickly, looking to where he would have to go to catch up.

"This isn't over," Reece let Hunter know as his feet found the pedals. A moment later he was gone. In Hunter's eyes Phil stood like a knight of old, those who saved the town's people from brigands or dragons. It didn't matter that Phil stood there with high footy shorts, worn down thongs, a beer gut hanging hidden beneath an old blue rugby jersey, a mullet and a cricket bat over one shoulder, Hunter could easily see the shining armour and mighty broadsword. In that moment he was so righteous.

"Are you alright?" Phil asked turning towards Hunter who simply nodded in confirmation. "It's probably a good idea if you go back inside, or you can come around to my place if you want, and your brother." Hunter thought about it. He had wanted to go around to his neighbour's house loads of times during school days but he had never been allowed.

"No thanks," Hunter replied with a smile. "We will just wait inside until mum and dad come back. Thanks though."

"No worries," Phil replied, waiting for Hunter to return inside before he walked away.

Hunter slowly returned to his home. Pressing the button for the automatic garage door as he stepped beyond its threshold. He was surprised by his current train of thought, with his mind swirling between shades of red and blue. The blue, which transformed into gold as well, showed the fun he was having with the skateboards, presented the regal and brave form of Phil as he rode into save the group. But the red, sometimes black image, reflected only three things. Reece arriving with his offsiders, James and Alex fleeing to avoid being a target for a much bigger kid, and Shane, leaving Hunter to his fate, and breaking a promise in the process.

"Didn't they want us to go over there?" asked Alex as he looked out of the front window. He had been watching everything that had taken place after he had escaped.

"No, they didn't," Hunter lied, before continuing on towards the solitude and safety of his room. Locking the external house doors as he went.

Hunter didn't go outside for the remainder of the week, nor that weekend. It was a glorious day but he just didn't want to. A foul taste in his mouth kept rising from the pit of his stomach, which he swallowed down only to feel nauseous. He was slightly worried that the next time he stepped out he would be met by the face of Reece. This proved to be true as one afternoon Hunter looked outside and saw the older boy circle the cul-de-sac a handful of times, clearly searching for them, before leaving the area. But the real reason was that Hunter didn't want to be seen with Shane. His heart sank at the thought.

The following week Hunter was introduced to his new soccer team. There were still kids who were not available yet as they had cricket commitments, as they had made the finals and couldn't play until they were finished. Hunter's cricket team had never been good enough to make it that far, but that didn't mean they didn't have fun. It was quite the opposite, they had nothing but fun, they just weren't successful. Hunter was introduced to a couple of other players and found that he was drawn to one who he became friends with quickly. That player's name was Greg and his older brother was the coach, though they were told that his dad would sometimes coach instead due to availability.

Hunter found a combination between himself, James and Greg and he quite enjoyed it. He had a gratifying time at training and he was not as bad as he thought he would be. The only downer had been that he had been avoiding Shane throughout the training, but he pushed it to the back of his mind.

The first game arrived in no time. Hunter had no idea who the team was, but he didn't really know any of them anyway. His excitement levels were up. He had been placed as the right back because his leg was a canon and he had shown in one training session that he was capable of clearing the ball a long way. Another new player, also called James but was affectionately known by his last name of Bowie, played on the other side of the field as the left back. Hunter liked him because he was a bit of a larrikin, but he was actually a really nice kid. James and Greg were in the midfield and, luckily for Hunter, Shane was way up the front in the forwards.

The first half went by without any negative incidents. Hunter fell back into the game reasonably easy and found that although he wasn't the best in the team he certainly wasn't the worst. Hunter had gotten involved early to calm his nerves, clearing several balls at least half the length of the field while also providing cover defence when opposition players broke through the line. Both teams were evenly matched and no points had been scored. When half time came Hunter threw himself to the ground next to a Tupperware container full of oranges. He devoured several as the coach started giving his interpretation of what was happening. Hunter didn't really listen to what was being said, he had gotten involved in an unsaid competition between himself and Bowie of who could eat the most oranges. The juice was delicious and thick, and it flowed down Hunter's arm as his teeth grabbed hold of big clumps of pulp. He could feel the strands get stuck their but he paid it no mind as he enjoyed the competition of orange eating and the taste of the fruit. When they finished Hunter had to use his water bottle on his arm, hands and face to remove the sticky feeling which clumped together his hair follicles and glued his fingers together.

"Oh no," James groaned as they returned to the field. Hunter hoped he wasn't hurt because their team had no substitutions, and weren't even fielding a full team. James simply pointed towards the other team.

"Reece is a Ranger," Hunter groaned as the bully appeared on the field for the opposite team. One of the other boys who had flanked Reece with his intrusion to Angus Place was also taking the field.

"We have got them Hunter," said Bowie as he watched his team mates take the field. "Doesn't matter who they put on we have got them." Hunter nodded and returned to his position on the other side of the field this time. Hunter hoped that Reece would be a defender for the other team, and therefore not have anything to do with the bully. He had no such luck. Reece and his friend were both midfielders, meaning they could go anywhere on the field and near any opposition player. The bully smiled as he saw Hunter and James notice him.

It took only moments for Reece to show his intentions for that game. The Waratahs would kick off and would have the possession of the ball. Greg tapped it forward to start the second half before passing it to James. James was immediately tackled by Reece, who slid along the ground with sprigs up and took out James. James toppled over as a result, pleading for a penalty from the ref. The referee was young and was either not informed of the rules or too scared to enforce them. Reece got away with it. Greg was in pursuit. Reece tapped the ball too far forward and Bowie struck by clearing it down the other end of the field.

"I have a canon," Bowie said to Reece. He was as tall as Hunter and as big also, and Bowie was not intimidated. "It's probably a good idea if you stand clear." The ball went sailing back towards the forwards where it got stuck in a fight up there.

"Are you alright?" Hunter asked James who had been hobbling around after finding his feet. The boy looked shaken but nodded in reply. There was some time before the ball came back towards Hunter. James got it early this time. He went straight at Reece, determined to show the bigger boy how good he was. James feinted left and then went right. Reece fell for the move, almost tumbling over in the process. James laughed as he shot past him but Reece wasn't beaten. The bully shot an arm out and grabbed at James's collar, dragging him to the ground roughly by the neck. It was a clear foul. Both teams reacted it was so obvious. Most of the Waratahs went up in protest, while the Rangers dropped their head showing their frustration in the move.

A penalty was called in which Reece went over and patted James on the back saying he was sorry. James was in tears. He was intimidated and he was hurt. He tapped the ball resuming play and passed it to Shane who had been calling out for it. As everyone watched Shane work some magic Reece struck again. He tripped James over when no one was watching and stepped on his hand while he was on the ground. The sprigs grated on the bones beneath his foot and James rolled over, holding in a yelp of pain as he was clearly in anguish. Hunter was on his way to run over to him when Shane scored a goal. The crowd applauded the act but Shane ran to his brother as he headed back to halfway.

"What are you doing?" Shane asked his brother with little concern.

"He took me out," wailed James, pointing his eyes towards Reece as he clutched at his damaged hand. "He stepped on my hand." Shane looked over at Reece who was smiling as a result of the claim, not even trying to hide his actions.

"Get back on side, you are embarrassing me," Shane growled.

The comment stunned several players, on both teams. The opposition team started play again. Reece tapped the ball forward this time and went straight at James. His target was so obvious that he paid little attention to those around him. Greg snuck in and stole the ball away from him.

"What man?" called out Greg as he ran off with his prize. Reece scowled at him but he also didn't stop running. He ploughed straight into James, knocking him flying through the air to land in a crumpled mess. Hunter and Bowie ran in to help him, Shane saw what happened but got involved with the play up field instead.

"Pick on someone your own size," Hunter barked at Reece, entirely fed up with the older boy.

"Yeah come at me instead," Bowie backed him up. "If you touch him again though I will deal with you."

"Ha," laughed Reece. "I don't have to." He pointed towards James who was crawling his way from the field, grabbing at alternate injuries as he went. Hunter's heart sank, he knew he could have done more to help his friend. The target of James had been the easiest of the three boys who had opposed him earlier.

"And now you are going to lose," Reece laughed again. With Greg helping Shane in the forwards, James slinking away from the field defeated, and Bowie and Hunter standing up for him, there was no one apart from the goalkeeper to stop a goal being scored. The Rangers made a runaway and that is exactly what they did. The ref blew his whistle and the game was concluded. The Rangers winning with a two to one goal difference.

"Losers," Reece said as he was joined by his friend. He didn't continue his insults as he left to join the rest of his team. Hunter looked around at those surrounding him. He glanced at Bowie who looked angry and bewildered by what had happened, at Greg who was completely gassed by the amount of work he had gotten through, at James who had collapsed completely shattered at the sideline unable to join his team, and Shane who didn't seem to care about any of it. Hunter couldn't help but agree with Reece at the moment. Yep, he thought with a snarl, losers.

But he wouldn't let it end that way.

"Cooking?" questioned Hunter's mum.

"Yep cooking," Hunter repeated.

"Why are you cooking again?" his dad asked this time.

"James has to do some cooking for class at school and his mum said that she would show us as well if we wanted," Hunter replied. Alex nodded in agreement. There was a couple of crates of eggs in their hands, as well as flour, food dye and some vinegar.

"I will pay you for these," Hunter offered, pulling out a couple of dollars from his piggy bank as compensation for removing the cooking ingredients.

"No it's okay," his mum shook her head. "Just let us know next time so we can get extra stuff in advance."

"Sure thing," said Alex way too enthusiastically.

"We will try," Hunter said, offering the more usual response as to avoid unwanted attention.

"Be back before dinner," dad said as Hunter and Alex left.

"You have about an hour and a half," mum shouted out behind them.

"Oh boy," Alex squeaked as he almost danced around with excitement.

"Cool it," replied Hunter with a whisper. He walked out the door and straight into the Spigot's garage. He waited there for a few minutes along with Alex, whose heart was beating so hard Hunter thought even he heard it beating.

Shane and James were not home, but Hunter could still see them. Their parents had gone out while they had remained behind. Sort of staying home. They were hiding on the top floor of Raul's house which was still a construction site. Hunter gave it a few more minutes, imagining that was the length of time that either of his parents had ventured to watch them from the front door or nearby windows, before deciding that they were safe inside and doing the right thing. Hunter spied some elastic rope with hooks nearby in the Spigot's garage and picked them up while he waited, just in case.

Finally, cautiously, but quickly, Alex and Hunter made their way over to the wooden framed incomplete development. Hunter checked to see that there were no shadows hidden within the curtains or glass at his home's front windows, as his expedition would have been over before it begun. There was none. His pace quickened nonetheless, expecting his house door to burst open at any second. Alex and Hunter arrived undiscovered but still hid behind the fence that stood between the construction site and their home, just in case.

"It took you long enough," James said as the brothers climbed to the top floor. "We don't know how long our parents will be gone for." The access to that top floor had been hard and hazardous. There were no stairs up to that loft, and the scaffolding that would have provided access to the builders had been dismantled due to their inactivity. Hunter and Alex threw up their materials to James who waited on a ply wood floor laid out above, before scurrying up the timber frame. They had to carefully select which timber beams to stand on as some were able to take significant load while others were just there to prop up temporary beams and were flimsy.

"I don't know what I am even doing here," Shane added from his seat inside a wall cavity.

"That makes two of us," Hunter said under his breath. He avoided the eyes of Shane as he knew he had been overheard, but set about outlining his plan. It was clear that James had as much desire to get on with this as his neighbours with his vast array of ingredients that were laid out. Buckets of water, water pistols, and sling shots amongst countless other things.

"We know he is coming," started Hunter, "but we need to make sure he really gets it or it is a wasted opportunity."

"Who is 'he'?" demanded Shane.

"Reece," Hunter and James declared in unison. "Reece is coming." Shane's eyes widened noticeably but returned to a look of nonchalance a moment later.

"How do you know he is coming?" Shane asked crossing his arms. "And why are we up here?"

"You would know if you cared," James scowled at his brother. Everyone waited for the admission that Shane didn't care as was usual when trying to sort out an argument. It didn't come. "When we got off the bus he was waiting with his mates again. Your mates," James continued looking hurt. "And once again they tried to pick on me. You didn't do anything, typical. But you wouldn't know because you were too busy staying away from us, doing your own thing and avoiding us. Hunter stepped in and called him out. Alex helped too. He told us when he would be coming so we are going to wait for him. He will no doubt bring his friends, but we are going to take all of them out."

Hunter picked up as soon as James finished. "And it is going to be fun. We are committed to this, win or lose we will enjoy how this plays out."

"What do you mean?" Shane asked with a look of confusion. It was easy to tell he was ready to remove himself from the others.

"This is going to be our fort and we will defend it from any siege," Hunter nodded, slamming his hand down on the fibreglass board in front of him.

"That's a bit babyish don't you think," Shane said getting up and moving to the space that he had climbed up. "We are a little bit old to be playing these games don't you think?"

"You don't believe that," Hunter boomed, he too had reached his endpoint. He had simply had enough. "Your so called friends believe that, not you. I understand that they don't do what we do, that is their loss, and I understand that you think you will look foolish by telling them, so don't, but this is fun. This is what you like to do. If you deny it you are denying yourself. I know this will not last forever, but as long as we have it why not relish it. I would fight all the people who would try to persuade me otherwise. I would fight all those who would try to deny me my fun and imagination with my friends. And," Hunter took a step closer to Shane. "I would definitely fight those who pick on my family." Shane looked away before answering the charge given him.

"I didn't have a choice," he shouted back, "and he is my family not yours."

"You are wrong," Hunter blasted back. His usual calm and collected demeanour completely gone. "You always have a choice, and despite the short time we have spent together I think of both of you as closer than friends. All but family. So you can walk away from this. You can make that choice. But if you do you are choosing far more. You are choosing to stand beside the bullies, you are choosing to inflict pain and fear on your own family, you are choosing to lower yourself when we hold you in such high regard, and you choose to never play with us again, to explore, run, imagine, create, or have fun, with us again. You will choose to remain king of your domain, or to let it collapse around you."

Shane had stopped and was looking off towards the grass mound and the creek beyond it.

"It is childish," Shane whispered.

"Choose," James demanded.

"We are in high school now," Shane continued speaking to himself.

"Choose," Alex echoed.

"It is time we grew up," Shane said once more. Hunter walked over to him and placed a hand on his shoulder.

"With us or against us," Hunter stated simply. Shane looked him in the eye. Conflict still raging inside him. He met the icy stare of his neighbour and saw the fire that reflected in that ice. He knew what the right choice was for him, but not for reality. He also felt like Hunter would throw him from the skeleton framed house if he declined the invitation. He looked around the incomplete room. He saw the sky in the background, trees which swayed lazily there, he saw the faces of his friends and family nearby, and he saw the kingdom he had help create.

He looked down at the ground.

He took one last step towards Hunter.

Shane shot out his hand towards him.

"Together," he said softly. Repeating what he had said to Hunter the first time they had met. Remembering the promise he had made there. Hunter smiled. There was no hesitation for him to respond, despite what had happened lately.

"Together," Hunter repeated and was joined by Alex and James who added their hands and voices. "Together." They all looked around the circle, letting an infectious smile spread between them.

"Okay," Hunter said finally. "Here is what we have to do."

Hunter was in position. He was ready. So was James. So was Alex. Shane stood beside him, knowing the role he had been set but still questionable as to whether or not he would fulfil it.

Hunter's imagination had once again taken over. The construction site had transformed into a glorious medieval fortress. Formidable and unassailable. Not only a fortress, but *The* fortress. Camelot. They had met against a round table, which was made by a carpenter's tool with ply board resting upon it. Around it the four knights had gathered listening to Hunter's plan.

Hunter had taken on the role of Sir Gawain, the right hand man of Arthur, the formidable one, true in values and brave. Shane in Hunter's mind took on the mantle of Lancelot, not King Arthur like he previously would have assumed. Hunter did not fully trust him and if he abandoned the group he would stay true to name, if he didn't he would be remembered for his strength and valour. James was Sir

Galihad, who was the son of Lancelot. Hunter thought it would be good to keep the relationship somewhere in the imaginary world. Alex had taken the name Sir Mordred. In legend he was Arthur's son and enemy. Hunter knew Alex would do his job at this moment, but he was also painful a good portion of the time. None of them knew the names they had been given, just Hunter, but they took on those roles where they stood. They sealed their plan with clasped hands in the centre of that round table, each calling out their name proudly.

"Creek Crew," they cheered bravely before setting about their tasks.

Each of them wore great armour, and each stood next to the weapons they would use. Hunter was proud of what they had assembled in such a short time. James, being the shortest, hid beyond the entrance to the cul-de-sac. His job was to warn the group when Reece was on his way, or if he saw his parents return which would mean the end of the ambush. If the plan played out correctly he would also pepper the bullies retreat with eggs and a dye filled super soaker. Alex was in a similar position, but he would remain out of sight until either Reece left or he attempted to scale the building frame in pursuit of Shane and Hunter.

Hunter and Shane however had created something formidable and were excited to use it. Using buckets, elastic rope and hooks, and the building frame itself, they had constructed projectile launchers. They took on the form of catapults or trebuchets and would launch all the extra ingredients from the top floor down to the road below. There was a pile of eggs already broken on the road where they had tested the range, marking on the ground nearby how far they had to pull back to achieve each distance. The more Hunter thought about it the more he had a hybrid theory. King Arthur's knights holding guns and using 12 pound canon in a defensive effort.

They held their breath and waited.

Finally James turned within his hiding spot and gave the secret signal that told them Reece was on his way. The signal that followed revealed that there were more than one. The Creek Crew hid out of sight. They could see the intruders but the intruders could not see them. Reece came into view first, flanked by two other boys. It was clear they were looking for Hunter already, they never looked the other way, for if they had they may have noticed James hiding behind a collapsing real estate sign. Hunter's heart hammered away. He was paying close attention to only two things, the approaching bullies and how far away they were from reaching the mark on the road. The catapults were already pulled taut, loaded with a bag of flour. Hunter looked over at Shane as the impostors approached the spot and gave him a silent nod. Shane replied in kind. This would reveal where his loyalties would lie.

Hunter released his bucket and watched as it slung hard, vaulting the contents out over the edge of the building. Reece hadn't seen it, which gave Hunter the opportunity to reload in secrecy as Reece hadn't seen him launch it, but that also meant he never saw it coming. Hunter had suspected that he would have to empty most of the contents of their storage of ingredients and ammunition, but that was not the case.

His first shot had been straight and true, smashing into Reece's chest and launching him from his bike. The packet had not exploded as it sailed through the air, nor when it made contact. It hit Reece like a brick. Every one stopped to watch the bully flounder after the impact, all of them stunned at what had happened. Hunter gritted his teeth and looked over at Shane who was yet to launch.

"What are you waiting for? Lay it on, no mercy," Hunter spat as he made the demand. Shane smiled and did not hesitate. His own small bag of flour went hurtling through the air. The boys who accompanied Reece saw this one fly. Instead of pointing out where it came from they turned their bikes around and fled. Shane never aimed for them though. He had launched it at Reece as well. His bag slammed into the frame of Reece's bike and exploded. Clouds of white spread into the air and covered the road. Reece still lay on the ground. He hadn't really moved and now it looked like he had been punched by a marshmallow, white spreading everywhere.

Alex and James jumped into action and they showered the escaping duo with everything they had. Water and dye was pumped out aggressively as a hail of eggs were thrown hard across the street. The retreating boys never looked back, simply making a meek call to get out of there and soon they were gone. Alex and James didn't chase them, they advanced on the still crumpled form of Reece. He convulsed as he moaned in the street but the abuse he received was relentless. Hunter had been ruthless but he still kept some ingredients held back. That didn't mean he stopped. More eggs were launched, along with slops of butter, a bucket full of milk, a bag of sugar and a few other ingredients. Reece was well and truly beaten. Hunter climbed down and made his way over to the downed boy. He waved away the younger siblings as they excitedly danced around, triumphant in their victory.

"You don't seem to get it," Hunter said as he bent over Reece as he turned to face him. "I don't like bullies, especially those who pick on my friends or my family, or pursue me to my home. You are not welcome here, and if you come back it will be worse for you." Hunter had laid down his threat and then left, along with a bag full of ingredients. Alex and James went with him. Reece eventually got his feet and looked at Shane who had remained there.

"You are dead meat," Reece spat, clearing egg yolk and white powder from his face.

"I don't think so," Shane said in reply. "You are all alone here. We can easily take you, this is our territory. You don't belong here."

"I am going to come back and get you," Reece said shaking. There was no conviction in what he said. It was clear that he afraid and hurt.

"Sure you can," Shane replied with little care. "But nothing will change, except that I would be happy to tell other's about how you got beaten by primary school kids, how you got knocked off your bike by flour, how your friends abandoned you," Shane smiled, "and how you cried." Reece sneered, audibly sobbing as he retreated slowly back up the street. He had only just gone out of sight when Shane heard a car horn blast.

"Get off the road you punk," yelled out the voice of Shane's dad. Shane couldn't hide the mess that was left on the road, but he also knew his parents would know exactly what had happened after seeing Reece. The car came around the corner, avoided the pile of ingredients laid out across the road and stopped beside Shane.

"What happened?" his dad asked. Shane thought for a moment and told the same lie that Hunter had told.

"We were cooking," he answered simply with a shrug. His dad looked over at the mess, shook his head, and then turned back to his son.

"Not enough eggs," his dad said, "it looks like you spoiled it." Shane smiled, realising what they had just gotten away with.

"Clean it up," his dad said. The car drove off and parked in the garage.

What they almost got away with, Shane thought.

CHAPTER 10 – SOCCER SLAM SHOWDOWN

Just because Hunter wasn't good at soccer didn't mean he couldn't try and get better. Almost every evening after Reece's destruction consisted of all four boys, with the addition of Raul on occasion, going outside and using a soccer ball in all manner of scenarios.

The previous wet winter was being repeated which meant that they couldn't utilise the back paddock area as much as they had before, but that didn't mean they weren't outside. All of their parents had formed the opinion that despite the risk of catching a cold and getting sick they were doing something they wanted to do to improve themselves. Whether the rain was pouring down or the weather was just overcast with a slight hint of a chill they could go outside and practice. It meant a massive change to routine which now consisted of going outside and playing, then come in and have a hot shower, get into nice warm pyjamas, drink some hot chocolate, and then chill out before dinner. Homework preceded all of that, but Hunter was smart enough to either do portions of it at school or on the bus, leaving the bare minimum to do at home.

The games they played were as, if not more so, creative and imaginative as they had been while out near the grass mound. Each one lasted some time, but inevitably all were cancelled by the intervention of their parents at some point.

The first one they began was born due to necessity. Seeking shelter from driving rain, not being able to kick a ball around inside, not that the idea of that was that productive anyway, and neither house having an undercover outside patio area of considerable size, they took it upon themselves to train on Raul's abandoned construction site next door. The crew started by playing normal soccer where there were goals at the back end of the house and some more near the front door.

Play would commence as normal, but, with the added difficulty of wooden posts, cross beams and braces impeding them, it resulted in some very creative play. They would always try to return the ball to open areas to improve the flow of the game but everyone figured out how to do that effectively so the ball didn't advance that much, choosing to instead fight their way through the jungle of timber.

Always trying to make their games harder they decided to take the game upstairs to the skeleton and bare bones construction area. After having a really good look and noticing that the floor didn't exist in many spots the idea was abandoned. Occasionally when the risk of getting hurt far outweighed the prospect of fun these things happened.

They ended up just doing trick shots all through the place. Lobbing it off their foot and over certain beams, in between gaps in the invisible walls, and bouncing them off particular targets into other areas or making it to a certain spot. This was fantastic fun until the builders came back and finally resumed their work. Immediately, and understandably, the whole area was off limits. The boys were glad that there was some life in that construction site as it meant that Raul was closer to hanging around on a more permanent basis. It just sucked that their play was affected.

The next plan was to kick the ball against the garage door. It had to be at Shane's house because Hunter's driveway sloped and when they kicked it there was more likelihood of the ball ending up on the roof rather than on target (that was a fun game in itself, but not useful to their improvement at all). The argument was made that they could simply aim down, but whoever took shots into the ground when playing soccer? That game didn't last all that long.

The boys had used wheelie bins as the goal posts to reduce the size of the goal and to make the shots more realistic. The game was fine while ever the goalkeeper was stopping attempts at goal or the person kicking the ball missed and hit the bins. But whenever there was a wayward shot it would crash into the aluminium garage doors with an enormous metallic bang that left the whole frame shuddering. This was okay in small moderation, the occasional loose shot being largely ignored by the adults residing inside. When Alex jumped into goal though the goals became more frequent and so did the noise.

"Hey you lot, cut it out," Shane's mum yelled from the front door, terminating the game and making the boys move on in the same instance. They didn't argue, they simply obeyed. The possibility of being pulled inside as a result of dispute too great to be risked.

The game resumed just as before but this time using the iron fence panelling. The boys were oddly shocked when this game was called off in similar fashion shortly after.

One day Raul accompanied his parents as they looked over the new progress since the building recommenced. He didn't care about what was happening and just jumped into playing with the others.

"What about over the fence?" he advised after hearing the stories of some previous games.

"Hey yeah," James agreed enthusiastically. He and Raul had already become fast friends due to their similar age and it wasn't uncommon for one to agree with the other. "Like soccer volleyball." It sounded fantastic and the teams were split. The two older boys verse the three younger boys. May and Alana tried to play as well but were dismissed by their older brothers, running away to tell on them, but more likely to play somewhere else together instead. The younger boys all talked massive games saying that between them they were going to win because they could cover more space, Hunter and Shane just laughed.

"We can dive on this nice soft grass," Shane whispered to Hunter. "If they do that someone is going to land on a nail or a brick or something." He mouthed the word ouch as he considered the consequence. There was probably worse things hidden under the dirt than those that were visible sitting on top. Raul's house now had roof tiles, bricks, windows (some of which had been broken by clumsy builders) and internal walls with insulation were starting to get put in. Any number of those things which had been frequently cut or broken could impale or maim any of them with the slightest of effort.

The game was basically hacky sack with volleyball on a larger scale. One team would kick the ball up and by only using your feet you had to return it back to the other side. If it came straight to them all the boys could all easily volley it back towards the other side. If it was just out of reach it was a different story. The ball still had to land within a set boundary making it harder to score points but it never stopped either team from attempting something sly.

The scoring was reset several times throughout the afternoon as parents talked to the builders and amongst each other. Finally Raul got given a time limit.

"Ten minutes and then we are going," his mum called out. That was not just a confirmation of a reduction in numbers but an announcement that the game would be over. When all the parents ventured back inside they would surely drag their kids in with them.

Hunter and Shane, like they had for the majority of the games throughout the afternoon, took the lead early. Once they were winning they would simply try and hold it, allowing the other team of three to collapse under pressure or try riskier shots than they would otherwise attempt usually.

"You're going down," Alex called out.

"Sure thing," Hunter replied with a laugh.

"We're way better," James added.

"Whatever," Shane replied.

The score stretched further ahead in the older siblings favour. After minutes there was a near unassailable gap between them.

"Alright, we're going," Raul's dad called out this time.

"Last play," Raul cried out in reply so everyone could hear. The ball was kicked high up into the air, easy to get to by Shane. He attempted a bicycle kick to show a little bit of flair (despite Hunter being the only person who could see him) and comfortably flicked it back over his head and the fence as he slid to a stop on the ground. The calls of anguish from the other side revealed that the younger players had failed to pick it up in time.

"One more," called out Alex immediately.

"Winner takes all," Raul added, trying to convince Hunter and Shane who were already the clear winners, "last point wins."

"Unless you're scared," James barked finally. Hunter and Shane each rolled their eyes.

"Fine," Shane bellowed back before turning to Hunter. "They are going to cheat, you go forward, closer to the fence, just in case they just throw it over the edge. I will go back. Hunter nodded and took his position. He could hear voices on the other side of the fence but not what they were saying. As he waited he pulled away random blades of green grass that had attached themselves to him as he slid along the ground. They had not been noticed, which was vastly different to the grass he had become used to that grew in the back paddock. "They are sneaking up the fence," Shane whispered. "Get ready." Hunter soundlessly crept towards the fence. He would not be able to kick it back over from here without hitting the fence or making it to go straight up. Hunter gestured to Shane that he would simply flick it with his foot back to his friend who would launch it back over towards the others.

"Ready?" James asked loudly. Hunter heard the other team scrambling at the fence and knew they were up to mischief. As soon as he saw movement from above it he moved in with his right foot out ready to flick the ball on. Something quickly dropped over the fence towards the ground. Hunter was already under it and had prepared to take action. His foot came up. Hunter saw that it wasn't the ball that had been flung over and immediately started to retract his foot. He was too late.

"AAAAAARRRRRRGGGGGHHHHHHHHHHH," Hunter screamed. He felt like he was about to run around the backyard, the action somehow easing the pain that raced through his body, instead he fell to the ground clutching at his right foot.

"What is wrong with you?" Shane roared at the others as he rushed to Hunter's side. "Why would you throw a brick over?"

"Did it get him?" James called out suddenly concerned. Hunter saw the smaller boys' heads pop up over the fence and then drop back immediately.

"Let me see," Shane said as Hunter continued to roll around on the spot in agony. Hunter reluctantly drew away his hands which he felt were covered in blood. His eyes remained shut tight for a long time before he finally started to ease himself up onto his bottom, resting on his outstretched hands.

"What did they get?" Hunter asked grimacing, constantly fighting the pain with pulsed seemingly everywhere.

"Your toes," Shane replied frowning.

"How bad?" Hunter ventured further.

"Oh," said Shane with the tiniest of unintended laughs. "Those things are broken." At the news Hunter slumped back onto the grass. He had never had anything broken before. He felt sick to his stomach, suddenly resisting the urge to vomit. He tried to wriggle his toes but it was no use, he couldn't feel them, apart from how hurt they were.

"Looks like the game is over then," Hunter stated, before waiting for someone to come and assist him.

Out for a month. It was possibly some of the worst news Hunter had ever received. That along with the fact that he could no longer continue playing soccer or any other sporting activities. Three of his toes had been broken requiring surgery, while another had been jarred hard and been forced into a crunched or rolled up position.

Alex had been the culprit who had concocted the braindead idea to lob a brick over the fence, and he had been punished as a result. When he wasn't at school or his own soccer training he was relegated to his room. Alex liked to be active and hated sitting still, he despised his punishment. His isolation would only end when Hunter could finally resume sport.

Hunter was on crutches for several weeks, and then, when they were finally taken away, he still had another week of limping or hobbling along before he even started returning to normal. When the month finally finished he eased his way back into playing games. Allowed to play outside once more it took him another few weeks of only playing goalkeeper, as they played cul-de-sac soccer, before he could resume training for weekend sport. Whilst at home they would fluctuate between playing on the road and playing on the path besides Shane's house. The path was bordered by fences on both sides now as another house had almost finished being built on the path's other side. Hunter was only allowed to use his hands not his feet. He couldn't use his right foot until he had another check-up and got the all clear from his doctor, but he couldn't use his left foot either as it would put excess pressure or strain onto his already weakened toes. It was frustrating but Hunter followed the direction to the letter, not wanting to add more time to his already restricted existence.

The all clear was given and Hunter's sporting life started almost immediately again. On Wednesdays he returned to training. The afternoons were immediately better. Alex had his soccer training on another day in a different location. Hunter couldn't keep an eye on his younger brother while he was training so Alex would walk the short distance to their grandparents place and wait to be picked up by their parents. Hunter on the other hand couldn't make it all the way to training by walking and his parents couldn't take him. This meant that he got to go with Shane and James. All three caught the bus home before sprinting down the hill on their street so they could get changed quickly and go. Hunter squirmed as his still ginger toes took the impact, but he persevered. He unlocked the front door, threw down his bag in his room and got changed as quickly as he could. He had already laid out the gear he needed including shin pads and plastic studded boots. Hunter was panicking in the back of his mind, certain that he would be holding up his neighbours and they would be waiting for him angrily. He grabbed his boots and ran with socks on his feet only. He jumped up the retaining wall and ran over to the Spigot's front door. Hunter waited patiently for a minute, expecting the others to come storming out at any time, but he was relieved that they weren't waiting for him.

His expectation was wrong.

"Come in," Shane's mum said opening the door for him. She looked Hunter up and down smiling. "It's good to see someone is organised." Hunter left his boots at the front door before walking through the house. He had been inside so frequently lately that it had almost become a second home. Hunter was quite certain that when he looked back on the houses he had lived in, despite them being numerous, he would be able to remember the interior of that house just as much as any others that were his own. May sat there with Shane and James all eating some afternoon tea which consisted of some fruit, a small packet of chips and a couple of biscuits. Hunter sat politely before accepting Judy's offer of food with enthusiasm. He enjoyed the snack as the boys were chased from room to room by their mum. Ten minutes later they were on their way.

When they arrived at training Hunter found that there were a few new faces in the team. It was fantastic news because it meant the team was complete, regardless of ability. Every position had someone playing in it and there were reserves that could be used for substitutions. Hunter got to know most of them pretty quickly, as well as reconnecting with Bowie, Greg and the others who had already been in the team. There was only one new player who had not introduced himself.

"Who is that guy?" Hunter asked Shane and was greeted with a sneer. The boy in question was in the process of attempting to juggle a ball, flicking it up off his toe and tapping it on towards the goal while still in the air.

"That's Ross," Shane answered grumpily. "He thinks he is pretty mad. It is probably best to have very little to do with him."

"Why?" came the obvious question.

"There are a couple of reasons," Shane admitted. "He is a representative player, for basketball. I don't know why that makes him a better player at soccer, but apparently it does. Another reason is that he doesn't like me, and he won't like you." Shane avoided the why question again and simply continued. "He is one of Reece's friends from primary school, they are still friends now, even though they don't go to the same school, and meet up every now and then. Ross is the reason Reece knew where we lived. Ross lives in one of those houses on the other side of the creek." It was a lot of information for Hunter but he understood. All the doors seemed to open at once revealing everything. Ross, seeing that he had drawn attention came over to them.

"Who are you?" he demanded looking in Hunter's direction. The boy was tall with a mostly shaved head. It was slightly longer around the crown of his head and on top. He also had a husky voice, like when he spoke he dragged the words on a brick wall before releasing them.

"I'm Hunter," Hunter answered, offering his hand. It wasn't taken, all Hunter received was a glance up and down.

"So, you're one of the backs," Ross continued to analyse him. "Are you any good?" Hunter thought about how best to answer that comment. He didn't like the word good at the best of times as he thought it meant satisfactory, mediocre, or average.

"Nah," Hunter replied with a smile. He didn't justify his answer, and neither did Ross chase it. The other boy gave a dirty look to Shane and moved over towards the others. He swaggered as he went, but his shoulders jutted forward deliberately with every step, trying to reinforce his presence.

It wasn't long before Hunter could see what was happening. Ross continually tried to undermine Shane's position in the field. Ross was one striker and Shane was the other. Hunter did his best during training to help out his neighbour but even that wasn't easy. It was clear that Ross was the better shot at goal. When he lined it up he would thump at the rubber covering and send it sailing into the back of the net. He was also skilled with dribbling it between his feet, but he wasn't a fan of the contest. Shane on the other hand would take the ball into the fight and come out triumphant on the other side, but with the added pressure of defenders around him his aim could be thrown out. Training would end up being a contest of who got the most balls and put them in the goal.

That was only initially though, because every week the contest expanded and became even more bitter. Extra points started coming for who touched the ball more, how many shots were made and how many times they got to head the ball from a corner. Those were the simple ones though. Eventually it became a contest of who was the favourite player between them, each jeering at the other whenever they got the ball.

"Greg likes me more than you," Ross would declare as he received the ball from one of the halves. "If James wasn't your brother you would never get the ball up here." Ross was usually the one who delivered the insults more, but then eventually he was the only one who was giving them out.

"Do you know why Bowie and Hunter clear the ball to me?" he scorned on another occasion. "It's because they know that there is more chance in me scoring than you." It wasn't true. In most cases both of the backs would simply kick the ball as hard as they could to remove it from their half of the field, and on the rare occasion where either of them went for a run they would force their way through a pack and then toe the ball forward to whoever was there, the recipient wasn't even on the same team half the time. Most players couldn't care less about the jibes, mostly because they weren't the receivers and Shane was a pretty tough individual, but eventually that changed too.

Trainings started to turn sour as the insults started flying. Where the boys, and girls as there were some on the team, started to enjoy coming to training less and less when it had initially been one of those things they all looked forward to. Hunter and some of the other's still persevered. Despite the internal conflict the team was somewhat successful, and the players were getting better all the time. Hunter, Bowie and Greg had become peacekeepers amongst the group. Originally they were impartial, telling anybody off who required it. Now they just ripped into Ross while picking up others.

"Lay off Ross," Greg said as he stood up to the other player. Another tirade had been let loose after a younger player didn't deliver the best quality of passes.

"Wake up Greg," Ross screeched back with his odd voice. "Do you want to win or lose?" Greg didn't pursue the conversation. He had stood up for another and that was it. It was obvious that they didn't want to lose, no one did, but it was more obvious that how that occurred mattered.

"Pass it here James," Ross continued his verbal spray. "Just like your brother, useless."

"Bowie what are you doing? What is the point of being able to kick hard if it goes out?"

"Hunter, I know you play favourites but I thought you were smart. Another dumb decision."

"Don't you want to win, you won't if you don't give me the ball."

The fact that the team could hardly hear Ross made it almost tolerable. He didn't act out at anyone, he just stayed running around in a position where he wasn't marked demanding for the ball. He was a member of the team now, but not a team member. Everyone ignored him, even if it meant that they would fight harder in a game and eventually lose.

One training session turned especially nasty. It was clear that he had been talking to his friend Reece. The verbal spray that he had delivered for months during the soccer season turned personal. There were things said about Hunter that were mean, but mostly not true. But what Shane was having said about him was not pleasant at all, and that was putting it nicely. Anything that it seemed he had ever done wrong was being yelled out on the field.

Finally it came to a head. Shane walked over to Ross and stood toe to toe with him. Ross was marginally taller, more athletic looking and leaner, where Shane was more solid and continued to slouch. It looked like Shane was going to punch him, and no one was going to blame him. But Shane didn't. He never even touched him. He just left the field completely and walked towards the carpark.

"That's right walk away," Ross bellowed croakily. "You know that you aren't a winner like me. That I am the best. We don't need you." He smiled triumphantly. But only for a moment. James walked after his brother. Ross shrugged as if it was inevitable. Hunter followed them without a second thought. Ross must have assumed that would be where it ended, but he was wrong. Bowie and Greg left the training field. Then everyone else did as well. Ross stood alone. He was no longer triumphant, but still held onto his defiance.

"We have a game that will get us into the finals this week," he yelled after them. "You will all be there. You know you will."

Ross was right. Saturday morning came and it was wet. The game was all but called off due to a waterlogged pitch but they were allowed to play. The rain which usually spelled misery to the players was at the bottom of the list of things that they didn't want to be there for. At the top of the list was the internal wretchedness which was from the presence of Ross. They couldn't play with him, but wouldn't win without him. They had lost games before because of it. But this game was to get into the finals, and it was a rematch against Reece's team. To make matters worse Ross and Reece arrived in the same car, late so everyone saw them. All of the players' heads dropped at the sight.

"Shane," Hunter whispered as he came closer to his friend.

"Yeah mate," Shane replied unmoving.

"Something needs to be said," Hunter told him. "Look at them all. Some will fight on no matter what, but the rest are beaten already."

"What can be said?" Shane asked, he was evidently one of those who was defeated. "And why me?"

"I don't know, something," Hunter responded. "And it has to be you. You are the Captain of the team."

"That's not true," Shane snapped back. "We all share the captaincy role."

"Fine, maybe you're not the Captain," Hunter agreed. "But you are the heart and soul of this team. The players follow you, regardless of what has happened and probably even more. You also have the most to lose."

"I am no Captain, and I can't lead this team," he said pointing out players. "I am no leader."

"You're wrong," Hunter growled back. "You are a King. I follow you, and others look up to you." Shane thought about it for a second resisting the urge to return to the grown up mentality he had spouted about months before.

"Why would they follow me into a match they can't win?"

"Because they can win it, the opposition knows it. But also because you have the most to lose." Players continued to gather. Some treading lightly on the puddled grass while others trudged amongst the slop. Shane just watched them for a moment. He watched as Ross and Reece dawdled towards the field, still some way away.

"Get them in," Shane demanded and left Hunter to gather the group. It didn't take long. Despite their sense of foreboding they were all keen to get something started to remove the fear they felt. They walked over and formed a circle without hesitation or command. Shane kneeled on the wet grass, his knees sinking into the pitch, and beckoned others to follow him. James did so first, usually the last who would have done so. Hunter followed, then Bowie and Greg, and then the rest. Shane waited for those who were squirming at getting wet to stop before he addressed them.

"Today is the day," he said softly. He looked at each of them in the eye before he continued to talk. "I for one am proud of what we have done so far this year, regardless of what happens today. I am proud at all of you for what you have achieved and the progress you have made. Some of you were not soccer players before the season started, but now I couldn't tell the difference." He hesitated a moment, allowing the glory of his words to sink in before he addressed the opposition. "While I am talking you have been thinking of them. It's okay. I have been doing that too. But in a different way. You are probably thinking that they beat us before, they play dirty and you might get hurt, and that without Ross, who is our best player even I will admit, we don't stand a chance. But that is not what I am thinking about. I am thinking of facts. They beat us last time, when we didn't have a full team. They beat us last time, when we were green and didn't know much about how we play. They beat us last time, because they are bullies and are intimidating. That was last time. They beat us last time because we were divided. Now we have a team, now we have pride, now we have skills, now we are strong. Together." Shane's lipped quivered. He glowered at them all. Suddenly the air had changed. The feeling was different.

"You are here to play soccer, to have fun, and to get wet," Shane smiled suddenly. "I will do what I have to do. I will take it all on because no matter what happens I get to play with you. This isn't a grand final, but it may as well be, so let's enjoy it and have fun."

"Together?" Hunter called out, louder than Shane had spoken, and stuck his hand into the centre of the circle. James was the first to take up the call knowing full well what it meant, but the rest enthusiastically followed throwing their own hands into the pile.

"Together," they all yelled which received a cheer from their families who watched on.

"What's going on?" Ross asked as he arrived nearby and the team dispersed to get ready.

"Don't worry about it," Shane replied with a smile. "Team business."

It wasn't long until kick off and Hunter could feel the difference now. There was a buzz around the team when there had previously been a lull. All of the Waratahs were welcoming the wet weather and drenched field. Jumping and slopping the cold liquid everywhere. They had embraced it. The Rangers had not, many of them stood with arms pulled tight around their bodies trying to keep in the heat.

The whistle blew and the Rangers kicked off. The ball had been touched only twice before Greg swooped in and stole it. He laughed with glee, his face beaming out more radiance than the sun, and then took off down field. He knew what he was doing but was still caught up by the puddles on the field, which slowed down his progress. James was ready and pounced, demanding the ball and then carrying it off downfield. He managed to barge through the opposition who were all bigger than him. He twisted and turned, twirled and burned them all before emerging out the other side. He had a defender to beat and did so with some difficulty. He was almost overcome when he heard Shane sprinting down the field with giant muddy slops. James passed it perfectly. Shane took one step before he hit that ball. The goalkeeper had no fight in the initial stages of the game, he quivered in the corner of the goal. He did nothing to stop Shane's fury.

The whistle blew.

"Goal," Hunter called out from the back of the field. It was more than he thought would happen and if he wasn't part of the frenzy then he wouldn't have believed that the miserable group that had walked over to the field had been so full of energy. The Rangers were the opposite. They were hesitant to return to the centre of the field for the restart. All stood shivering in disbelief. It was their ball again.

Reece was one of the only ones with fire in his eyes. He tapped the ball forward and it begun again.

He ran straight at James. Laughing as he went, trying to intimidate the younger, smaller boy. That wasn't going to work today though. James dug in, remembering all the games that he had played in the backyard with his brother and Hunter. He waited for the right moment and then he struck. James was in and out in a flash. He slid forward trapping the ball, flicked it away mid slide and then found his feet to take off after the ball. Reece turned scowling still within reach to lash out with his feet but he missed his attempt at tripping the boy. Not because he didn't want to, but because he was face down on the ground. As soon as he had turned to assault James Shane had appeared and sent Reece flying with a slight knock from his shoulder.

"Not today," Shane informed Reece as he followed the play. "Not ever again." Reece spat mud but didn't follow.

"You shouldn't have done that," Ross finally said to Shane.

"Do you want to swap shirts, go onto their team?" Shane blasted him. "I don't mind putting you on the ground next to your mate."

"I am here to win," Ross dodged the statement, looking down at Reece but not helping him.

"Then do something," Shane left him to think about it, and hurried off to help the others. A few seconds later another goal followed.

"Oh yeah," Greg called out as he punished it into the back of the net. "What man?" he yelled into the face of an opposition player who had decided to abuse him.

"Let's do that again," James declared as he gave his centre partner a big wet hug. The opposition stood back more, the fight was almost gone. Reece wasn't going to allow that so soon.

Reece started the play again but ran over towards Ross as he walked back into position.

"Get me the ball so I can score," Reece said casually to him.

"You are on the other team," Ross said with confusion. "I can't just give you the ball."

"You will if you know what's good for you," Reece threatened. "I am going to run at you and you will let me past, or else." Ross looked stunned by what he had just been asked to do. Shane had heard the whole thing, but he didn't let on.

Reece started the play and ran straight towards Ross. Reece attempted some tricky steps before stepping past Ross unopposed. Everyone was stunned by that, with a few Waratahs stopping dead at the movement while Rangers started following down field after some positive motion. Shane walked over to Ross and placed a hand on his shoulder.

"Despite everything you have said about me," Shane paused. "Despite everything that has happened and the animosity between us . . . I still thought you were better than that." He left him there. Ross bent over on his haunches and started to shake. He sobbed, and then he cried. Reece had passed the ball to one of his forwards. Despite Ross giving the ball up so easily it was not something that was going to happen in defence. Hunter slid in from the side, dislodging the ball before Bowie pumped it downfield.

"Yeehaw," Bowie cheered, which received laughter from the players and the crowd. "Not today brother." Bowie's positive energy was infectious. The team lifted immediately. Reece could see that he was losing his team and the game and put another plan into action. He gathered the ball as it landed nearby and started attacking immediately. He ran back past Ross, he hadn't moved, his eyes swollen red from his tears.

"Come with us," Reece demanded, as one of his other friends ran beside him, before adding. "Loser." Reece was quick and used his team mates as a shield to make it down the field so quickly. Ross stood up, glaring at him. He breathed deep and then sprinted after his would-be friend. His strides were wide and he slid slightly as he landed but he was upon him in seconds. Ross came in from the side and jumped forward. He trapped the ball under his foot and sent Reece flying in the process. Ross got up and continued to play, but Reece did not.

"Owwww," he screeched as he rolled on the ground, "I think he has broken my ankle. Come on ref." The referee was marginally older than the one they had during the last time they had played. He saw the action and did not hesitate in pulling a yellow card from his pocket and pointing it in Ross's direction, awarding a penalty within shooting range to the fallen Reece.

A chorus of boos rang out from the crowd. Many of Reece's other friends, both boys and girls, who had either been threatened to turn up or chose to watch him had crowded the sideline. Ross felt his heart plummet. He had become unanimously hated by everyone on the field despite his natural talent. He dropped his head again but that only encouraged those who were already berating him.

"What do you lot think you are doing?" Hunter ran forward racing towards the sideline, ripping into the hostile crowd. "Who do you think you are?"

Someone said something in the crowd which just got Hunter angrier, yelling at the person to 'prove it' by getting some footy boots on. Hunter continued until all the heat had been taken off Ross and had either been transferred to him or dispersed. Ross looked on.

"Are you alright?" Hunter asked as he returned to the field. Ross simply nodded despite his glowing eyes and dribbling nose stated otherwise. "You are a great player, and you don't deserve that." He said to the tall athletic young man. "Show them, show all of us." Ross said nothing. He was hurting inside, which was amplified by the cheer that rang out as Reece scored a goal from the penalty he had been awarded. His ego had been bashed, his pride dragged on the ground, and the popularity that he had attained was diminished.

"Throw it," Reece cackled towards Ross as he made it back onside, referring to Ross giving the game over to Reece, "or else."

It was the Waratah's turn to start. Greg took it this time. He ran forward, flicked it to James, who then passed it to Shane. Shane looked over and saw Ross in the open. He had no other options, for if he did he would have taken them regardless of the risk. Shane passed the ball and then followed his pass. Ross took off towards the goal. He was fast. They couldn't catch him. He had one defender to beat and he did so easily. From outside the goal box he struck the ball hard and watched it sail sweetly into the net. The crowd boomed again, but this time with enthusiasm. Ross was cheering. He ran into the crowd of players seeking anyone to applaud his actions but received nothing. His heart fell some more as he returned to field without acknowledgement, but then a second later so did he.

"I told you, or else," Reece said, spitting on the ground beside the fallen form of Ross. He had been taken out amongst the throng of the opposition where the ref couldn't see him. His body ached as he lay there sobbing.

"Take your time, get up when you are ready," a calm and almost soothing voice came from above. Shane kneeled there with his back to the ref and the others. Ross rolled onto his back before sitting up slowly. He sat panting as he regained some composure. "That was a hell of a goal, you're good." Ross looked up at Shane who now offered his hand. Ross took a moment to observe Shane, then took the hand and was promptly pulled to his feet. The pair looked at each other for a moment before Ross broke the silence.

"I'm," he said, trailing off for a moment. "I'm sorry."

"Me too," Shane said.

"What are you sorry for?" Ross asked in confusion, knowing full well what he had done over the last period of time had been despicable. "You haven't done anything to me."

"I am sure I have somewhere," Shane replied sombrely. "We probably didn't welcome you like you wanted. But we can fix all of that now."

"Despite everything that I have done?"

"Despite all of that," Shane agreed. "You can turn it all on its head right now, and show everyone how good you are, on and off the field." Ross nodded, a tear creeping from his face again."

"Thank you," he sniffed, his already raspy voice struggling to get the words out. He received a hard pat on the back which became a wet slap due to the water residing there. He followed Shane as they went back to their starting positions. He shot Reece a look of disgust before running a finger across his own throat.

"You're dead," he mouthed, and was happy to see Reece prickle at the response. He turned again to Shane. "What were you sorry for?" Shane smiled at him openly.

"I am sorry because I am going to get more goals than you," he smirked.

"You're on," replied Ross with a smile. Then the flood gates opened, and the goals started flowing.

"Are you sure about this?" Shane called out. Ross nodded from the other side of the creek, the weekend after they had beaten Reece's Ranger team. All of the team mates that lived close by had gathered in the space that was shared between them. James, Shane and Hunter were gathered on one side of the creek, while Ross and Bowie, who also lived nearby, were present on the other.

"What exactly are we doing though?" Ross called back perplexed by what was happening. Hunter answered his question this time.

"You two are having a shootout, to see who the better goal scorer is once and for all," Hunter declared. "But instead of doing this at training you are doing it here, doing it my way."

"And what is that exactly?" Ross was still confused, his questions had gone unanswered.

"There is a King of the Creek, if you want the title you have to beat the King," Hunter continued as if it was so obvious. "Ross, you will shoot from your elevated position on the hill and you will try and score a point by shooting into Shane's goal over the water and onto this side of the creek which is lower. Shane. . ."

"The opposite I get it," Shane interrupted his friend.

"So we are doing this?" Ross asked as he started stretching, accepting what was happening. "And why do I want to be called the King of the Creek?"

"Yep, we are," responded Shane. "And we are doing it because it is fun, which is something I think you need to remember to have more often, but also because claiming the title of King tells everyone that you have beaten me."

"And is this what you guys do?"

"Yep," Shane replied with a smile, "this is what we do." Ross proceeded to stretch until he was satisfied that he was finished.

"Okay then," he said as he approached the ball nearby. "I am ready to be called the King of the Creek. Bring it on."

CHAPTER 11 – THE GREAT GRASS GRAND PRIX

Spring is the time of year when nature seems to explode. There are massive thunderstorms which drench everything, before the sun comes out and humidifies the air. There is an aroma as flowers burst into bloom, inviting people to come out of their homes and breath deep. Hunter's mum had been planting like crazy and although some things were coming along slowly some plants had thrived. A shooting star jasmine hung along one fence, showing its bright white flowers and spreading its intoxicating scent. Almost as if at war with it a potato vine was doing likewise from the other side of the house.

In spring sport comes to an end, as was the case with soccer. The Waratahs hadn't made it into the last week of the final, but they had given it their absolute all, those lasts weeks of the competition were some of the best the team had participated in all year. As those sports came to an end it also made way for new sports to start. Cricket was Hunter's summer sport. His team rarely won but it was the most fun you could have while standing out in the sun on a thirty degree day for hours.

The warmer months also brought out the smell of barbecues in the evening. Sitting outside or playing usually brought with it the heavenly smell of meat or veggies cooking on the outside grill, beckoning you home as the sun lingered and dropped lower from the sky. Ice cream from the freezer, steam escaping from its frost bitten container, also accompanied the meal. Families would lounge around for hours after dinner simply because they could, because the sun was still up, or because they were too full to move.

But as fantastic as spring was with all the joy it brought, it also conveyed something else out as well. Something so horrible you hide when you venture outside. Something so terrible that you jump with the slightest of cries. Something so sinister that you become instantly concerned when walking under trees. Something so terrifying that the most unfit person can become an Olympic sprinter at a moment's notice. Something so scary that all your worries evaporate in the face of it.

Birds come out in spring.

Those like rosellas, rainbow lorikeets, superb parrots, and kookaburras are not the sort that are being talked about here. The birds in question are magpies, and plovers.

"Do you see them?" Shane asked in a whisper. He along with Hunter, James and Alex were lying sprawled across the ground as they hid below the shade of a young banksia bush.

"I see them," Alex confirmed. "But what are they?"

"If you don't know what those are then you are lucky," James snorted at Alex's ignorance. Hunter hadn't seen them before either but refused to let the others know.

"Those are plovers," Shane told them all, graciously sharing the abundance of limited knowledge he shared about the birds. "They have bright yellow masks on their faces, and under their wings they have yellow barbs hanging there."

"Yellow barbs?" Alex said with concern.

"Yep," established Shane. "They know how to use them too. You probably have seen these birds around before, but usually they will just call out at you and fly away. No harm done."

"But now it is spring," James added. It sounded like he was trying to scare his neighbours but the look on his face revealed his own fear.

"Why does that matter?" Hunter asked.

"Because they are like magpies in the spring," Shane said to him. "They go crazy. Except instead of laying their eggs somewhere safe like a tree, they lay them on the ground wherever they think is good. Then they hang around them, and if you come too close they will scream and swoop you, digging in with those barbs until you run away. I have heard stories," Shane trailed off. It seemed like they were too horrible for even him to repeat. With great difficulty he continued his sentence. "I have heard stories of people being pecked and barbed, so hard that blood was drawn. One boy even lost an eye."

"I heard another boy had his nose bitten off," James added. "Then there was that girl who lost an arm."

Shane shook his head in disbelief. "Tragic." Hunter said nothing. The loss of an arm seemed pretty intense, but the other injuries sounded more plausible. He watched from his hiding spot the birds in question. There were just two of them. They stood to one side of Raul's house, guarding a small stack of discarded sticks and wood. Raul's house was all but finished, the boys assumed that they would be moving in soon but had not been informed of when that might be yet. The plovers walked towards the driveway, then pivoted and walked back towards the road. They were both on full alert.

Hunter noted that he could hear the breathing of all of them as they hid. He also imagined that it would have been comical to see, all four of them, some of the bravest young men in the town by his assumption, pressed hard against the earth lest a bird detect them. They stayed for an age but none knew why. Hunter supposed they were waiting for someone to walk past so the birds could showcase their wrath, but there was no walking track nearby or any other reason for someone to walk down this far. That was the same for cars. Nothing happened.

It seemed odd that his heart beat as fast as when they were riding bikes over jumps, when all he was doing was watching a bird. The more he waited the more he delved into his own mind. Hunter envisioned the sort of chaos one of these plovers could unleash. It started off as a simple scratch when a postman ran too close to the nest, but then became far more elaborate and creative. The next time it was a group of bike riders who simply got swooped, followed by an ice cream truck that got its huge Popsicle prop on its roof ripped off, and then a police car that had responded to trouble, only to be carried high up in the air and dropped. His vision finished when the plovers tipped the finished building of Raul's house on top of an army tank. Probably not that dangerous.

The engine of a car was finally heard from far away, and the sound grew louder as it gradually got closer. The boys saw this as an opportunity and pressed down even further into the ground. As the car rounded the corner they saw that it was a new white four wheel drive ute that belonged to Raul's dad. Hunter sucked in air and held it deep in his lungs, not wanting to make a move or a sound as he saw what could happen. He breathed out a moment later. The ute drove past unscathed, the plovers hardly moved.

"What are you guys doing?" asked Michael, Raul's dad, as he jumped from the car.

"Just playing hide and seek," James replied quickly, instantly realising it was a dumb answer.

"Oh," came the interested and confused reply. "Who are you playing with?"

"Oh, someone," James replied rolling his eyes. Michael reluctantly accepted the answer before walking slowly around the front of his vehicle. Raul jumped out, saw the boys hiding under the bush, and ran over in a half squat prepared for whatever was happening. He slumped loudly down beside Shane who waved him into silence. It must have been confusing but he just watched like the others. Their focus was enhanced again. Raul's mum and sister accompanied his dad as they made their way along the edge of the road curb and towards the driveway. The plovers noticed them and the boys noticed the bird's simple bobble of the head that showed them that Raul's family had been marked as a threat.

"Cree, cree, cree, cree, cree, cree," one of the birds screeched as it took off into the sky. The sound was followed in reply by the other bird, but the second added formidable clicking sounds as it cracked its beak shut in quick bites. Hunter watched as the reaction was sudden. Raul's family stretched their arms up to cover their faces and head, their necks were sucked into their body, their spines crunched into their pants, and they ran in a bizarre defensive fashion. Alana ran to where Raul was hiding whereas his parents made it to the doorway which was on the opposite side to the plover's nest. The birds continued to scream and threaten to swoop, hovering high up in the air watching everything below them. Raul just laughed but everyone else was astonished. The birds stayed there for several minutes longer before returning to their sentry like stance.

"That was cool," Raul declared. He received a nod from the others in agreement. The boys all looked at each other making faces showing their silent delight and amazement. They watched for a short time longer but nothing of interest happened.

"I brought my bike," Raul finally stated, getting the crew to their feet instantly.

"Me too," Alana said as well. Shane looked back towards his house and pointed towards the door.

"May would be in there somewhere," he told her. "If you go and ask I am sure she will come out and ride with you." Alana smiled with delight and, after looking to ensure that no cars were coming into the cul-de-sac, she ran over to find out. It sounded like Shane was being kind but he was simply informing her, plus it would most likely get the girls away from them while they played.

Hunter and Alex already had their bikes lying in a pile nearby alongside James and Shane's. They had been riding for most of the morning up and down the upper parts of Northstoke Way, listening to all the people who had pulled out their unused lawnmowers and whipper snippers to give them a run on the aggressive grass that quickly popped up. They were happy to ride, but not where they had already been. It was also better to not go that way due to the fear of the swooping plovers.

"Out the back," Alex stated, and without answering everyone walked in that direction. Alex walked in front, swaggering as he went as if he had come up with some grand plan. After they waited for Raul to get his bike they all made their way to the path. Shane's parents had come outside after Alana had shown up at their door, with Hunter's parents joining them. The boys just waved, pointing to the back paddock which was approved with a nod.

"Watch out for those plovers," Phil called as May dragged out her bike, "they will rip your face off." The boys laughed at the comment, before laughing more when Phil got hit hard in the ribs by Judy as he received a glance of horror from May.

They walked quietly down the other end of the path and found the paddock beyond. It was similar to how Hunter remembered it when he had first ventured into the area. The grass was overgrown to a height that was just above his head. Standing on the tips of his toes Hunter could still manage to see where he was going. He assumed Shane would be able to as well but the other boys stood no chance. The lanes that formed the labyrinth were more manageable but you could still get lost or have trouble leaving if you weren't careful.

"Are we going to ride in this?" Raul asked with bewilderment. Hunter wasn't sure if that had been the plan. The ground was hard enough as there hadn't been any rain in over a week, and despite the razor grass ripping at their flesh it would be manageable to ride between the massive clumps. He imagined that Raul wanted to try and jump over them but that would be almost impossible. Before any of them could answer they saw Ross waving from his backyard beyond the creek.

Ross had become friendlier, without actually being an overly active member of the group. The crew discovered that his house backed onto the creek from the opposite bank and that it was quite easy to get from his house to the grass mound that they played on frequently. When the season changed he went back to playing basketball more often because of his representative responsibilities, which meant despite him being close enough to join in he was hardly ever there.

His competitive edge hadn't changed though. Ross and Shane still had shoot-outs but otherwise they just stood next to each other talking up their various, and sometimes fictional, deeds. The crew moved over to see him following Shane's lead. The bikes were abandoned at the mouth of the path for the time being. It was probably the case that they would all return and continue riding up the street afterwards anyway.

Ross had jumped his fence and walked along his boundary line before hiking down to the creek. The tall eucalypt trees had once more been full of blood curdling magpies who would dive bomb at a moment's notice. The crew had discovered that if you walked around the tree at a certain distance or you avoided most parts of the grass mound and the rise leading up to it you would be mostly disregarded. Ross took a running start and leapt the full distance of the creek. It was easier from the other side as there was a slight elevation away from the creek, but the display was entirely for Shane's benefit. Hunter already knew what the response would be.

"Good jump," Shane shouted to Ross as they arrived next to him. "If you keep training one day you might be the best player in whatever team you are playing for." Shane smiled and Ross returned it. Shane was referring to the presentation awards for their soccer team. Ross hadn't got any of them whereas Shane had got a few. Shane received the best and fairest award because of how well he played. That was awarded from the referees so it was unlikely Ross would have gotten that. Shane also got the highest goal scorer award for the entire junior club, plus best forward. Bowie had got best back, Greg had got the player's player award and Hunter had even received the coach's award. Shane and Ross hadn't even had time to jump into their playful mockery of each other when a call came from Ross's home.

"Ross," his mum called out. "There are some boys here who want to see you." Ross curled his bottom lip in surprise, clearly he wasn't expecting anyone.

"I'm down at the creek," he yelled back with his husky voice. "If they want me they can come down here." He turned back to the others with a shrug as they all waited for the visitors to show themselves. When they did there was a unanimous groan.

"What a pleasant surprise," Reece called out as he walked down the path from the hidden street beyond. "Fancy seeing you here." Neither Hunter nor Shane had anything to do with Reece much anymore. Neither Shane nor Reece played a summer sport so they didn't meet up there, school had never been a thing since the intervention of the big polar bear looking Jono, and Reece never ventured down towards Angus Place after his knockout encounter last time. They had nothing to do with him. Clearly that was not the case for Ross.

"What do you want Reece?" Ross grunted in reply.

"I want to know why we aren't friends anymore," Reece pleaded as he walked closer. "It hurts to know that we used to be so close and now we aren't." As always Reece was flanked by two other boys, Hunter didn't know who these ones were though.

"Did you run out of friends Reece?" Shane called over. "Is that why you have to get your cousins to follow you now?" It was clear that the jibe had done damage as Reece's nostrils flared wide at the quip.

"You have nothing to do with me now Shane," Reece barked. "If you want to keep it that way then stay out of this."

"I don't want anything to do with you," Ross stated simply. "We *used* to be friends. Back when we were in primary school. When you used to be fun, you used to be a good sport and had some skill. You have changed though. You are not like you were. You use people, or you bully them. I am busy. I don't have time for you." Reece looked furious but Ross didn't care. For the first time since Hunter met Ross he saw the figure that he had originally claimed to be. Tall, strong, confident, and powerful. He wasn't scared of Reece. The bully could have left but for some reason he wanted to fight it.

"Fun?" Reece spat. "I am so fun. Name a game and I will beat you. Any game." Ross turned his back but Hunter saw an opportunity, noticing that Reece and his cousins had dumped their bikes back up near the street.

"How about a race?" Hunter asked.

"A race?" Reece boomed with a smile. "Kid you clearly don't know who you are talking to. I am the best street racer for my age. I will have your race." Ross who still looked away from Reece glanced at Hunter and nodded his agreement with his eyes, which were also filled with concern.

"Not a street race," Raul yelled back. "Anyone can do a street race. This is a different race."

"Who are you?" Reece asked insulted. "I can win any bike race."

"I am Jeremy," Raul called back. "You won't win this race. It's the Great Grass Grand Prix, and you play for the King's Cup."

"The King's Cup?" Reece repeated getting some laughs from his cousins. "Who is this king?"

"Shane's the King," James stepped forward, "and you are looking at his kingdom." Hunter watched as Shane rolled his eyes with embarrassment. He remained standing unmoved otherwise.

"You're a king, Shane?" Reece guffawed. "I am so sorry that I haven't bowed down to you before." He started a mock bow which was copied by the others.

"You will," Ross stepped in again, turning to look at Reece for the first time since his arrival. "Shane has never been beaten in his kingdom. When you are beaten you will have to bow to him. How many times does he have to beat you?" Ross was fully aware of what had happened in the past between Reece and Shane, it had been highlighted by James on another post soccer encounter.

"I ain't doing that," Reece blasted. "That sort of play is for babies."

"I thought you said you were fun," Ross replied. "Or maybe it's that you are scared." Reece looked like he was about to break something.

"I thought you two were enemies," Reece added calmly, his rage simmering down to a small bubble.

"No, not enemies, rivals," Ross said smoothly. "I know that. But the question is what are you? A man, or just a mouth?" There was no response for some time before finally Reece agreed to all the demands.

"Meet us at the path over there," Shane demanded pointing to where his bike still remained near his house. "I am sure you still remember where that is. There is a big mound of white dust just inside the entrance of the street." Reece growled but turned away towards his bike and left on the road, not wanting to get his bike wet in the creek. As soon as he was out of sight the crew turned and ran.

"I am coming too," Ross called out as they ran. "I will just get my bike and see you over there, okay." None acknowledged him, they just sprinted back as fast as they could. When they arrived in open space Shane started talking to all of them about his plan, but first questioned Raul.

"Jeremy?" he asked, "why Jeremy?"

"Jeremy McGrath the famous motorbike racer," he sounded hurt that they didn't instantly know who he was talking about. "Just call me Jeremy." They left it at that but agreed that they would. James was sent to grab some cordoning off tape that Shane had acquired on a previous occasion, Alex was sent as well to find some items. Neither of them would compete in the race. They would instead be prepared for the shenanigans that Reece no doubt would plan during the journey to Angus Place. Jeremy, Shane and Hunter made it to the bikes last and found May and Alana playing down the alley.

"What are you two doing?" Shane asked soothingly. Despite how much he complained about how irritating his little sister was he was frequently caught doting on her.

"We were told to find rocks that look like plover eggs," May answered. "The small white looking ones."

"Why?" Hunter asked.

"Because my dad is going to confuse the plovers with the fake eggs, lead them away for a minute, then place the nest somewhere safer off of our property," Alana added. Shane smiled at their task.

"I have work to do right now, but as soon as you find those egg looking rocks come and show me, please," Shane asked kindly. They agreed. While they waited for Reece they jumped to work.

"Here they come," Jeremy announced as the boys rolled around the bend. They were watched indiscriminately by all the parents as they arrived. Each of them had already been informed of the race and so let the teenagers through undeterred, but made sure that their presence was a warning to ward off trouble. James and Alex were nowhere to be seen, each had grabbed what was needed to create the track and maintain a status quo. That included an odd sounding sealed bag that James refused to reveal what the contents were inside. Shane leaned in his bike seat alongside Hunter and Jeremy in the middle of the cul-de-sac, not concerned at all about cars that wouldn't come. It was essential for the first stage of his plan. They saw Ross roll in behind them but immediately positioned himself near Shane. The numbers said it was three on four, the odds finally in Hunter's favour.

"Where is the track?" Reece asked, not waiting for any formalities.

"It's all marked," Shane stated simply. "Our starting spot is here, you go along the path, follow the tape that goes through the long grass, ride up the grass mound, come down the other side and then back here. The winner is the one who finishes first. Simple."

"So simple, I thought you said this was fun," Reece said with sarcasm.

"It will be so much fun," Hunter remarked with seriousness. Despite the conflict within the group he was already imagining music that had started in his head as they got organised, and was prepared for that select tune to change once the race started. He wouldn't be racing a bike in a paddock despite that being his reality. He would be racing a go kart in the all-encompassing Great Grass Grand Prix, a bonus level in a kart racing game which he had played countless times with the others. His excitement was palpable.

"Whatever, let's get this done," Reece said with annoyance. All seven racers lined up in the middle of the street. As they prepared to start James came running over from Jeremy's house.

"Wait," he called as he came. He initially ran backwards with his back towards them, before turning and wishing them all luck. He spent extra time with each of the cousins before Reece lost patience.

"Go," he yelled while no one else was prepared. Reece shot off from the rest and turned to smirk at James. To his surprise James smiled back and waved fondly at him. He had no idea why. Then he reached the path to the paddock and raced away. A cry rang out from nearby and Shane looked to see that all the parents were rushing for cover.

"Cree, cree, cree, cree, cree, cree," the screeches rang out. Both of the plovers were in the air and in pursuit of the boys on the bike. James had shown them the decoy eggs and placed those small stones in the backpacks that the cousins each wore. The birds were ruthless this time. Instead of just flying in the air as a warning they were swooping and clicking their beaks. The rest of the Creek Crew took off leaving the cousins to their own demise. Hunter felt slightly bad, they had been caught up in Reece's nonsense like so many others, but he had the hope that perhaps this race would finally end it. The cousins were as bright as they looked however, they didn't move at all and were almost resigned to the fact that they were going to be bludgeoned down by them.

"They're after your bags," Hunter's dad called out, appearing to take pity on their stupidity. "Take your bags off." The pair listened, throwing them off as if they were a swarm of ants. The boys continued to get assaulted until finally Jeremy's dad arrived. He had taken the opportunity to move the plover nest and held a couple of fake stones above his head. The plovers reacted accordingly and changed their focus towards the eggs they thought they saw. A minute later they were guarding a new location on the other side of the street where both fake and real eggs resided.

The route that the Creek Crew had chosen went back on itself a couple of times before leading up over the grass mound. Reece was firmly in the lead followed closely by Shane. Next came Hunter and then Ross and Jeremy. The path was only about as wide as a bike and considering that even Shane, who had help make it, didn't remember the track that well it caused frequent bank ups of riders, which reduced the gaps between them. Jeremy was easy to hear as he made dirt bike sounds every time his tyres found any amount of air, but so was Reece who frequently called out abuse from his spot in the lead. Hunter didn't know where the cousins were until he couldn't hear Jeremy making motorbike sounds any longer.

"Hey," Jeremy called out, "no fair." Hunter knew he had been the victim of foul play without seeing it. Ross was taken out a moment later in a similar fashion.

"Cowards," Ross yelled after them with his coarse voice. Hunter was upset that his friends had been knocked down but knew they would keep going. He also knew that Shane had prepared for this. Just up ahead he saw the smiling faces of Alex and James as they poked their heads out of the long grass. James motioned Hunter to remain silent by pressing a single finger to his lips. Hunter rode on, noticing the buckets that sat at the boys' feet filled with sopping wet sponges. He kept riding to catch up, realising that there was now a race behind him and a far more important one ahead.

"What the heck," called out one of the cousins as the loud slapping sound of wet sponge hitting a body could be heard.

"Hey wa-," the second rider started to cry before getting hit in the face. Hunter silently hoped his mouth wasn't opened, then he smiled and changed his mind. Hunter heard the triumphant call as Ross and Jeremy pushed past the cousins.

"Where did those small twerps go?" one of them yelled out revealing that Alex and James had disappeared as quickly as they had arrived. Hunter looked ahead and saw that he was catching up to Shane who had almost managed to pass Reece. They had raced up a straight before turning the last bend. In front of them was the slow rise up to the grass mound. The race was on. Hunter ducked his head down a little. In his head, that was filled with racing music, he told himself it was to streamline his bike and make him faster, but in his heart he did it out of fear.

The whistling that would have been beautiful if it wasn't so deadly cried out from above. Down they came, three magpies in total, bombarding the race. Hunter smiled as Reece got clipped, he had refused to wear a helmet as he was too cool for that, and as a result he fell from his bike as he tried to evade being sheared.

"Hey they are trying to cheat," Ross called out from behind, clearly referring to the cousins again.

"Not today," Alex called out with excitement. Hunter caught a glimpse of the younger brothers nearby. They ran into the long grass where the cousins were trying to take a short cut and dropped that mysterious bag down beside them, which was no longer sealed.

"What was that?" one of them called.

"It's just a bag," the other replied. "But what is that sound?"

"Is that buzzing?"

"AAAAAArrrgh," the other replied in anguish. "Wasps." Hunter chuckled to himself, remembering the wasp nest that had existed on Jeremy's vacant block of land at their first meeting.

"Poor buggers," Hunter said to himself. All of this happened in a blur. The cousins were attacked by wasps only seconds after Reece fell off his bike. Shane shot past him and as he did Reece regained his feet with a medium sized rock held firmly in one hand.

"Shane, duck," Hunter bellowed as Reece released it from his grasp. Shane flung a hand out over his head to avoid impact there, it was a trigger reaction as Shane was already wearing a helmet. The rock missed Shane but hit the handlebar where his palm would have been nanoseconds before. Shane fell off his bike as it jolted and jack-knifed, tumbling hard into the razor grass. Hunter sped past Reece who had not regained his bike yet, slowing down slightly as he made it to Shane.

"Keep going," Shane yelled from his back, "Just beat them." He powered on past him accepting his friend's demand. He looked back and couldn't help but be impressed by Reece despite his benevolent ways. He had regained his bike and despite pedalling uphill on grass he had accelerated quickly and was catching Hunter fast. Hunter thought initially as he passed Shane that he had a chance to win, to be called King of the Creek, but by looking at Reece now he knew he would be caught, and that meant that they would all lose and Reece would win. That couldn't happen. Hunter looked for anyway out, anyway that he could gain an advantage. There was none. His brain flicked over to its imaginative state. He was racing through the castle on his go-kart wishing there was some sort of hidden passage or booby trap.

Then it hit him. Hunter picked up speed suddenly. He pedalled harder and faster than he had ever done before. He looked back at Reece as he flashed away and opened his mouth. Hunter didn't like abusing people, to egg them on in a negative way. He had been told early on that retaliation or instigating was usually worse than the reaction you received. There were always exceptions.

"I thought you said you were fast," Hunter blurted out. "I am probably the worst rider and you can't even beat me." It was simple but effective. Reece's head dropped as he pushed harder to catch up, fire now burning in his eyes. "You don't stand a chance." Hunter knew he had done enough as he spat out the last words. He was not really religious but decided it was as good a time as any to say a silent prayer.

"Please let me be safe," he said silently before turning back to Reece. "This is a kingdom, you are riding through the castle, and just like every castle there is always. . ." Hunter waited for a moment until it was too late for either of them to stop. "A trapdoor." Hunter launched down over the edge. He sailed through the air and prepared for the pain that would follow. In his last action he had thrown himself clear of his bike and just waited to hit the ground. Reece had no time to stop. He hit the empty air full speed. He caught his shins with the sharp spinning pedals as he tried to brake, but it was no good. He wailed loudly as he fell, but was greeted by a loud thump as his bike hit the ground and he bounced from the seat, his whole body jarred.

Hunter sat up. He had landed relatively softly with no major injuries. His body hurt from the impact and there was no doubt that he would be nursing bruises for some time, but he was alive. He returned to his feet in time to see Shane ride past on the top of the mound and safely down the steep slope. A few seconds later he was down and sprinting his way back towards the finish line.

May and Alana who had remained unseen the whole time appeared on the side of the dam wall, cheering with a violent squeal as Shane hurried by. The race was over. Shane would win. Hunter jumped up and down for joy and then looked over at Reece. The bully was on his feet, blood poured from his head, upper arms and his legs. Not only was he on his feet, he was also on his bike. Reece had his teeth gnashed together but there was nothing he could do, he couldn't catch Shane for he was already out of sight. His anger would mean nothing. Unless.

"Girls, watch out," Hunter yelled out with urgency sensing they were in danger. Hunter was nowhere near his bike so there was nothing he could do except watch on as if he was seeing a car crash. Reece, despite his obvious injuries picked up speed as he belted towards the girls. May and Alana huddled together, petrified about what was about to happen. They screamed and wailed at the same time, eyes shut tight as tears exploded down their faces. Reece was almost upon them. They were about to get hit. A cloud of dust caught Hunter's eye.

"I've got you," Ross called out as his bike raced down the side of the grass mound. He had gone down so fast that you almost didn't see him. One second the girls were there screaming, the next they weren't. Ross had managed to grab both of them in one arm and bounce them only a couple of metres out of the way. It wasn't far but it was enough.

For the second time in minutes Reece overshot his mark and sailed through the air. He tried his brakes but they slid on the loose dirt on the dam wall and were completely ineffective. He screamed, and then he splashed. James and Alex arrived next, followed by Jeremy. James took May away quickly and Alex walked Alana back towards home.

"If you two come down here I am going to deck you," Ross called out with a previously hidden ferocity to the two cousins who had appeared at the far side of the dam wall. Hunter had no idea how they managed to get there, perhaps they had hidden there for some relief from the wasps. Several sore bright red spots were present across their faces, despite the distance between them, and other uncovered patches of skin. The fight was gone. It was easy to see they had never wanted to be there in the first place. They both trudged glumly back into the grass labyrinth. Hunter never actually saw them leave though, he supposed they may have even gotten lost.

All eyes returned to Reece. The boy had landed hard within the water of the dam, despite its great depth in the middle it was quite shallow for several metres along its edges. The handles of his bike protruded from just beneath the surface as Reece stumbled to his feet. Before him stood Hunter, Ross and Jeremy. All stood glaring at him, blocking his path out of the dam. He said nothing to them and remained almost frozen in place, taking their stares but never returning them. Ross was pushed aside by Shane who had returned after hearing the yelling. He moved to the edge of the water and just looked at his former friend.

"What will it take?" Shane asked simply. "All year this has gone on. You have held a grudge on others because they wouldn't take your nonsense, because they stood up against you, and what has it gotten you? You are standing cold and alone in the middle of a dam that you have no purpose of being anywhere near. Your friends have abandoned you. One by one you have driven them away because of the choices you have made. Even your own family no longer stand by your side." Shane stopped as Reece had not once turned to look at him.

"Is putting others down who you are now? Is threatening young girls what you want to be known for?" Reece didn't answer and as a result Shane's voice rose in anger.

"Is it?" Shane boomed. Reece finally turned at him, nose quivering in defiance.

"No," he stabbed back.

"Then why?" Shane asked, returning to a more subtle tone. "This person who stands in front of me is not the kid I remember when we first met, because if it was we would never have been friends."

"Nor me," Ross added. Nothing was said for some time. Nobody moved. Finally Shane stepped forward. He stepped out into the water, his shoes instantly filling with brown and dirty water. The others shared a look of surprise between them, the only sound was the squelching of his shoes as they suctioned into the mud. He walked over to Reece slowly. When he arrived he extended a hand towards Reece, and he did so in a manner which looked like he was off balance.

Looking on Hunter could see that Shane had put himself into a vulnerable position, one where he could easily be pulled over into the water. Hunter understood that Shane had presented an opportunity, and evidently so had Reece.

"Why are you trying to help me?" he asked. "There is four of you here, and I just tried to take out your sister, as well as all the other things I have done. You should be punching me in the face, all of you."

"But I am not," Shane responded simply.

"Why not?" Reece demanded.

"Because it won't help you, or any of us," Shane said calmly. "If we hurt you, who are you going to run to now? Who is going to help when you have driven them all away?" The questions hung in the air for a moment. "I learned recently that I have to make choices that affect me and the ones that are close to me, and I did that the hard way by almost losing those people. The person I am is the one who stands with his friends, in the best times and the worst. Reece you are now standing in your worst." The pair looked at each other for a moment. Reece started to cry. The tough high school bully façade disintegrated before them, replaced with a sad and sorrowful kid.

"That's why instead of showing you my back I am offering my hand," Shane finally whispered. "Please take it." Ross, Jeremy and Hunter relaxed their intimidating and opposing stances, watching as a mournful and trembling hand reached out and grabbed Shane's. Shane held it for a second before wrapping an arm around him instead and leading him out of the dam. Ross walked in and past them, retrieving the bike that was mangled from its treatment.

When Reece finally managed to reach the edge of the dam it became obvious just how hurt he was. Blood seeped in wet streaks from open wounds and injuries that he had sustained. Some were recent while others were not. Hunter thought that there was a hidden secret about Reece's life that none of them knew, but he suspected that Shane was fully aware of what that was.

The girls ran off ahead of the small groups, no longer frightened by the presence of Reece. He was broken and everyone knew it. No one said a single word. There was no complaints about his behaviour, no snarls for what he had done, and there were no sorrys. Hunter felt like he was in a funeral procession by how slow they all walked as they returned to the path. He wondered about fairy tales at that time though, and how frequently they were resolved with the happiest of endings. This was in no case happy, it was quite solemn and glum. Hunter couldn't help but understand that he knew what every one of them felt at that exact moment, because he felt the same.

Relief.

The threat had gone, the circumstances were not great but the problem had been resolved.

And that had become another reason to love spring.

CHAPTER 12 – THE LOST DAMSELS

Jeremy, formerly Raul and actually Matt, had finally moved into his house. Due to the fact it was spring and that it had worked out so well on the last occasion the three households got together and attempted to complete some landscaping. At Hunter's house they were wheeling barrow upon barrow of red rocks into the garden beds that had been created. Shane's house had piles of woodchips that were being placed in a new vegie patch and upon long surviving dirt and weed patches in the backyard. Jeremy's house was getting all of it.

Fences were being erected, the ground was ripped up with a rotary hoe before turf was thrown down over the top, garden beds were being both created and filled. The parents relished this immediate neighbourly help. The mums all worked together in the gardens, planting flowers and directing the others. The dads mostly talked nonsense from beside the pallets of grass or piles of soil, bark and rocks, but they did also shovel the majority of the supplies. The five boys all had a wheelbarrow and they were running tirelessly between start and finish countless times.

A friendlier competition had begun in comparison to last time. Hunter and Shane had started it up, both claiming that they would win, but neither really partook with much interest. It had been an attempt to get Alex and James to do more work than their older brothers and it had largely succeeded.

Alana and May were busy doing other jobs and weren't expected to help out at all. Those other jobs consisted of looking after Jeremy's two younger brothers, which the rest had never seen before and due to Jeremy never talking about them Hunter assumed they didn't exist. One was a toddler while the other was in his first year of school. Hunter would have hated occupying the younger boys so was definitely happy to be doing the hard yards instead. Besides there was an incentive to their work.

When it was all finished the three dads had promised to pull out their lawnmowers, hand held slashers and trimmers and clear a spot for a cricket pitch in the back paddock. There wasn't much to do as Phil had gotten in contact with the local council who had sent a tractor down to clear most of the grass. It was still overgrown but the dads could handle that. The idea was that all the work got done on the Saturday, including the mowing, and then when Sunday came all three families would be out the back playing cricket together celebrating the developing cul-de-sac and friendships.

Once more falling down exhausted at the end of the day every single person had done their job effectively, all satisfied by the effort they had delivered. A fresh new lawn was laid and that had been a task in itself. Having a corner block meant you had to lay the heavy wet dirty and worm riddled turf out the front of the house, out the back and also along the side next to the road. Fences had been erected and garden beds placed along those with fresh lively plants and flowers dug into them. Stones and bark had been separated into the designated locations and a pitch had been mown.

The hot shower, warm meal and long sleep swept by as excitement drove the boys towards the cricket match. Both Hunter and Alex had their own cricket kits which they gladly shared with the others. They were only using a tennis ball but the stumps, bails, wicket keeping gloves and bats were all put to good use. To Hunter's surprise and delight there were more people who attended the day than he had envisioned. His, Shanes, and Jeremy's families were all there, which was fifteen people straight away. They were also joined by two other families who had built nearby. One from the house on the other side of the path which was not yet complete, and the other from the house that been built behind Hunter's and Raul's. That was another eight people, four adults and four children although the children were also quite young and weren't really interested in cricket. Ross had walked over from his house and Bowie came across as well. There ended up being a solid dozen playing at any one time with all the boys and the dads playing. The mums and some kids jumped in and out frequently, and the dads stood mostly together with a drink firmly placed in one hand at all times, but they were still there. Everyone got a turn of batting but when any of the dads had a turn it was more a game of fetch as they sent the ball sailing to the furthest reaches of the paddock over and over again.

The game continued for a few hours in that morning session before it was abandoned. A small lunch was given to all the kids before the parents left. Several of them drove to the local shops for weekly groceries, while some went to get supplies for that evening. They had all decided to get together at Hunter's house for a bit of a housewarming party for the entire cul-de-sac and a barbecue was the best course of action. Most of the younger kids went along with them but the boys all stayed to play together.

"Keep an eye on your sister," Judy called out to James and Shane as she walked towards the open back gate of Hunter's house.

"You too Matt," added Jeremy's mum, Janelle, as she followed.

"It's Jeremy," he mumbled under his breath, waving grumpily to show he had heard her request.

"We will be fine," Alana said as she started skipping over longer tufts of grass with May at her side. The girls were able to play by themselves nearby as they usually did. Shane and Jeremy both knew their sisters would be fine until they were summoned as long as they stayed within the paddock.

"You had better be," Jeremy replied. "We have important things to do and I can't be looking after you all the time."

"There is a storm coming," Hunter's dad yelled out as he skipped off to start the barbecue. "If it starts coming over you have all got to come inside." Hunter nodded in reply. It was an easy request because chances were that the food would be ready by that time and he would sprint to get his fill.

Ross and Bowie had sprinted away shouting that they had something that they could do and to meet them near the eucalypt tree on the other side of the creek. The rest of the boys walked slowly behind. Each of them only too happy to take their time and relax. Every one of them held a can of soft drink they had been given after the cricket match and they each savoured it. Hunter was enjoying the spring time smell. Freshly mown grass was thrown into his nostrils by a steady breeze which revealed the presence of the approaching storm by the way it dampened the aroma it spread. Hunter could already see that approaching tempest. A deep blue bubble had appeared on the western horizon which stood out against the pale blue cloudless day. A trickle of sweat flowed down hunter's neck which became cool as the wind hit it, giving him a prickling sensation.

"We have heaps of time before that gets here," Shane declared as they had all taken turns of investigating the approaching shadow.

"I reckon it will get here pretty quick," James replied. He was no longer looking at the storm though, instead glancing up at the top of the eucalypt tree which guarded the creek crossing. A snort of amusement was heard from Shane.

"They aren't up there anymore," he informed his younger brother. "I thought you knew that. They flew over to that big dead one in the middle of the swamp. No doubt they didn't think it was safe because we play here all the time."

"Or maybe they were poisoned when they got James last time," Alex chimed in.

"Ha ha," James boomed with sarcasm. "Very funny." The small group all chuckled, and eventually so did James. They all made it over the crossing easily as the creek had been running a little lower lately due to the lack of rain. Hunter knew it wouldn't take much for it to rise again, and wouldn't be surprised if that afternoon's storm made it swell if it actually eventuated. As Hunter waited under the tree he noticed the apparent lack of temperature. It appeared like there was none. He was warm but a lot of that heat had come from high intensity effort during the game of cricket. Now that he was cooling down he could feel the chill of the breeze as it floated by, but also the sting of the sun as he stepped out of the shade and into its stare. Hunter felt like he was in the Goldilocks Zone, somewhere in the middle of not too hot and not too cold, but he didn't feel just right either.

"We have got them," Bowie yelled out excitedly. He was running at pace down the pathway from the road, struggling to slow down. He held a large amount of long strong rope which also trailed through the grass behind him. Ross walked behind him, far more casual than the other boy. He carried what appeared to be a big circular rope seat that had ropes woven across its diameter resembling a spider web. All the boys allowed their jaws to hang in wonder at what was before them.

"Okay, this is what I am thinking," Ross began as he arrived. "We are going to swing on this rope chair, from this big eucalypt." It sounded so simple to all of them, but so obvious that they all wondered why it had never been thought of before. "The hard part is trying to get the rope up over the branch up there so we can actually do it."

"That's not the hard part," said Hunter.

"That's the fun part," finished Alex. They were proven right, well at least in part. For the best part of the next hour they all took it in turns to achieve that goal. Each would attempt to get the rope over the solid branch which hung about five metres above them. Several different strategies had been tried and failed but laughter rather than anguish had followed every attempt.

Throwing one end from below hadn't worked, nor had the idea of running and jumping from a higher part of the hill. Attaching it to something hard was better but still ended in disaster with Ross copping a ball to the head. Surprisingly it was Bowie who came up with a grand idea. He grabbed the rope and tied it all together after rolling it into a proper coil. Then he leaned forward in front of himself, before throwing his arms back and sending the whole thing backwards over his head. He monstered that throw and everyone was pleased to see that when he attempted it a second time he found the mark which allowed the rope to flop over it. Everyone cheered at what he had achieved. Ross fixed it so that there was enough space for the rope chair to swing from a higher spot on the hill without touching the ground and allowing some clearance below. Then he smiled as he gave the rope back to Bowie.

"It needs to go over at least twice more," Ross said to him. Initially annoyed Bowie continued his attempts. Several minutes later he was exhausted but the job was done. He slumped down on the hill with his arms flailing out comically in his act of exhaustion. Hunter laughed at him at his antics, but then exploded with laughter as Bowie launched up off the ground and into the air, scrambling to reach his back as he had collapsed on top of an active ant's nest. Bowie ended up jumping into the creek, releasing a moan of glee as the biting subsided.

"I am going first," Shane yelled out as he grabbed hold of the chair. Ross didn't argue as he was too busy making sure the thing was tied down properly. Hunter was with him, being shown how to untie Ross's knot should the need arise to pull the chair down. Ross had told them that his parents had bought it for all of them to play with so he was happy to leave it up.

"Why do you get to go first?" whined James.

"Because I am the king," Shane answered quickly.

"Fine, your highness," James replied with a sarcastic bow. "But you can't just swing on it, that would be lame. You have to swing over to the other side of the creek and jump onto Ayer's Rock." Shane looked at what he was being ordered to do, analysing if he could do it. The top of the grass mound wasn't too far below the upper trajectory of the chair's swing.

"Unless you're . . ." Jeremy started saying but Shane interrupted.

"I'm not," he said, starting to walk back up the hill for an extended run up. "Just watch me." He breathed deeply a couple of times and then he started. He took a few big steps, running with the swing hanging loosely behind his rear, and then jumped onto the chair. He swung fast and high, observing all below him. At the upper part of the swing he could see his parents along with Hunter's gathered together in the backyard of his neighbour's house. He could also see the full extent of the storm clouds that were almost upon them. The faraway flash of lightning had been hidden by the low hanging foliage of the tree that covered them.

"You're a chicken," James yelled out, "You won't jump." Shane returned to the job at hand. He leaned back in the chair as it swung back to where he started, before leaning forward to build some momentum. Part way through the pendulum like swinging he managed to climb to his feet. He picked a target, gulped down his fear and jumped. He did it quickly like ripping off a bandage so it didn't hurt as long. The wind whooshed past him and his stomach gave an uppercut to his lungs as the freefall panicked all of his muscles.

There was a loud rustling as he landed directly in the middle of a large grass clump. His movement stopped almost immediately with the grass acting like a giant cushion and taking all of his energy. He climbed out with only a couple of small cuts from the grass and lifted his hands in triumph. The crew just looked at him stunned, shocked that he had actually carried out the deed. Then they jumped into argument.

"I am so next," they all cried out in their own way, jostling for dibs on the next turn of the swing. They all gave way to each other with minimal whining. Shane walked slowly back over, his adrenaline still making the space between his ears as well as his heart thump wildly. He managed to watch three of the others swing before he returned to the other side. Ross had landed in a similar fashion to Shane, Hunter had landed in a softer patch of grass which was not as far as the one Shane had landed on, and James was the same. They were all successful with their first couple of swings each, every one of them telling a story of their fall. None of those stories were true but all started with similar comments.

"Did you see me?" one of the crew said.

"How cool was that?" told another.

It wasn't until their energy subsided and the effects of adrenaline had worn off that the real stories started to appear. James had let go too late and fallen onto the lower level of the grass mound, which was a fall of several metres more than the others. Bowie in his ridiculous manner attempted a belly flop as he jumped, only to find the path between some grass patches, badly bruising his ribs. The best one was Alex who caught his foot in the ropes and fell into the creek with an enormous splash. Luckily it was one of the deeper sections that still held water even when there was less flow. The crew only realised that later though, they had immediately erupted into a roar of hilarity as they fell all over the place. Hunter lost his wits completely, rolling around on the ground unable to stop the fit of giggles which continuously rolled from him.

Jeremy had taken on the name Tarzan, insisting that everyone call him that now which no one did this time. To his credit he upheld that name to some degree, attempting trick jumps every time he leapt into the air. He was successful in landing a front flip on one occasion, and then a three hundred and sixty degree turn during another. Despite all that everyone still insisted on calling him by his actual name, not willing to give him the luxury of knowing he was in this sense actually as good as he claimed to be. Bowie, James and Alex refused to jump after their incidents so the rest tried these for a short time longer until their bodies were so beaten they couldn't take another landing like the previous.

James and Alex found a whole bunch of the abandoned tennis balls on the mound and proclaimed a classic catch competition, with the idea taken from test match cricket television coverage. They were all allowed to get wet, and figured that now that the storm clouds had all but covered the sky above them they were about to get wet anyway.

The crew moved to the side of the dam which was easily accessible due to the cut grass. The game consisted of someone throwing a ball up high above the water of the dam and one person at a time doing a running leap and catching it in the best fashion possible. All sorts of tricks and hilarity were attempted. Bowie followed up his previous attempt with the swing, diving into a huge belly flop as he reached for the falling tennis ball. The resulting slap of skin on the surface of the water made every single observer bend over and clutch at their stomachs. Apparently even one of the parents had heard it as Hunter could hear a cry of anguish erupting from the back area of his house.

Small drops of rain started to fall amongst the countless dives in the game, the warmth disappearing almost instantly. The boys had started to shiver with the wind starting to howl as small flashes of lightning became more frequent from the dark sunless sky above. They made the decision to stop the game and return home through severely chattering teeth before their parents made that call for them. Bowie and Ross ran back towards their own homes while the others returned through Hunter's open back gate. Each of the boys were talking about one of their better dives when the parents met up with them.

"Alright boys," Hunter's dad said first. "There are warm showers waiting inside, you can take turns using them, get dry and dressed. We have towels for you in there already. Then the barbecue should be ready to eat." They each nodded.

"Where is your sister?" Judy asked Shane, who immediately looked confused.

"Same with Alana?" Matt's mum added.

"I thought she had come back already," Shane replied, a terrible feeling settling in his gut.

"Well they haven't and you were supposed to look out for them," Phil said as he came forward. A big flash of lightning lit up the sky followed by a window rattling sonic boom.

"Get inside kids," Matt's dad said next. "You can't go out in this. Have a shower while we go and find them. It's not safe for you."

"We can help," Shane offered, knowing it was at least partially his fault his sister was missing.

"No you have done enough," Phil replied gruffly. "Go and get warm before you catch your death." The boys could do nothing but watch as the parent's split up to search for the two missing girls. Hunter's parents had stayed to watch all the kids including Matt's two younger brothers, as well as make sure the food that was being cooked didn't burn and go to waste. Shane's parents walked south towards where the cricket game was played and where they had all sat about eating. Matt's parents went out towards the road to see if the girls had returned to the front area.

"We need to go and help too," said Shane to the rest of the boys.

"But we aren't allowed," James stated, "we will get in more trouble if we do. Besides Hunter's parents are still here. They will stop us."

"What do we do then?" asked Matt.

"I have an idea," declared Alex finally.

"Those aren't usually good though," Hunter retorted.

"This one is, but you won't like it," Alex replied, "I know this will work. Just play along and get ready to go. Are you ready?"

"Are you going to tell us what it is?" James asked.

"Sorry," Alex said shaking his head, "it will be better if you don't know."

"Fine then," Shane agreed, more worried about his sister "anything's worth a shot."

"Okay, here goes." Alex said stepping backwards. He yelled loudly in a high pitched fashion, then punched Hunter in the face. Hunter groaned and hit the grass hard. Everyone else looked stunned.

"What do you think you are doing?" Hunter's dad boomed. He power walked over towards Alex and dragged him off by his collar. At the same time his mum came over and saw Hunter clutching at his cheek.

"I will get you some ice, stay there," she said with worry, "come on kids this way." She hurried off with Matt's two younger brothers in tow, Alex was already out of sight.

"Let's go," Hunter said as he looked up with difficulty from an already closed over eye. None of them waited and immediately broke into a run.

"You two go back around the dam and up to the swing," Shane ordered James and Matt. "Don't be seen by the parents, then start making your way back down towards the house on both sides of the creek." They obeyed without hesitation, both equally worried by the disappearance of the girls.

"What about us?" Hunter asked. Shane stood motionless. His eyes were darting to every nook he could think of along the creek, deciding in his brain what the best spot was to search. There were too many. He froze, oblivious as to the direction they should go, aware that if they went the wrong way it could mean tragedy.

"Shane?" Hunter asked the question as birds called nearby, big ibis and heron which were hidden in the lower parts of the creek had taken flight to avoid the storm.

"I don't know," Shane snapped back. Hunter saw out of his partially collapsed eye that for the first time Shane had lost all of his strength. Hunter wanted to help his friend, imagining what he was feeling but knowing that he couldn't understand completely. A bolt of lightning flashed bright above them. The rain was still almost non-existent but there was a dire and eerie feeling surrounding them, the dark sky mixed with orange and red as the sun was blotted out entirely. Hunter searched the sky for more flashes and watched as the magpies reeled from the roar of the thunder before swooping back down to the ground.

"What are they going after?" Hunter asked almost unthinking before immediately exploding into a run. "Shane follow me." He didn't check to see if he was being followed, and despite not being able to see out of one eye and the storm swirling around them he could see with amazing clarity. Hunter remembered reading about seagulls hovering around massive schools of fish when they were hungry, and it was second nature to know that magpies defended their territory against anything when it was a certain time of the year. That also meant that they had to be defending it from someone.

Hunter groaned as he heard the rain start to fall down. He turned back to the house and saw it teaming down from above like a plane was dumping it in a sheet as it flew overhead. They ran past the dam and past the mound, always being guided by the swooping birds who maintained their barrage despite the weather. Hunter kept running until he made it to the edge of the swamp, which was evident as the ground underfoot transformed from solid ground and then into mush. An extra step was a step too far and Hunter's leg was immediately drawn down and away from him. Pressing off the ground from a crouch he managed to pull his leg back and clear of the mud. His leg from his hip down to the bottom of his shoe was completely covered in brown sludge.

"There they are," Shane said as he arrived, pointing first to May and then Alana. Both were amongst the swampy part of the area where there was more water than bog around them, but considering neither could swim it didn't help the situation. They also were not together. Alana was closer to them but still well out of reach. While May was further away and closer to the far bank. Both girls were neck deep in the water with one hand clutching a collapsing grass clump and the other shielding their faces from the attacking birds.

The ground in front of each of the boys was not crossable. The bog was too thick and Hunter and Shane had no chance of accessing the girls that way. The girls would have been light enough to skip from grass island to grass island but Hunter couldn't, and nor could Shane, as their weight would surely collapse the platforms. The rain got heavier and Shane searched about for something to use to help them. He found sticks and discarded building materials nearby but they were no use. He didn't know what to do.

"What do we do?" Shane asked Hunter. Hunter looked at Shane through his one good eye, then turned and ran. Shane didn't follow. He just watched in disbelief as his neighbour disappeared without a word. Lightning raked the sky followed by booming thunder. Both girls screamed, and as they did so water entered their mouths, revealing why they had never called for help, or rather why Shane had never heard them.

"I am here," Shane called out uselessly but trying to reassure them. "I am going to get you out of there, stay calm." The girls finally noticed that he was there. Alana broke into tears as she held a hand out towards him. Her grip slipped and she slumped into the water. She flailed about for a moment, her arms thrashing trying to find a hand hold on something to keep her above water. They finally grasped another grass platform but she was still unable to pull herself out.

"Don't let go," Shane called out. He wanted to go find help but now that they knew he was there he couldn't leave them. His eyes widened as he watched with horror. The rain had become torrential quite fast, as was the norm with large storms like this one, but as a result the heavier drops splashed water up into the girls' faces causing them to shut their eyes completely to resist the water from below and the birds striking from above. But that water was also rising, several grass platforms disappearing in seconds. His heart beat faster. He was lost as to what to do.

"I'm coming," Hunter cried out through the howling wind. He was on the other side of the creek and running with a full length of rope. It was from the rope swing they had assembled a couple of hours earlier. Hunter had managed to pull the knot out and was dragging it towards May. As soon as Shane saw him so did the magpies. They stopped bombarding the girls and flew off to defend against the bigger foe. It didn't stop Hunter as he rushed to get as close as he could, but he was not alone. James was with him brandishing one of the sticks that they had used as oars some time before. He swung out defending his neighbour from the assault.

"Shane," Matt called out from behind him. He had his own rope and soon Shane realised it was the one that he and his brother had used to scale the steeper side of the grass mound, the same one he had used to save Alex with a long time ago. He thrust the rope towards Shane while calling out to his sister to hang on.

"What are we doing?" Shane asked him, a force from within him jumpstarting every muscle.

"Hunter said to make a big loop, like a cowboy lasso," Matt reported.

"What for?" Shane hadn't followed the train of thought. "It won't be able to go around them without them going under."

"He said something about an axe and said you would know what it meant," Matt continued. A lightbulb went on in Shane's head and exploded with the amount of energy he had given it. His hands started finding their way along the rope searching for the end as his eyes searched the swamp for something else. Another flash of lightning and he found it.

"There," he said to himself allowing Matt to hear him. In moments he had formed a loop. He could see that Hunter had managed to do the same, already flinging the noose towards one particular grass island.

The rusted axe still stood tall, protruding from where Shane had thrown it months ago. If he managed to get his rope around it then he could pull it tight and get Alana to drag herself along it and to safety.

The first few times he missed and grimaced at his failure. He was stressed with the pressure. The water was already rising and in a few more minutes the platforms to which the girls hung would be gone. He looked over to Hunter and was surprised to see that even now he appeared to have disappeared into his imaginary world. Hunter was almost doing a square dance as he twirled the rope above his head and then he let fly. Shane's heart leapt when Hunter found his mark and the loop wrapped around the rusted axe.

"Why isn't he pulling it tight?" Matt asked showing panicked concern for his sister's safety. Shane wondered as well, but found the answer quickly.

"Because he might pull it over," Shane said aloud. "He is waiting for me to get it as well." Shane couldn't fight his frustration but thought of something that might help him. He did what Hunter did. He closed his eyes, envisioning that he was something else, somewhere else, doing something else. He fought the voice in his head that told him that what he was doing was childish and just went with it. He opened his eyes and almost everything changed.

No longer was he in a swamp in a grassy green paddock. Now he was in the American old west. There was no more rain, he was still wet but that was due to the sweat he was pouring out thanks to the intense heat of the sun. He was facing a canyon with deep ravine's running through it, amongst this were two damsels who were hanging on as the rocks they clung onto teetered dangerously.

"It's now or never," Hunter called out from the other side of the chasm, wearing a slouch hat and a stone shirt that was stained with still damp white salty sweat.

"Here goes nothing," he said softly to himself. Without dropping a whole bunch of cowboy phrases he swung the rope over his head. Around and around it went until he was satisfied that he could hit the target. He lobbed it high up in the air, feeling the pull on the rope as it took more with it. He held his breath, somehow feeling the dust that was near him. Then the rope found the mark. The desert area that surrounded him vanished and he was returned to the tormenting storm that flashed all around.

"Pull tight," called Hunter almost instantaneously. Shane obeyed without question and then started shouting orders to Alana as Hunter did the same to May. The axe stayed firm under the new pressure but could be seen moving to the will of the ropes who sought its hold. The girls took some convincing to listen, but slowly and surely they obeyed. They each leaned out to grab the rope that was pulled tight. After a few feeble attempts they managed to hold on and carefully pull themselves back towards their rescuers. Encouragement flew from everyone until the girls were almost half way back.

A sudden crackle was heard after the last lightning strike. Magpies screamed into the air as the large dead stump was struck by lightning and burst into flame. Neither Shane nor Hunter had been that close to a lightning strike before. The fear that another would fall and hit them rose up inside. The storm was right on top of them, but neither carried any metal to be a conductor. Shane's eyes rose with fear. The axe was a massive target for lightning.

"Go faster," he screamed in panic recognising the peril they were all now in. "Go, go, go, go." Hunter repeated the warning to May. Neither girl asked what was happening but they reacted rapidly. Their rate increased and they covered the space quickly. Shane saw May get pulled clear on the other side and his insides leapt. She was safe. But Alana was not, and neither were Shane or Matt. Shane just waited for a bolt to strike him, his fear profound. Alana would find it hard to make it through the bog easily without help. Shane made a decision to end it quicker.

"Matt come here and get ready," he ordered. "Alana, hold onto the rope tight and don't let go. Hold tight." Shane saw her spit water as she nodded her understanding. "Ready, pull." Shane heaved with all his might as did Matt from behind him. The first effort was fruitless, but the second brought the rope clear of the axe which stayed standing straight in the air. The danger was still real as Alana was still in the water. Shane dragged the rope back, fist over fist not actually noticing if Alana still held firmly there. A moment later her safety was confirmed as she fell sobbing into the arms of her older brother.

"We're not safe yet," Shane hissed and urged them away from the bog at pace. There was no sign of Hunter, James or May but Shane had trust that they were safe. As they cleared the dam it became obvious that the parents could now see them and they called out in various tones. Shane heard none of it, just the white noise in his ears and the pound of his heart. Alana fell dragging Matt down with her. Shane instinctively threw himself down upon them urging them to get up, knowing that sanctuary lay inside the house before them. He glanced back towards the tall dead tree which was flashing like a lighthouse as the fire struggled to reignite. Smoke smouldered from the top as if the tree was actually a slim volcano.

Shane swore he saw a spark leap from within the swamp area and squinted his eyes through the dark to see.

Vroom! A spear of lightning impacted from the sky right in the middle. Everyone was gasping in astonishment, knowing only so well how lucky they all were. Shane knew there was only one thing that strike could have hit. He squinted once more to where he had seen the axe only moments ago.

The axe was gone.

CHAPTER 13 – A FEAST OF FRIENDS

Grounded for life had transformed into grounded for a month, then only two weeks. Even then the amount of force that the parents were all imposing on that consequence was very slim. They could all still do everything they could normally do except go outside and play with each other. There was no anger or frustration or cries of being unfair at the result, it was just accepted by all parties.

On the Saturday when they were allowed to go back out together they were accompanied by a massive picnic basket and a few other bags as well. The three households had been told to go and have a picnic and relax in the back paddock but go no further than the top of the grass mound. There was still some small lack of trust but the terms were accepted. The purpose was to get the kids away from the house as the families tried once again to have a joint barbecue as it was so unceremoniously high-jacked during the last attempt. But the grass mound was the boundary and therefore it was the destination.

Upon arrival they found the most usable area where each of them could recline into a grass clump and still be in the immediate vicinity of each other. Even though it was a picnic Hunter once more imagined he was within the castle, like he had been told it was on the first visit to the area, but he was now within the great hall preparing a feast for all. They were all lords and ladies sitting beside each other. The meal which consisted of multiple wrapped sandwiches, some muesli bars, a bucket of apples, and several jugs of green and orange cordial, instead turned into tables of roast beef, suckling pigs, row upon row of glazed donuts and assortments of soft drinks. It was magical. Each of them shared what was on offer retelling their favourite stories that had happened since they had moved in, or informing Matt of all the things he had missed so far.

After that there was no desire to play. Each collapsed into their grass hammocks and relaxed under the soothing afternoon sun. James and Alex were locked in discussion as they collapsed peacefully next to each other. May and Alana fell asleep holding hands. Matt jumped between several different spots until finally settling on one and immediately snoring.

Hunter had chosen a spot where he could see out over the creek and the farmland beyond. It was so tranquil that he too imagined he would fall asleep soon. The castle seemed to flicker like it had bad reception, but then it vanished completely. Hunter no longer had to imagine he was somewhere better because he was already there.

"Hey mate," Shane whispered as he crawled to a spot nearby.

"Hey neighbour," Hunter smiled back, knowing full well that Shane couldn't see that action. There was silence for a time. It wasn't awkward, it was just nice. Finally Hunter had become comfortable with others around him that weren't his family.

"Hunter?" Shane probed.

"Yep, what's up?" Hunter replied.

"I never thanked you for what you did."

"You don't have to," Hunter replied, "It was no big deal."

"Yes I do," Shane responded somewhat startled. "It was a big deal."

"I know it was," Hunter said quickly, trying to restore the calm. "What I meant to say was it was nothing extra on my behalf. You would have done the same for me. In fact you did, and back then you hardly even knew me."

"Still," Shane said after a moment. "You saved a family member, and knew what to do when I completely froze. So I have to thank you."

"Your right," Hunter agreed. "I did save a family member, but not just yours, I also saved mine."

"What do you mean?"

"I mean that before I came here I was searching for something. I had lived in a dozen houses in more places than I can remember. I had no friends to show for that then, even though I have more now. I expected that this place was going to be the same. I hoped that I could make friends here, but I had no trust that that would happen. It is actually me who needs to thank you."

"What?" asked Shane still confused.

"I have a family, a great one in fact. They give me everything I need. Then they gave me an opportunity to make friends, but that didn't happen. Instead of making friends I added onto my family."

"Instead of making friends I found a home."

Once more there was nothing said for a long time. Alex and James had stopped talking and there was just the sound of nature. Hunter believed that he had made Shane feel uncomfortable but silently hoped that wasn't the case. Eventually Shane cleared his throat.

"That's cool mate," Shane said considerably choked up. "That's what we wanted too." More silence, but not as long.

"So I also discovered some things earlier," Shane said changing the subject. "Do you want to know what they are?"

"Sure," Hunter replied. His eyes were now firmly shut tight.

"The first was that I went looking for that axe," he started explaining. "The water has gone down but it's not there anymore, it's gone, vanished without a trace."

"Probably vaporised," Hunter suggested.

"Probably," Shane agreed, "there was one more thing though."

"Yep what was that," Hunter was on the verge of sleep.

"Dad told me that during the week the council approved the continued expansion of Northstoke Way. They are finally going to continue the road down the street." Hunter sat upright immediately and looked straight at Shane.

"You know what that means right?" Shane asked.

"It means we have a kingdom to expand upon," Hunter replied, the stone walls of the castle reappearing like a mirage around them, "it means you, lord king, will have a larger domain to rule and explore."

"No, not me," Shane said shaking his head. "Us. Together." Hunter smiled for a moment and then offered his hand towards his friend and agreed.

"Together."